This edition has been lightly revised from the 2010 original. Previous readers won't find significant additions or deletions, just some authorial tinkering.

CONTENT NOTE:

This novel contains violence, sexual situations, themes, and language some readers may find objectionable.

The Forsaken Boy

The Forsaken Boy

a werewolf novel by Troy Tradup

TOUGH TIMES PUBLISHING
SHOREVIEW, MINNESOTA

TOUGH TIMES PUBLISHING
Shoreview, Minnesota

© 2010, 2021 by Troy Tradup

ISBN 978-0-615-40914-6

Cover image by: KimSongsak / Shutterstock

Everything in this novel is complete and utter fiction. Any resemblance to actual persons, events, locations, businesses, or circumstances is entirely coincidental.

For additional information about this novel, or if you just want to say hey, contact troytradup@gmail.com.

This one's for me.
Someone else can have the next one.

I fear your charity,
I fear you have an affection
too human for me.

Saint Ignatius of Antioch

Contents

Prologue: May

Freak, they called him. Weirdo. Queer. Rez rat.

Brandon leaned against the windshield of Chad's Jeep and tried to visualize the derogatory names as tiny, parchment-winged bats. He pictured them flapping out of his head and rising into the night sky. The May full moon floated directly overhead, round and golden, and Brandon wished it might somehow absorb the names, render them powerless.

Daryl Reisling had started the names back in elementary school, and the other kids had caught on fast. From Brandon's first day at their school, they'd hated him. Hated his patched clothing, hated his shyness, hated that he'd been thrust into their midst with no explanation. No one had bothered to explain it to him at the time either.

One day he'd been living with his mom, going to the rez school in Mille Lacs; the next, he was riding in a pickup beside a glowering white man he'd only ever seen in a photograph. Then he was in a new town, in a new second-grade classroom, and the kids had taken one look at his coal-black hair and eyes, the small Ojibwe medicine bag he wore around his neck, and the names had started and never stopped.

Names and punches and whatever else they thought they could get away with. Just yesterday, Daryl had slammed Brandon against his locker hard enough to dent the metal door. "Didn't see you, Chief," he'd said, loud and overly friendly in case any teacher was nearby. Then he'd leaned close, breath steamy and foul against Brandon's face, and whispered, "Do you really think we're gonna let you out of here alive, faggot?"

That was another of Daryl's favorites.

Still, here he was. Even after ten years of their hatred, he'd come to the pre-graduation bonfire anyway. First, because who knew when they might all suddenly change their minds and decide to like him? And second, more importantly, because Chad had asked him to come. He smiled. Maybe he was a *little* queer—at least where Chad was concerned.

Chad had been his best friend, his only friend, since that terrible day he'd been unceremoniously relocated to Talbot. They were closer than friends—brothers, almost. Brandon didn't know why, but Chad had never succumbed to the cloud of suspicion and distrust that had instantly enveloped the other kids in their class.

He realized he wanted to say something about this to Chad right now. He wanted to find Chad and thank him for ten solid years of friendship in the face of everyone else's unwavering hostility. Then he remembered that Chad was off in the bushes with Nikki and settled back to continue pleading his case to the moon.

"What are you thinking about so hard, Brandy-man?" Nikki asked from behind him. Brandon jumped a little. Had he conjured Nikki simply by thinking about her?

Her pretty face bobbed in front of him as she teetered on the fender of the Jeep. "You look like you're a thousand miles away."

"Farther," Brandon said. He pointed to the glowing golden orb hovering above them. "Seems close enough to touch, doesn't it? Like you could reach up and pull it right down out of the sky. But really it's more than two hundred thousand miles away."

"Oh," Nikki said. "The moon." She hopped up and sat next to Brandon on the hood of the Jeep. "I didn't know you were such an astrology buff."

"Astronomy," Brandon said. He allowed himself the barest flicker of a smile. "I must have been paying more attention back in Mr. Iverson's class than I thought."

Nikki sighed. "You *always* pay attention in class."

Coming from Nikki, Brandon didn't know if this was compliment or accusation. She settled in beside him, snuggling close as if she were cold. Brandon knew that Nikki didn't like him any more than any of the other kids did, but during the time she'd been going out with Chad she'd at least come to tolerate him. Openly touching him was a different matter, however, and she couldn't *really* be chilly right now. The last several weeks had been unseasonably warm and even this late at night, even this close to the lake, the temperature was still in the seventies. But Nikki continued to press against him, nuzzling his neck like a puppy, until finally he relented and wrapped one arm around her shoulders. Despite the distraction, he found it nearly impossible to pull his gaze away from the moon.

"If I didn't know better," he said, "I'd think I was a little drunk." A small laugh bubbled up inside him, like an amusing secret he could no longer keep to himself.

"Like you'd even know what that felt like," Nikki said, but Brandon didn't hear any judgment behind her words.

She was right, though. He might smoke a little weed with Chad now and again, but he never drank. Not so much as a sip of beer. Not after what had happened to his mother. Not after what had happened to send him off with the glowering man in the pickup—that had marooned him here in this snakepit full of assholes.

Still, his thoughts were hectic and disjointed—exactly how he imagined he *would* feel if he'd been drinking. And the moon seemed to be laughing at him. And there was something he really wanted to tell Chad, something right on the tip of his tongue, but whatever it was kept getting lost in the night sky.

"Hey," he said. His thoughts ratcheted momentarily into focus. "Where *is* Chad, anyway?" He wrenched his gaze away from the moon long enough to scan the clearing. "And everyone else?"

"Chad passed out over thataway about an hour ago," Nikki said. "Everyone else went home two hours ago."

"Is that why you're sitting here with me?" He thought he had looked into her eyes when he said it, but realized he was staring at the sky again.

"I'm right where I want to be," Nikki said. "Besides, it's time for your present. It's not every day a guy graduates from high school, you know."

Brandon found this irresistibly funny. He laughed and felt Nikki lean away—annoyed with him already. This was even funnier for some reason, but Brandon made himself bite the laughter back. Hiding his laughter suddenly seemed tremendously important, although for the life of him he could not have said why. "Graduation's technically not 'til Sunday," he said. "Besides, I didn't get you anything."

Now it was Nikki's turn to laugh. Her own laugh was smooth and slippery, voluptuous as Nikki herself. Her face bobbed into focus again, blocking Brandon's view of the moon as she kissed him. Her lips tasted of campfire smoke and brandy. *Brandy-man*, she'd called him. Apparently, Nikki wasn't exactly sober tonight herself.

Brandon gently pushed her away, and now he did manage to look into her eyes. "What would Chad say about this special gift you're planning to give me?"

"Chad's asleep," she said. Before Brandon could respond, she lunged forward and kissed him again. An image popped into his head just before their lips mashed together: the hungry velociraptors from *Jurassic Park*.

Brandon's whoop broke the kiss like a dousing of ice water. He slid down the Jeep's hood and crumpled to the ground, waves of laughter engulfing him.

Nikki hopped down, face contorted and eyes blazing. "Do you think it's funny I'd lower myself to kiss you? I felt sorry for you! I don't know why Chad insists on being friends with you—you're just so damned weird!"

She stalked away. Brandon tried to stop her, tried to call her back, but his laughing jag would not subside.

So Nikki had thought she would kiss him and...what? The frog would turn into a prince? The leper would throw off his bandages to reveal fresh pink flesh and a sharp white smile? He pictured her velociraptor mouth plunging toward his lips and a fresh wave of laughter rolled over him like an incoming tide. So much hatred, so much disgust—and even now he had no idea why they all despised him.

Slowly, awkwardly, he tried to stand. He needed to get moving, get walking, but he stumbled almost immediately and sank once more to his knees.

Maybe he really *was* drunk. Or something. He tottered a bit, leaned against the Jeep to steady his balance, and finally managed an upright position. The maniacal laughter hiccupped itself out and he stood beneath the moon, breathing hard, trying to clear his head. His brain was growing fuzzier by the minute.

Walk it off—that's what he needed to do. Get his blood pumping, get some oxygen flowing into his soggy brain cells. He wandered over to the area where he'd last seen Chad and found a scattering of empty beer cans fanned out around a worn pair of sneakers. He kicked at the bottom of one of the shoes. "Chad, man, wake up. Walk with me." But Chad answered only with a loud, wet snore.

Brandon wheeled around. This was some wicked buzz. He wondered if someone had slipped something into his Red Bull earlier. Ecstasy? Speed? Whatever people slipped into other people's drinks at parties because they thought it would be funny. He thought of all the people who'd been at the bonfire— more than half the senior class. The same people who'd hated him for ten long years. The same people who'd shoved him against lockers, or smashed his books out of his hands in the hallway, or simply found him alone on the street and punched him and punched him and punched him. Any one of them would have been more than happy to put something in his drink. Anything to make him look stupid yet again. Anything to show how much better than him they thought they were.

Hey, look at the freak—stumbling around drunk just like his squaw mama. No wonder they kicked his ass off the rez.

Brandon stumbled away from Chad's prone form and headed toward the edge of the clearing. The bonfire felt too warm, too bright through the oily prism of anger and betrayal misting his field of vision. Why was he always the punchline, the freak, the weirdo, the queer? Why was he always the one who ended up alone?

He moved into the forest and the moon cast a long black shadow ahead of him until it looked like he was walking into himself—or into some larger, darker version of himself. This image thrilled Brandon in a way he was hesitant to think about.

He started to laugh again, laugh for the sheer joy of moving alone through the moonlit night, but found he no longer quite recognized the sound that issued from his throat. He realized immediately that he liked this new sound better.

The buzz in Brandon's head grew more intense the farther he moved from the clearing. What had they given him? He stumbled down the rutted dirt tire tracks that were the only easy access to the clearing, and far ahead on the path he saw Nikki, still pouting, still pissed off and stomping away from their scene on the Jeep. He knew he should go to her, apologize for being rude, but he had the distinct impression Nikki would not want to see him right now. Would not want to see him like *this*, he thought, but wasn't exactly sure what that meant.

Nikki disappeared around a curve in the path, and Brandon thought it was just as well. He didn't feel like comforting her anyway. A storm was raging inside his head, his thoughts windblown leaves almost impossible to catch or hold. He stopped for a moment to concentrate, to breathe, to bask in the mellow, glowing beauty of the night.

The night was a living thing all around him. The gentle breeze, the scent of budding green life, and over everything else the moon, round and full and watchful. The moon and the scent of the green and the wind through the trees—Brandon felt like dropping to the ground and rolling in the night's intoxicating perfume.

The crunch of footsteps on gravel told him Nikki had given up being offended in favor of a ride back into town. Nearly a mile to the main road through the dark forest and another six into Talbot proper—much too far for a mere pout, even for Nikki. She was walking with her arms folded and her head down, watching the path, so she hadn't seen Brandon yet. He thought about calling to her, or clearing his throat to make her aware of his presence, but instead, without quite knowing why, he crept backwards off the path until he was deep in the shadows of the forest. *Safe*, he thought, although that didn't make any sense. He wasn't afraid of Nikki. Still, the word kept playing through his head as he lowered himself into a crouch and waited. *Safe, safe, safe*—like a neon sign blinking red in the window of some dilapidated roadside motel.

Nikki was only a few yards away when an even stranger thought popped into Brandon's head. Perhaps *he* wasn't the one who needed to worry. He stared at Nikki, walking down the path, completely oblivious to his presence there in the shadows. Moonlight cascaded through her blonde hair and created darker golden highlights that shimmered as she moved. Even from this distance, he could smell the campfire smoke on her, perhaps a whiff of brandy. And he was aware of another scent now as well. Indefinable, yet familiar at some deep, elemental level. Like the scent carried on the whispering wind, the scent of the budding trees, Nikki's scent made him think of life itself. The very essence of life, tangible and complete, right there in front of him. His mouth filled with a metallic taste that both thrilled and terrified him.

He bolted. He crashed through the brush and darted across the path directly in front of Nikki. She screamed, but quickly recovered and offered a hesitant, querulous, "Brandon?" to the darkness.

But Brandon was already gone. He was running, loping, moving wildly through the trees. *Away, get away, just get far away*, he told himself. *Safe, safe, safe*, blinked the neon sign.

Now he was a part of the night. He was the night itself, running through the night and into the night to become the night. He ran, and the night howled to catch up. Ran, and the trees bent back to offer a clear path through their dark tangle.

The moon shone down to illuminate the path, and the warm night breeze spoke to him in shades of green and in other shades now too.

The breeze told him things. The big oak to his left held a nest of baby raccoons. The creek he was running beside would soon curve around in front of him and he would have to jump it

(now!)

if he did not want to get wet. The breeze told him that the bonfire back in the clearing was dying down, little more than embers now, and that Nikki was still walking, walking down the path, only walking faster now. Anxious to be back in the clearing, anxious to be back with Chad, anxious especially—for reasons she could not quite articulate—to be back near the Jeep.

Brandon laughed to know these things, and the sound of his new laughter echoed through the darkness. It made Nikki freeze in her tracks at the edge of the clearing. Made Chad bolt awake and stare at Nikki by the last red glow of the dying fire. Made lights come on all the way into town, and parents there rise to check on sleeping children and jiggle door locks or fasten window latches.

After a time, Brandon left the forest. The trees thinned and disappeared, and then he was running through a field of scrub and thorns. He realized he was barefoot, although he couldn't remember taking off his shoes. He knew the field must be cutting his feet to bloody ribbons, but he couldn't feel a thing. Or rather, the leaves and pickers and rubble under his feet felt strangely invigorating. Liberating.

At the other end of the field, a farmhouse stood in vivid relief beneath a blanket of stars and the extraordinary moon. Why he should want to go to the farmhouse right now, he had no idea. The image of the place had bubbled into his thoughts unbidden, an idea whispered on the night wind. He'd been here before, quite recently even, but he couldn't remember much about it, or why the idea to return felt so compelling.

As the image in his head loomed up out of the night to become the real place in front of him, Brandon slowed to a jog and then to a walk. He panted a little to catch his breath and the tongue that could no longer quite translate thoughts into words lolled from one corner of his mouth. A string of saliva descended from it and hung suspended for a moment, glistening in the moonlight.

The Call of the Wild
(Five Months Earlier)

He looked over, and there stood the wolf as big as a calf against the horizon, its tongue out, and its eyes glaring like marsh-fires.

Sabine Baring-Gould

Having reached the solitude of the country, he howls aloud, and in vain attempts to speak; his mouth gathers rage from himself...his garments are changed into hair, his arms into legs; he becomes a wolf.

Ovid

Presently I looked back after him, and saw him strip and lay his clothes by the side of the road. My heart was in my mouth in an instant, I stood like a corpse; when, in a crack, he was turned into a wolf. Don't think I'm joking: I would not tell you a lie for the finest fortune in the world.

Petronius

On the feast of the Nativity...such a multitude of wolves transformed from men gather...and then spread to rage with wondrous ferocity against human beings.

Olaus Magnus

The natives were a pastoral people, and would consequently suffer very severely from the attacks and depredations of wolves. They would naturally institute a sacrifice to obtain deliverance from this pest, and security for their flocks. This sacrifice consisted in the offering of a child.

Sabine Baring-Gould

All true werewolf stories begin on Christmas Eve.

Lewis Graydon

December

He was already late, but at the T in the road where the drive home presented its usual choice—glide a single mile over straight, level, well-lit streets through the middle of town, or cowboy seven miles over snaking, dusty, unlit country back roads—Brandon turned without hesitation toward the darkness.

Instantly, the blacktop grew rough. Within a mile, blacktop gave way to gravel. Another mile, and the trees on either side of the road began to display such a blatant disregard for anything but their own wildness that Brandon felt every hair on his body stand on end as he entered their dark embrace.

Gunning his ancient Mustang down the thin strip of gravel that cut through the trees, Brandon jabbed the volume control knob of the car's stereo to illuminate a glowing orange clock. 11:23 PM. Nearly an hour past his curfew—even on a holiday, even on his birthday—and still early enough for his father to be waiting up in his easy chair, nursing one last Jack and Coke and absently caressing the fraying edges of his thick leather belt.

But Brandon didn't give a flying rat's ass about his father—*or* his father's belt. He didn't care about the sour, hangover-fueled recriminations his stepmonster was certain to spew at him the next morning, or the inevitable threat of revoked driving privileges. He cared only about the night, and the throaty rumble of the Mustang, and the dark country roads that would lead him away, however briefly, from all the pain and frustration of his stupid, pathetic life.

People were supposed to be happy on their birthday, and people were supposed to be happy on Christmas Eve. For Brandon, the two events invariably canceled each other out. He felt cheated out of his birthday by the holiday, and cheated out of the holiday by his own "special day." Even when he was little, about the best his father and stepmonster ever managed was some cheap plastic toy from the hardware store and maybe a new pair of socks.

Every year, Chad and his mom tried to make the day better for Brandon. Kate would bake Brandon a cake and she would make Chad wait until Christmas morning to open his presents because Christmas Eve was reserved for Brandon. Chad had never tried to make Brandon feel guilty about this, but the guilt stuck in Brandon's throat anyway—like a splintered chicken bone.

Every year, he forced himself to suffer through Kate's delicious dinner. Every year, he choked down two pieces of her extraordinary cake and smiled like an idiot while she and Chad showered him with birthday presents he never could have afforded himself. Every year, they begged him to stay overnight, stay for Christmas morning (*more* presents, for crying out loud), but every year he found some excuse to beg off, to leave that house of love and happiness and escape into the frigid December darkness alone.

This year, because he was turning eighteen, Chad and Kate had gone even crazier than usual. Kate had made a big production out of needing to send Chad into town for some last-minute dinner item, and Chad had made an equally big production of needing to borrow Brandon's Mustang for the trip. When he returned, nearly an hour later, the Mustang had sported four new tires that crunched down the frost-coated driveway like something alive. It had taken all of Brandon's resolve not to bolt for the door that very second.

Remembering that moment, Brandon stomped on the Mustang's accelerator and let the car fishtail wildly. He'd driven these roads a thousand times, but still he liked to imagine a violent, tire-screeching death around every curve. A big whitetail buck leaping from the ditch and crashing through his windshield. A massive blowout, sending him careening into a tree or down an embankment or into an oncoming vehicle.

Except there were no oncoming vehicles. Brandon drove these roads alone. The Mustang's engine was loud enough to clear the road of deer or moose well before he might have reached them; his tires were new, thanks to the Bowmans (and the only decent thing on the car, when it came right down to it); and the trees were all far enough back from the gravel that a wreck would only land him in the frozen muck that lined the shallow ditches on either side of the road.

Brandon sped through the darkness. Overhead, a gauzy meteorological haze turned the December full moon into a pale silver disc that did little to illuminate the frosty night. Wisps of greenish fog rose from the ditches and floated lazily across the road. *Ghosts*, Brandon thought innocently, but immediately the cynic in him took over and he said, out loud, "Swamp gas." Human shit from one of the new housing developments, leaking all the way back here into the wild places.

Brandon grimaced. *Wild places.* Just a quarter-mile back, a large wooden sign had materialized out of the darkness at the side of the road: *HUNDRED ACRE WOOD ESTATES—PRIME LOTS AVAILABLE NOW!* The sign had listed a realtor in Minneapolis, some big-city asshole trying to turn the north woods into one giant condominium. Brandon had noted with satisfaction that the sign, up for only a couple of weeks, was already riddled with bullet holes. *Hundred Acre Wood. A.A. Milne must be turning over in his—*

Without warning, an enormous gray blur loped up out of the fog on the west side of the gravel and crossed directly in front of the Mustang. Brandon stomped on the brake pedal with both feet and sent a plume of dust up behind the car like an enormous rooster tail.

"What the—?"

Brandon rolled down the driver-side window and squinted into the darkness. *Probably just some stupid old farm dog,* he thought, although something about his brief glimpse had seemed too sinewy or graceful for a dog. The sleek heft of the body, the smoky grace of the stride...

Of course, a wolf wasn't out of the question either, but Brandon could count on the fingers of one hand the number of times he'd seen a wolf in the wild, even here in the very heart of Minnesota's wolf country.

A low growl drifted toward the Mustang from the ditch on Brandon's left. The sound was just loud enough to register over the car's engine, the timbre perfectly pitched to settle in the very center of Brandon's chest. He stared out the open window and listened, willing his pulse to stop pounding so hard in his ears so that he might *hear—*

The growling thing moved closer but not close enough, careful to avoid the small circle of light thrown by the Mustang's headlights. It moved off to one side, then back to where it had been. Up and back, up and back—quieter, louder, quieter, louder. *Doppler effect,* Brandon thought, although he wasn't sure that was correct. Chad would have known.

After a bit, the growling moved toward the back of the car, and Brandon automatically shifted his eyes from the window to the rearview mirror. The Mustang's brake lights painted the night behind the car a striking neon red, but still the animal remained hidden.

Mindful of his ever-increasing lateness, Brandon slid his foot across the brake pedal toward the gas. The animal edged into the perimeter of the brake-light glow.

A wolf.

It *was* a wolf.

Just a big gray wolf.

Really big, Brandon thought, but so what? Wolves were just like people—some big, some small. And some, like this one, freakish in one direction or another. This one was perhaps twice the size of any of the wolves he'd seen previously, either in the wild or at the Center when he visited Chad, but otherwise it looked pretty much like any other big gray timber wolf...except that it was sitting in the middle of the road, staring at him.

The big gray wolf—the big, *big* gray wolf, Brandon said to himself—was sitting in the middle of the frosty gravel, at the very edge of the brake-light glow, calmly staring at the back of Brandon's Mustang. *Specifically* staring at the back of the Mustang, Brandon realized, and his breath caught in his chest. The wolf cocked its enormous head, padded a few steps closer... and *smiled* at him.

Brandon's heart began a weird, dry *thump-thump, thump-thump*, loud enough to drown out the Mustang's engine. The wolf stretched luxuriously, smiled again, and padded closer.

Brandon stared into the rearview mirror, not quite able to take his foot off the brake and move it onto the gas pedal. This was not the way wolves were supposed to act around people or cars. Chad's mom ran the Talbot Wolf Research Center and Chad worked there part-time, and they were both willing to talk about wolves until the whole world fell down around them. So

Brandon had plenty of information about the way wolves were *supposed* to act, and this one was not making even the slightest attempt to appear normal. As if to prove this definitively, the wolf abruptly stood and began walking toward Brandon's open window on its hind legs.

Brandon's mind took three seemingly endless seconds to make his foot stomp on the gas pedal with as much force as he could possibly exert. The rear tires spun, the engine screamed, and finally the car caught the road and bulleted away. Brandon's eyes never once left the rearview mirror until he was a solid half-mile distant, and it was only later, shivering beneath his blankets, that he finally let himself think about what he'd just seen.

Could something out of some schlocky late-night movie really be wandering the dark forests outside sleepy little Talbot, Minnesota?

And if something like that *was* out running around the moonlit countryside, why had that notion gone from terrifying to weirdly intriguing within the space of a few hours?

The first breathless tickle of possibility brushed Brandon's subconscious, and a tiny voice in the deepest recesses of his mind whispered, *"Be careful what you wish for..."*

But Brandon was finally tumbling down into sleep, and this was just the sort of bullshit warning he typically ignored anyway.

. . .

At breakfast, Brandon's father was a section of newspaper over a plate of congealing bacon grease and hardening smears of mustard-colored egg yolk. Brandon found a bowl, poured cereal, sloshed in milk, grabbed a spoon from the silverware drawer, and sat at the table. He took a bite of cereal, glanced at his nearly somnambulant stepmonster, took another bite…and the newspaper never wavered.

Brandon stared at the front and back pages of the sports section—pretty much the only part of the newspaper he ever looked at. Inside their loose V, the other pages turned periodically but always remained out of sight. Brandon took another bite of cereal. And another. He smiled at his stepmonster, but she was staring at her coffee cup as if she'd never seen such a thing before and didn't notice.

Three more bites, and he would be out of there. If the newspaper didn't drop before then, he could be reasonably certain his father had fallen asleep the night before and hadn't heard him come in.

Brandon took another bite. His mouth made a small slurping noise on the spoon that he immediately regretted, but the newspaper didn't budge. He took another bite, much more carefully, and looked at the final mouthful of soggy flakes in the bottom of the bowl. He scooped the flakes onto the spoon, inched the spoon toward his mouth…

"Did you have to be so goddamned loud last night?" his stepmonster said. She yawned hugely, extravagantly, and then narrowed her eyes into an even owlier squint than before. "You woke me out of the first decent sleep I've had in weeks, clomping in here in the middle of the night like you own the place—and on Christmas Eve, no less!"

Brandon stared at her. Without any input from his brain, his mouth decided to snarl out words: "Oh, is December twenty-fourth a day we acknowledge in this house now—for *any* reason?"

The newspaper at the end of the table lowered like a drawbridge about to release a dragon. Brandon saw the oily spike of his father's crew cut, the piercing gray eyes, the crooked boxer's nose, and finally the stubble-covered chin. An unlit cigarette bobbed between his father's lips as the newspaper came to rest on the grease-and-yolk-coated plate. Brandon popped the last spoonful of cereal into his mouth, silently cursed his cunt of a stepmonster, and looked at his father looking at him.

"What time was it this inconsiderate little bastard decided to wake you up?" The man spoke to the woman, but his eyes never left the boy. So much disdain that to look away and then have to reproduce it would have required too much effort.

"Twelve...oh...six," the woman said with more energy than Brandon had seen her muster in days. She might have been calling out a winning lottery number, or the combination to some long-locked safe.

"Twelve-oh-six," Brandon's father said. "That's funny, because my watch said twelve-thirteen." Eyes still staring, eyes still implacable as death, eyes still drilling directly into the middle of Brandon's head and finding the contents there sorely lacking.

Doesn't he ever blink?

After a moment, Brandon's father picked up the newspaper, opened the V, snapped the pages out once—efficiently—to smooth them. The second hand on the clock above the refrigerator logged sixty distinct *tk* sounds.

Brandon stood and moved to take his empty bowl to the sink. He took one step, then a second, and finally his father's voice oozed from behind the newspaper like rancid honey with bees still floating in it. "So you're eighteen now," he said. "Guess that makes you a man."

Brandon opened his mouth to respond, then shut it again. What would be the point?

"You've had your breakfast," said the voice behind the newspaper. "Now go pack your shit and get out of my house."

Brandon stood for a moment, stunned. For once, even his mouth didn't know what to say. He looked across the table to see if his stepmonster might inexplicably intervene, but she merely blew out a lungful of cigarette smoke and stared at him as if she couldn't understand why he hadn't already left.

Finally, he found his voice. He was pleased it didn't come out any more tremulous than it did. "You're kicking me out?" he said. "I still have five months of high school left. You know I don't have any money. You know there aren't any jobs in town this time of..." The utter perfection of his father's timing finally made it to the forefront of Brandon's mind. This time, his voice did crack a little—he couldn't help it. "But it's *Christmas.*"

The second hand of the clock carved another thirty seconds out of Brandon's life before the newspaper finally lowered once more. Brandon's father contorted his face into what Brandon supposed constituted a smile for him. "Well then," he said. "Merry fucking Christmas."

And up once again went the crisp V of the newspaper.

. . .

The logical thing would have been to go directly to the Bowman house. They'd certainly asked him enough times to come live with them. But something about showing up broke and homeless on Christmas morning felt too pathetic to contemplate, and Brandon decided he needed time alone to absorb what had happened. Another sudden upheaval in his life—and he'd had no more say in the matter at eighteen than he'd had at eight.

Christmas morning in Talbot was a quiet, thoughtful, lonely time. The only things open were the churches; even the Amoco station at the edge of town was closed that one day every year.

The bars would all open later in the day and do a brisk business with people fleeing their families and all of that happy Hallmark holiday bullshit, but at the moment the streets were deserted. Talbot might have been a ghost town, inhabited only by the slumbering dead.

Brandon hadn't been inside a church since...well, he couldn't remember *ever* being inside a church. His mother hadn't been religious, and his father and stepmonster certainly weren't. Brandon often wished he knew more about his Ojibwe side— that he'd had more time on the rez, more time with his mother— but his thoughts rarely centered on spirituality or nature or any of the other things he assumed an Ojibwe was supposed to care about. Church and faith, God or some Great Spirit—these were concepts for people who didn't need to spend every moment watching their back for attacks from one quadrant or another.

Still, after several circuits of the six blocks that made up Talbot's "downtown," Brandon found himself turning the Mustang and chugging up the hill to the parking lot of Saint Ignatius Catholic Church. The lot was full of cars and people. The church offered three Masses on Christmas day, and Brandon arrived just as the second was letting out. He pulled the Mustang into a spot being vacated by a family who looked like they belonged in a television commercial, and slumped in the seat to wait.

The lot took a long time to clear. Infused with Christmas cheer and the Glory of God, people stopped to talk to the priest outside the main entrance, then stopped again to talk to other parishioners in the parking lot. Everyone was scrubbed and dressed-up, exhilarated by the brisk December air and the knowledge that, thank the Lord, they were done with *that* for another year.

Finally, the last car but his left the lot, and Brandon realized the priest was looking at him, no doubt wondering if Brandon was going to get out of his car. He was a pale, somewhat soft-looking man of forty or so, dressed in opulent holiday robes. Brandon glanced down at his own torn jeans, faded Metallica T-shirt, ancient leather jacket, and grimy sneakers—his Christmas finest—and turned off the car. The Mustang's engine took a moment to shut down, and its rumbling purr was still echoing down the hillside as Brandon stepped out onto the blacktop.

Up close, the priest looked tired, perhaps a little under the weather. He had dark pouches under his pale blue eyes, and the eyes themselves looked a little bloodshot, as if he'd taken too much Communion wine already that day. His gaze, however, was open and welcoming. Quizzical, but pleased that a hint of mystery was presenting itself this fine Christmas morning. "I know you," he said as Brandon approached. Then his brow furrowed and he offered a warm, self-deprecating smile. "Or do I?"

"I don't know," Brandon said. "I've never been here before, if that's what you mean."

The priest shrugged. "Well, you're here now. Although if you're here for Mass, you're either late or early." He offered a handshake that Brandon found surprisingly strong. "Father Kevin Holloway."

Brandon introduced himself and scuffed one sneaker across the cold sidewalk. "I guess I'm not really dressed for church. I just..." He let the sentence trail off because he had no clue what he was preparing to say.

Thankfully, Holloway was always ready to jump into any conversational lull, awkward or not. "I can't say that the Lord really cares one way or another what you wear to Mass. And I certainly don't care if you wear a Metallica shirt, so long as you don't make me listen to any of their music. Let's go inside and warm up a bit before the next happy flock start making their way toward the fold. I can find us some hot coffee, and you can tell me why you're here."

"I don't really know why I'm here," Brandon said. "Except I've got nowhere else to go."

"Well, you're not the first lamb to show up at a church for that reason," Holloway said. He opened the door and Brandon let the gentle outward rush of warm air usher him inside.

. . .

Chad and his mother were appalled, intrigued, and more than a little flummoxed. Appalled at the abhorrent behavior of Brandon's parents—a new low even for them; intrigued that Brandon had taken it upon himself to go to church; and flummoxed by the news he brought with him when he arrived for Christmas dinner that afternoon.

"You're kidding," Chad said. "You're going to live at a *church*, for Christ's sake?"

Brandon laughed—the first genuine spark of happiness he'd felt in days. "I'm not sure I'm ready to live there for *Christ's* sake yet. Let's see how the whole handyman thing goes, then we'll talk about the priesthood."

Chad's mother took the news even harder. "But there's so much room right here!"

"I know," Brandon said. "And I knew that I could come here and you'd take me in, no questions asked. But something didn't feel right about that. I didn't want to impose—"

"Impose!" The word was a call-to-arms for Kate Bowman. She searched the counter for something to throw at Brandon, but found only a dishtowel and a half-eaten Christmas cookie in the shape of Santa's bottom. Since neither matched the level of her bewilderment, she polished off the cookie and used the towel to wipe a few random crumbs into the sink.

"Dude, you're family," Chad said. "You could never impose."

"I really do appreciate everything you guys have done for me," Brandon said. "But Father Holloway made the offer—a job and a place to live—and it just felt...*right*. Like the universe was throwing me a bone for once."

"Speaking of that," Kate said. "You know, you *are* a good-looking young man. And this *is* a Catholic priest we're talking about..."

"Mom!"

Brandon laughed again—the look on Chad's face was priceless.

"What?" Kate said. "It's in the news all the time."

"That's not what I'm talking about," Chad said. "Where do you get off telling Brandon he's good-looking?"

This time Kate did find something to throw—a bedraggled-looking apple that Brandon could have sworn had been sitting on the Bowman counter since Halloween. The apple arced across the kitchen straight at Chad's face, but Chad snatched it out of the air and took a massive bite out of it all in a single motion. Brandon laughed again, felt as if he could continue laughing all afternoon and into the rest of his life.

Since driving away from his father's house that morning, a sort of lightness had been overtaking him bit by bit. Or perhaps it would be more accurate to say that a certain heaviness had been leaving him. First rising from his forehead, where it had lain like a clammy damp washcloth; then lifting off his shoulders; finally floating away from his chest like the relief that must come to someone who's survived a terrible case of pneumonia. All day, the heaviness had been lifting and the lightness had been taking its place.

He'd lived with the heaviness for ten years, since the day he'd been whisked away from the reservation. Or really since the day the trash collectors had discovered his mother's body in one of the dumpsters behind the casino. The first eight years of his life, changed irrevocably in a single moment. So why not another change now, ten terrible years transformed over the course of a single day?

There in the Bowman kitchen, with his two favorite people in the world, Brandon watched a pink and silver dusk fall on the crisp afternoon outside and wondered if his life might actually turn out okay now. Perhaps his father had done him a favor that morning, releasing him from a house in which he'd never been welcome in the first place. Perhaps his father had inadvertently set Brandon upon an entirely different path today; perhaps Brandon had already taken his first steps toward some previously unimagined, happier future.

Well after midnight—after a wonderful dinner, after several rounds of Trivial Pursuit and Yahtzee, after a sleepy viewing of Kate's *It's a Wonderful Life* DVD—Brandon finally took his leave. He didn't immediately head for the church but, pondering the mysteries of change and transformation, steered his car toward the dark country back roads.

What lonely creature besides himself, he wondered, might be roaming the forest on this happiest of all Christmas nights?

January

In January, Chad started dating Nikki Langley. They'd known each other all their lives, but probably hadn't passed more than five words directly between them in all that time. Then one day Chad said something funny in sociology class and Nikki laughed. The next day Brandon saw them holding hands in the hall. The day after that, they were officially a couple.

The only thing remotely unusual about their pairing was the fact that Kate Bowman and Nikki's widowed father, Davis Langley, had themselves been known to "go a round or two now and again," as the locals liked to say. Nothing serious, just dinner once in a while, or a late evening somewhere private. Two busy single parents, enjoying each other's uncomplicated company. Kate wondered if the kids were somehow trying to bring she and Davis closer together. Davis wondered if they were trying to drive them farther apart. For their own part, Chad and Nikki hadn't given the matter a single thought.

Of course, the person most affected by Chad and Nikki's pairing-up was Brandon. Nikki wasn't Chad's first girlfriend, but she quickly proved the most demanding. She had endless ideas for ways in which Chad might benefit from doing something for her, and Chad had his job at the Wolf Research Center as well. Brandon's job at Saint Ignatius took up still more time, and so for nearly a month his friendship with Chad whittled itself down to little more than a random "Hey" or "What's up?" as they passed in the hallways at school.

Brandon felt Chad's sudden absence from his life more deeply than he would have imagined. He thought he could live the rest of his life without seeing his father or stepmonster again, but losing out on regular interaction with Chad and Kate—that was another matter entirely. Now that Chad was always with Nikki, Brandon thought it would feel too weird to visit Kate on his own. He felt like he'd been pushed away, set adrift, and although it was something he'd been expecting all his life, once it happened he was woefully unprepared. All of a sudden, Nikki was just always *there*, taking up every minute of Chad's spare time—and Brandon was once again, for the second time in less than a month, effectively without a family.

His days became a routine of school and work and long, slow evenings in his room at the rectory. He read Salinger and Vonnegut and—although he never consciously realized what he was doing—watched the clock out of the corner of his eye and wondered if tonight was the night he would finally see the wolf again.

His obsession with the wolf grew by the day. His desire to repeat the encounter, combined with his new solitude, reminded Brandon of a story the staff liked to tell kids on field trips to the Wolf Research Center.

Because the Center was only a few miles out of town, it was an easy and inexpensive destination for a school district perpetually struggling with financial problems, and Talbot kids ended up visiting every year from kindergarten on. The junior high and high school kids got meatier science and biology lessons, but the elementary kids got mostly crafts and stories. Brandon's favorite story, not surprisingly, had always been the Ojibwe legend of the forsaken boy.

The forsaken boy is just a toddler when his father dies. On his deathbed, the father implores the boy's older brother and sister to care for their younger sibling, as he knows that his wife, their mother, will soon join him in death. (How the father knew this had always terrified Brandon—was the man going to drag the poor woman right down into the grave with him?)

Sure enough, the father dies and the mother soon follows. The older brother and sister care for the boy for a time, but soon grow bored and leave the toddler alone while they go off to seek companionship and adventure elsewhere. (At this point in the story, Brandon always had to force himself not to cry in front of his classmates. He could deal with the parents dying—he often wished such a fate on his own father and stepmonster—but the older brother and sister abandoning the boy pierced his heart like a rusty arrow.)

In the story, years pass, and eventually the older brother and sister begin to feel guilty about what they've done. They return to their old camp, expecting to find only their brother's remains. Instead, they find the boy very much alive. Grown now, and grown wild and feral, he's been cared for throughout all the intervening years by a pack of wolves. When the older brother and sister call to him, he transforms before their eyes. He sprouts fangs and claws. Fur covers his body and his nose elongates into a muzzle. With nothing but hatred for his siblings in his luminous eyes, he drops to all fours and snarls, "I am a wolf!" before bounding into the forest with a howl.

At the end of the story, the Center staffer doing the telling would pretend to howl, and someone at the back of the room would switch on a loud recording of a real wolf. The kids would jump and then fall back laughing. Brandon always jumped and laughed too, but his reaction was merely a performance—another attempt to make his classmates think he was like them. They never believed it anyway, and now that he was older he wondered why he'd ever tried.

But certainly he never could have shown his *true* reaction to the story. To Brandon, the story of the forsaken boy had always been less a fable about the consequences of forgetting compassion and more a tale of hope and possibility. Even the first time he'd heard the story, his first spring in Talbot, he remembered thinking: *that boy got away and maybe I will too.* His entire childhood, it seemed, had been one long dream of impossible escape.

There was a poem near the end of the story that some of the staffers incorporated into their telling and some didn't. Brandon had copied the poem into a notebook at one point, but had no idea where that notebook might be now. Not that it mattered—he knew the poem by heart:

Listen, brother—elder brother!
Now my fate is near its close;
Soon my state shall be another,
Soon shall cease my day of woes.

Left by friends I loved the dearest,
All who knew and loved me most;
Woes the darkest and severest,
Bide me on this barren coast.

Pity! ah, that manly feeling,
Fled from hearts where once it grew;
Now in wolfish forms revealing,
Glows more warmly than in you.

Ah, ye wolves in all your ranging,
I have found you kind and true;

More than man—and now I'm changing,
And will soon be one of you.

Brandon thought of the poem often, and his room at the rectory crackled with the dry electricity of waiting and the barely restrained desire—like an unreachable itch, like something growing inside him—to get behind the wheel once more. To drive. To escape. *To find the wolf.*

. . .

Despite growing up poor as dirt, and despite never having received so much as a single word of encouragement from his father or stepmonster, some quirk of fate had turned Brandon into a reader.

He remembered distinctly the thrill he'd experienced when letters first huddled to form words; when words clustered to form sentences; when sentences clicked together like pieces in a jigsaw puzzle to form a story. Everything else had become so much less important after that. Terrible parents, a tortuous home life, bullies in the school yard—all ceased to exist, at least temporarily, whenever Brandon found a quiet corner and opened a book.

At the end of his first miserable school year in Talbot, a sympathetic janitor had allowed him to take home a box of ratty paperbacks the elementary library was discarding, and he'd guarded those relics as if they were Incan treasures, reading and rereading the stories within until the pages literally fell from their bindings and crumbled to dust beneath his bed.

That summer he'd discovered the Public Library, three blocks from his father's house, and he went there as often as he could, sometimes two or three times a week. It was the first place he thought to go now, as he struggled to feed his obsession about the creature he'd seen on Christmas Eve.

Most clichés have at least some basis in reality, and the cliché of the prune-faced small-town librarian couldn't be argued in Talbot. Nola Fenster was tall and bony, her face indeed lined and wrinkled like a piece of dried fruit. Her skin had a bluish tint reminiscent of poorly-mixed powdered milk, and the prominent veins on the backs of her hands and at her temples appeared to contain a thin, amber-colored fluid instead of blood. More than one library patron had wondered privately over the years if Nola had perhaps been embalmed at some point and simply didn't know it.

Nola was generally disapproving to begin with—of Talbot and its residents, of summer people coming into her library, of any literature written after the 1800s—but she was specific in her disapproval of Brandon Turner. She was the type of person—Brandon had encountered a number of them over the years—who took one look at him and felt her blood (or whatever constituted blood for Nola Fenster) begin to boil.

As Brandon approached the checkout counter, he saw Nola's shoulders tighten and the corners of her mouth pull down as if attached to tiny weights. He smiled, and made sure he didn't lean against the counter because he knew Nola hated when patrons did that. "I'm wondering if you have any books on the supernatural?" he said.

A flush rose on Nola's pallid cheeks. "Why are you looking for trash like that?"

Brandon knew the dried-up old bitch might very well ask the same question of someone looking for *War and Peace* or *Moby Dick*, so he broadened his smile and continued as if she merely hadn't understood his request. "You know, goblins and vampires and witches—that sort of thing. Or maybe werewolves?"

Nola glared at him, then gestured with one skeletal finger toward a section of shelves across the room. "We'll be closing soon," she said. "So find what you need and be on your way."

"You're not open 'til five on Saturdays anymore?" Brandon pointed to the clock above the checkout desk: a few minutes past three.

Nola turned away and busied herself at some files, her jutting shoulder blades somehow more judgmental than her sneer.

Brandon wandered over to the area Nola had indicated and found a single shelf of books on the occult. Not very promising, but after a careful scan of the spines, Brandon found a handful of titles worth a closer look. He took the books to one of the reading carrels by the windows.

The Book of Were-wolves. Scary Creatures of the Night. Supernatural Beasts and Demons.

He felt ridiculous. He'd barely found enough sources at the library to write a term paper on Charles Darwin last fall—yet now he was hoping to find "real" information about a creature patently unreal. He flipped randomly through the books, amused by the garish illustrations, until his eyes fell upon a sentence in one of them that made him forget to breathe for a moment: *All true werewolf stories begin on Christmas Eve.*

Brandon placed the other books on a nearby cart—Nola tolerated no reshelving of books by civilians in her library—and carried the single tome to the checkout counter.

"*The Darker Heart,*" Nola said. "*Lycanthropy in the Modern World.*" She handled the book as if it might be radioactive; accepted Brandon's card as if he proffered a turd. "This volume must have been donated. I never would have purchased something like this."

Brandon smiled, anxious to have the book back in his hands.

"And I certainly would never *read* it," Nola said.

"It's getting me out of your library pretty fast, though, right?"

Nola narrowed her eyes, then turned and completed the transaction without looking at him again.

. . .

All true werewolf stories begin on Christmas Eve, claimed Lewis Graydon, author of *The Darker Heart*.

Brandon smiled at the apparent sincerity of the author's convictions—here was a man who believed there was a difference between "true" werewolf stories and false.

In older times, Graydon wrote, *people believed it blasphemous for a child to be born on such a holy of days—surely such a child would be cursed to walk the earth as a ravening, bloodthirsty monster throughout eternity.*

Brandon laughed, the sound sharp in the confines of his tiny room in the rectory.

Werewolf legends appear in virtually every culture, dating back well beyond recorded history. Here the book contained photographs of cave drawings depicting man-wolf creatures stalking ancient forests and plains.

Many scholars consider the story of King Nebuchadnezzar in the Book of Daniel the first written account of a werewolf, but the Epic of Gilgamesh featured a distinctly lycanthropic character some fifteen-hundred years earlier.

Scholars? Brandon thought. *There are werewolf scholars?*

According to the book, the founders of Rome had been raised by a she-wolf, and a werewolf had won boxing medals at one of the early Olympics. Saint Patrick supposedly found numerous clans of werewolves when he arrived in Ireland in 435 A.D., and 30,000 people had been charged with "werewolfism" in France between 1520 and 1630.

The book claimed "Little Red Riding Hood" was a werewolf story, as was "Beauty and the Beast" (*in each case,* Graydon wrote, *the werewolf gets rather a raw deal in the end*). The book said that Adolf Hitler was obsessed with werewolves (the term "Führer" loosely translates to mean the leader of a pack of hunting wolves), and sociologist Robert Eisler was quoted as saying that all werewolf stories stem from humankind's collective guilt over its violent past.

According to legend, there were nearly as many ways to become a werewolf as there were werewolf stories. You could be born on the wrong day of the year, sleep outdoors under a full moon, or wrap yourself in wolf pelts and plead with the devil to transform you. According to the movies, transformation invariably required a bite.

One can't help but wonder, however, Graydon wrote, *if any of these things is ever enough on its own. Perhaps a certain portion of the victim's very humanity must already be missing—dissolved by a lifetime of dismissal, absorbed into an endless river of disappointment with the world. Perhaps the potential lycanthrope must have been systematically worn down, over time, by a world that should have offered him more and people who should have loved him better, until a sort of internal pathway has opened. A raw wound, an expressway for contagion, and the essence of the beast is passed with no more mystery or hoodoo than a common disease like rabies. The pathway opens, the virus enters, and the dark heart grows ever darker, until finally humanity falls away altogether and only the beast remains...*

. . .

Near the end of the month, both of the Bowmans had a rare Saturday evening free. Davis Langley had taken Nikki to the

Twin Cities for the weekend to use up some of the gift cards she'd received for Christmas. The family on his deceased wife's side had never gotten it through their heads that Talbot was a five-hour drive from any of the stores in which they typically shopped, and this trek "down to civilization" to cash in the otherwise useless cards had become an annual event. The Bowmans used the opportunity to invite Brandon over for a night of dinner and board games. "A *normal* evening for once," Kate said when Brandon arrived, and Chad rolled his eyes behind her back and mouthed, "Not with *her* around, man."

Truly, it should have been normal—*like the old days*, Brandon thought—but for some reason the pieces wouldn't click into place. Kate was too enthusiastic, Chad too moony over his absent girlfriend, and Brandon couldn't sit still. He prowled the kitchen while Kate cooked; he picked things up and set them down again; he scribbled on the message board beside the door and then wiped the board clean again with the heel of his hand.

"Why do you have such ants in your pants tonight?" Kate asked.

"What do you mean?" Brandon's smile was without guile—or comprehension.

"He must be in love," Chad said. Because Chad thought *he* was in love, he wanted everyone else to be too.

"Who would I be in love with?" Brandon said. "More importantly, who would be in love with me?"

"You always think everybody hates you."

And so the evening slogged forward—moments of normality, glimpses of the old days, followed by odd hesitations and pauses of unexplainable awkwardness. A barrier had sprung up in the few short weeks since they'd last been together—a cloud or haze that muffled their natural affection for one another and made the conversation halting and stilted where it had once been easy and open.

When it finally grew late enough that Brandon felt he could leave without suspicion or hurt feelings, the three of them gathered in the kitchen with similar looks of befuddlement on their faces. Kate kept pressing leftovers on Brandon (she didn't believe him when he told her he was eating better now than he ever had at his father's house), and Chad stood back a bit, shuffling and tentative, wanting to say *something* to his best friend but completely unsure what. The Bowmans pressed Brandon with overly cheerful assurances that they'd all have to do this again real soon, and Brandon reiterated a few times too many what a great time he'd had, how awesome it had been to see them both again, and then finally he was back out into the night, able to breathe, able to release some of the twitchy foreign energy that had pricked at him all night and made it nearly impossible for him to enjoy himself.

Overhead, an enormous full moon floated high in a cloudless sky, its brilliance magnified by the biting January air. The first full moon since *that* full moon, Brandon realized, and all at once the awkwardness of the evening fell into place.

As much as he'd wanted to be with the Bowmans again, it was nothing compared to how much he wanted to repeat the experience of Christmas Eve. That night was a constant presence, a living entity almost, calling him, always calling, no matter what else he was doing. School had become a blur, his work at Saint Ignatius was mindless enough to hold no distraction, and his only friend in the world had given him space enough and time to adjust to an even more solitary existence than before. Brandon's entire field of focus had narrowed to that singular event—Christmas Eve, and the dark country roads, and the strange wolf that had smiled a terrifying invitation at him.

Climbing into his car, Brandon glanced back at the Bowman house. He could see Chad and Kate through the frost-edged windows, laughing, rummaging through cupboards for snacks, completely over the awkwardness of the evening already. Like so many before them, Brandon realized, the Bowmans forgot all about him as soon as he left their sight.

Chad and Kate would have been mortified to know that Brandon was thinking such thoughts. Either of them would have run after him, tackled him on the snowy sidewalk, thrown themselves over the hood of the Mustang to prevent his escape. But they were clueless—as people often are—at the precise moment they might have made a difference.

Brandon started his car and disappeared into the frigid darkness. The Bowmans made cocoa and watched an old movie on TV. High above them all, inscrutably distant, the moon shone down with a cold bluish glow that gave everything it touched a razor's edge. A solitary wolf filled the night with its lonely, mournful howl, but the Mustang's engine was too loud, and the wolf too far away, and on this particular night Brandon did not hear its ethereal plea.

February

For several days at the beginning of February, Daryl and his cronies reinvigorated their campaign against Brandon for reasons unknown. The bullying had always come in waves, rising and falling to the rhythms of some pattern known only to Brandon's tormentors.

The latest cycle began quietly. New graffiti in an upstairs hallway. A locker-room accusation of "queeritude" (whatever that might be). Some perceived infraction for which Daryl swore to "kick Brandon's queer red ass all the way to Duluth."

The ass-kicking never materialized, but Daryl did manage to blindside Brandon in one of the boys' bathrooms one afternoon with a shove that sent him careening into the room's persistent pool of urine. Several of Daryl's buddies pelted Brandon with soggy wads of toilet paper while Daryl ripped a soap dispenser from its mooring above the sink and squirted Brandon with pink, stinking glop from head to toe.

"Clean yourself up," Daryl said. "I don't know which part of you stinks worse—the queer half or the Indian half."

Sated, the mob dispersed. The outbreak ended as mysteriously as it had begun. Loud threats settled into whispers. Icy stares dissolved into something like selective blindness. Instead of hatred, the mob began to look at Brandon with a lack of interest that was almost more chilling. Moments after Daryl's latest outburst, Brandon ceased to exist for them again.

Until the next time.

. . .

"So what do you plan to do about school?" Father Holloway asked one night over dinner. Brandon's deal with Holloway and the church included room and board, and he had been thrilled to discover that "board" meant three square meals a day, prepared by Mrs. Dolores McGowan, a fat Irish widow who also lived at the rectory.

Brandon had his mouth full of Mrs. McGowan's amazing vegan chili, and wasn't sure he would have known how to answer even if he could. Father Holloway was pointedly *not* taking another bite of his own chili, however, and he'd leveled his calm blue eyes at Brandon in exactly the way he stared down inattentive parishioners during a sermon.

When Brandon finally managed to swallow, he said, in all innocence, "I'm not sure what you mean. I've been going to school every day. I may have cut out a bit early one day, but I needed—"

Holloway smiled indulgently, and Mrs. McGowan offered a gentle rolling laugh that floated over the table like the aroma of her fresh-baked morning pastries. "I think Father means the college, dear," she said.

Brandon flushed at Mrs. McGowan's offhand term of endearment. She was the type of woman who called *everyone* "dear" or "dearie" or "sweetheart" or "honey," and Brandon knew the words were little more than a tic. But that sort of thing always made him feel uncomfortable—like small beetles skittering up and down his spine.

Father Holloway snagged another biscuit from the platter in the center of the table. "I did mean 'the college' as Mrs. McGowan so charmingly puts it," he said. "I should have said, what do you plan to do *after* high school? I assume you've applied a few places."

Brandon felt a warm rush of blood first to his ears and then to the back of his neck. "I, uh…haven't really thought about that," he said. "I don't have any money for school."

Holloway leaned back in his chair and covered his empty bowl with his napkin, as if to physically distance himself from the temptation of a third helping. "Ah yes, the money," he said. "It does always come down to that in this world, doesn't it?"

"Afraid so, Father," Brandon said.

"Still, you're making a few bucks here at the church. You don't seem to buy a lot of things. Your appetite is too good for you to be on drugs. You must be able to save a little each week…"

"It's the car," Brandon said. He almost added a colorful expletive but he was getting better at not swearing when he was at the church. "It's paid for, so that helps. But the insurance and upkeep are just endless sinkholes."

"Ah, to be eighteen and paying one's own insurance," Holloway said. "Still, you can't expect to hang around Talbot doing odd jobs all your life. There are scholarships and grants, loans…maybe Mrs. McGowan could even be persuaded to dig into her casino fund for such a far worthier cause." He threw a wink at the old woman, who blushed almost as brightly as Brandon.

"I know," Brandon said. "There's always a way…"

"You don't sound like you much believe that philosophy."

"It's just been shoved down my throat by teachers and school counselors for so long…and yet every time I actually *need* help, it's like people can't move fast enough to slam their doors right in my face."

"You came here when you needed help, and we didn't slam the door."

Brandon smiled. "True," he said. "You've done nothing but right by me, and I can never even *hope* to thank—"

"Whoa there," Holloway said. "I hope it didn't seem like I was angling for yet another thank-you."

"Maybe a little," Mrs. McGowan said. She rose and started clearing dishes from the table. Brandon moved to help, but she gestured him back down with a stern, maternal head-nod and then gave a second nod toward Father Holloway that clearly said, "Get on with it, you."

Holloway laughed and watched Mrs. McGowan depart for the kitchen. "She scares the hell out of me sometimes," he said, but with such obvious affection that Brandon almost felt warmed himself by the second-hand glow. "Anyway, as I was saying, your teachers and counselors are right and there *is* always a way, even if sometimes it takes a while to find. I mean, we're not talking Harvard here, right?"

Brandon smiled, remembering his last report card—the last one he *would* receive, come to think of it, before he graduated in May. Nope, definitely not Harvard material.

"You know, there are three excellent community colleges each within fifty or sixty miles of here," Holloway said. "You could do a couple of years at one of them, maybe move on to the University system later. And then there are vocational or technical schools—"

"Last I heard, community college or vo-tech cost money too," Brandon said.

"Again with the damned money. I'm trying to tell you to make some plans, and *then* we'll worry how to pay for them."

Brandon traced the interlocking rings of moisture his water glass had made on Mrs. McGowan's linen tablecloth. How to make Father Holloway understand? He'd tried a few times with Chad and Kate—hell, he'd even given it a whirl once or twice with one badgering teacher or another. He knew they listened, but it was as if their life experiences had been so completely different from his own that his thoughts were incomprehensible to them.

"Come on, Brandon," Holloway said. "Talk to me."

"It just all seems so...out of the realm of possibility for me," Brandon said. "I know things work out all the time for other people. I know other people make plans and goals, have dreams, and that God or the Great Spirit or whatever lets those things come to pass on a fairly regular basis. But not for me. Never for me."

"No?" Holloway said.

It was the type of question Brandon easily could have interpreted as mocking, but he read only sincere interest and compassion in the priest's eyes. He took a deep breath. "It's like I don't exist on the same plane as other people sometimes. I walk by people on the street, and it's like I'm invisible. Or not invisible, exactly, but just a shadow they pass with barely a notice. They flick their eyes in my general direction, and then almost instantly dismiss me. And when something *forces* them to interact with me, like at school or whatever, that just makes things worse. All my life, so many people have taken one look at me and just hated me instantly. I can actually feel it as it's happening—like a chemical reaction or something."

"A pheromone?" Holloway said.

"I'm not sure what that is."

"A pheromone is a scent or a substance—some invisible signal—that many creatures in the animal kingdom give off for one reason or another. To tell others of their kind they're ready to mate, or fight, or whatever. It's believed people give them off as well, although the body of research in that arena is fairly spotty, so far as I know."

Brandon offered a wan smile. "So you think I'm giving off some scent that tells people 'hate this guy on sight'?"

Holloway's laugh was booming and genuine. Normally, being laughed at for something he was being serious about would have wounded Brandon deeply—or enraged him. But Holloway's laugh only made him smile.

"Not quite what I meant," Holloway said. "But who knows? 'There are more things in heaven and earth, Horatio, than are dreamt of in your philosophy'..."

"Is that from the Bible?"

"Even better," Holloway said. "Shakespeare."

From the kitchen, the sounds of Mrs. McGowan's efficient loading of the dishwasher were accompanied by her soft, almost tuneless humming of an old Irish drinking song. Brandon squinted at Father Holloway. "College, huh?" he said.

"College," Holloway repeated, his version more a command. "Stop worrying. Stop thinking this is going to end the second you finish high school. We're not going to throw you to the wolves, you know."

Throw you to the wolves. The expression made Brandon smile. Father Holloway interpreted this to mean he'd won Brandon over to all the possibilities that still lay before him— college, a real life, a chance to leave behind all the bullshit and pain of his first eighteen years on the planet.

"You know," Holloway said. "Someone was asking about you just last Sunday. A farmer—Joe Westcott, from out on County Road 6. Said he might have some work this spring for a willing and able young man if I knew of any. That would be some money for school right there. Then, of course, there's the Church—we should be able to scrounge up something. And I know a couple of businessmen in town who haven't been doing their part to pay things forward lately—"

"You do realize you're just plain browbeating him now," Mrs. McGowan said, swooping in from the kitchen to see if she'd missed any dishes on either of her last two trips.

"No, it's okay," Brandon said. "I probably need someone to browbeat me once in a while."

"Well, you definitely came to the right place for that, dearie."

Holloway cast the widow a dour look, but all three of them knew there was no real consternation in it.

"Farmer Joe, huh?" Brandon said. "Yeah, I know his place." He'd heard some stories about Joe Westcott around town, but he also knew people often liked to talk just to hear the sound of their own voices. Especially about anyone who was different from the norm in any way. He'd experienced that himself more times than he cared to remember. He'd certainly be willing to give things a shot with Farmer Joe—and who could say, this might even signal yet another step down the new path that God or the Great Spirit or whatever was so diligently trying to place in front of him.

Maybe, maybe, maybe, blinked a tiny neon sign in the back of Brandon's subconscious.

That evening, for the first time in weeks, he didn't take his nightly drive down the dark country roads, and February's full moon came and went almost unnoticed by the winter-dulled residents of Talbot.

Almost.

March

The first Saturday in March, Brandon went to work for Farmer Joe. He'd arranged to work at the church after school and on Sundays, and at the farm on Saturdays. Once the snow cleared and the weather warmed up, Joe would need more of Brandon's time to help get his fields plowed and his crops in the ground. Until then, he said, one day per week would be fine.

Brandon found it strange to be working on a farm while the ground was still covered with snow, but Joe assured him there was plenty to do on a farm year-round—a farmer's work was never done, according to Farmer Joe. This didn't necessarily jibe with Joe's own approach to work, Brandon noticed. Once Brandon knew what he was supposed to do for the day, Joe generally disappeared into the house for a few hours. He'd reappear at lunchtime, carrying sandwiches for Brandon and maybe a thermos of soup, looking sleep-creased and puffy-eyed. He'd sit on a stool in one corner of the shed and open the first of what would eventually turn out to be a goodly number of beers to be put away over the course of the afternoon. He sometimes puttered at something on the workbench, and he was always willing to show Brandon which part of a machine needed to be oiled, or which tool needed to be repaired or whatever. But generally Joe was either inside the house or over on his stool, drinking and yacking about whatever came into his head while Brandon worked.

Brandon didn't mind. He supposed Joe looked on Saturday as his one day off each week—who could blame him for wanting to slack a little? Besides, the work Brandon was doing was mindless and not even physically taxing—he got more of a workout shoveling snow off the sidewalk at Saint Ignatius, or carrying supplies from the church basement over to the rectory for Mrs. McGowan.

The shed where Brandon did the majority of his work was clean and heated and better organized than Brandon would have given Joe credit for. The barn—which Brandon liked even better—was quiet and dimly lit, almost a cave. Brandon found the barn calm and peaceful, full of an intoxicating mixture of foreign yet strangely familiar smells—hay, cow, gasoline, old wood. Small birds fluttered high in the rafters and every now and again a large, unseen owl would let out a low, tremulous *wooooooooo* that sent mice and other small somethings scurrying for hidey-holes.

Joe's scrawny cows were a constant warm presence in the barn as well, shuffling softly in the straw at their feet, swishing their tails against flies that wouldn't actually be there again until spring, and once in a while lowing out a vague bovine greeting or complaint in their deep, strangely melodic voices. Brandon assumed the cows were mainly there for Farmer Joe's own meat supply throughout the winter; Joe didn't seem to be fattening them up for market, and he never said anything about having to get up early every morning to milk them for one of the local dairies.

Brandon had little knowledge of what a farm was supposed to look like or how it was supposed to operate, but even he could tell that the Westcott farm had never been a particularly successful business proposition. Certainly not in the five years since Joe's parents had died within a few months of each other—

his father from a massive heart attack out in the fields one day, his mother of "the female cancer," as Joe called it when he told Brandon the story. Joe had inherited a dwindling family farm and dwindled it even further.

Brandon realized that Joe was more lonely than anything else, and he'd really been hired just to listen to Joe talk, but that was fine by him. The job paid fifteen bucks an hour, and Joe had even said he could use the barn or one of the outlying sheds if he ever needed somewhere warm to work on his Mustang. He could listen to plenty of the farmer's blather for a deal like that—he'd certainly listened to enough of it from his own father, for a lot less money (*none*, to be precise), back when he'd still lived at home and his father had made him help out down at the garage now and again "to pay his damned way for once."

If Farmer Joe sometimes let his hand rest on Brandon's shoulder for longer than seemed necessary, or if he reached around Brandon to get a tool off the workbench and ended up pressing his full body weight against Brandon for balance...well, he seemed as oblivious of it as Brandon was overly conscious. Brandon rarely liked to be touched—it made him feel shivery and exposed—but he knew this about himself, and figured he was being hypersensitive. Joe Westcott was the type of person who had no sense of anyone else's personal space, the kind of man who stood too close while talking, who touched and felt and patted and rubbed, and didn't even realize he was doing it.

No doubt it was exactly this ignorance of physical boundaries that had prompted the talk in town about Farmer Joe, but Brandon never felt any true menace, and there *was* the fifteen bucks an hour to consider. Fifteen bucks an hour was a big deal in a town like Talbot, and fifteen bucks an hour times the ten hours he spent at the Westcott farm every Saturday meant a hundred and fifty bucks in cold, hard, tax-free cash in his pocket each week. Brandon could put up with a fair amount of ultimately harmless touching for a deal as sweet as that. Besides, he thought, it wasn't like he was getting any action anywhere else.

. . .

Chad *was* getting action—almost more than he knew what to do with. Once his initial obsession with Nikki had cooled to a dull, not-quite-painful-but-not-quite-pleasant warmth in the pit of his stomach, Chad realized that what he wanted more than any additional action was to tell someone about the action he'd already experienced. Or, more specifically, to tell his best friend about the unprecedented turn for the better his previously Spartan sexual existence had taken seemingly out of the blue.

He found Brandon in the hall after classes one day and fell into step as smoothly as if it had been five minutes since they'd last spoken instead of nearly five weeks. "Dude," he said. "Walk with me."

Brandon darted a suspicious glance toward Chad, then focused his eyes squarely on the floor in front of him. "I have to get to work," he said.

"Who doesn't?" Chad said. "But we haven't talked in weeks, man. I need some face-time with my main dude."

Brandon thought about telling Chad where he could go and what he could do to himself there, but one look at his friend's open, smiling face melted his first rush of bitterness before he had a chance to truly enjoy it. "I guess I could use a ride to the church," he said.

Now that he was living at Saint Ignatius, Brandon was close enough to the school to walk. He'd done so even on the coldest days of the winter, not because he particularly enjoyed the daily potential for frostbite or the heart-healthy trek down the hill in the morning and up the hill in the afternoon, but because he otherwise spent too much of every day thinking about what might be happening to his car in the school parking lot. Even as high school was winding down to its final harried weeks, even now that his job at Saint Ignatius had made him even less of a presence at the school than he'd been before, Daryl and his cronies were always on the lookout for some new way in which they might torment him one last time before his path diverged from theirs forever. And when everything was said and done, that heap of a Mustang was really the only thing of value he had in the entire world.

He walked with Chad to the Jeep and they sat waiting for the defrost fan to clear the windows. Chad opened the glove compartment and brought out a joint, but Brandon only raised an eyebrow. "You want me to get baked before I go to work at the *church*?"

"They'll just think it's incense or something."

Brandon laughed, happy despite himself to be with Chad again after all their time apart. "I'll pass this time," he said. "But thanks."

Chad thought about making a snarky comment, but realized his mom wouldn't buy an incense story any more than the priest would. She never got all that worked up over a little weed—it was organic, after all, and *she'd* certainly smoked a joint or two in her day—but he didn't want to get all mellow and toasty if Brandon was just going to sit there and watch. *Later*, he thought. *Tonight with Nikki.* The image that popped into his head made him remember why he'd sought out Brandon in the first place. "Man, you wouldn't *believe* what's been going on in my life lately," he said. "My dick is so exhausted it's ready to fall—"

"If you're gonna sit here and tell me how amazing it is to be having sex with Nikki Langley every night while I'm sitting alone at the church, I swear I'll get out of the Jeep and just walk home."

Brandon's tone deflated Chad's enthusiasm instantly, and prompted a realization Chad knew he should have had weeks earlier. "Dude, are you *mad* at me?" he said. Even as he spoke, he realized how stupid he sounded. Of course Brandon was mad—Chad had abandoned him as soon as Nikki had entered the picture. That's how Brandon would see it, anyway.

"Who *are* you, anyway?" Brandon said. "I swear, I don't even recognize you anymore."

"Whoa, wait, hold up a minute," Chad said. "Let me catch up here." He held up his hands in surrender. "I knew things were kinda weird between us, but I didn't know it was anything serious. I would've been on you so fast—you know I would. You should have said something."

Brandon wanted to say something now, but his throat was closing, his brain shutting down. He felt oily, burning shame and anger welling up behind his eyes. All the hurt and betrayal of the past few months threatened to boil up out of someplace so deep inside him he hadn't been aware it existed. He thought he might vomit; was terrified once he started he might never stop.

"Oh man," Chad said. "Stupid fucking me, man. I am such an asshole sometimes."

Chad called his mom at the Center and told her he wouldn't be in to work that afternoon. Then he called Nikki and told her he wouldn't be able to see her that night. Finally, he called the church and told Mrs. McGowan that he was kidnapping his old friend for the evening and to please tell Father Holloway that Brandon would work double-time the next day to make up for it. "I would imagine the Father will do just fine lifting a finger around here himself for once," the widow McGowan said.

Chad threw the vehicle into drive and headed south out of town. "Seriously," he said. "I don't want to be another one of the jerks in your life. You gotta tell me when I'm not paying enough attention." He put in an old Springsteen CD and let the Boss sing loud while the Jeep ate up the miles that had built up between them. By the time they pulled into Duncton nearly an hour later, the young men were once again on solid footing with one another. "Twin sons of different mothers," Kate had called them once. "Two hearts—the darker and the lighter—sharing a single, solitary beat." No one who ever met the two of them, even for the briefest span of time, needed to ask which heart belonged to which boy.

At a restaurant called Pizza Portage, they ordered an extra-large garbage pizza and a pitcher of Coke. They talked about school, and graduation, and what might be waiting beyond. Chad had already been accepted to the University of Minnesota in Minneapolis, and was thrilled to hear that Father Holloway had convinced Brandon to get his own applications into the world. "Man, my mom is gonna freak," he said around a mouthful of burnt crust. "Both her boys going off to college at once."

They talked about the Wolf Research Center, and Saint Ignatius, and whether or not Brandon had heard from his father (he hadn't). They talked about pretty much everything except Nikki, and Chad was getting ready to bring up even that potentially taboo subject when Brandon said something that stopped the conversation cold.

"You're working for Farmer Joe now too?" Chad said. "You're working for that—" He stopped himself. He was pretty sure Brandon wasn't gay, despite what guys like Daryl Reisling said, but there was no sense calling Brandon's new employer names just when Brandon was getting back to relative normal tonight.

Brandon was way ahead of him. "Yeah, I've heard all those stories too," he said. "But it's not like he's tried anything, and he's paying me a fortune to do practically nothing."

"How much?"

"Fifteen bucks an hour."

Chad offered a low whistle. "Man, I'd let him blow *me* for fifteen bucks an hour."

Brandon laughed, and then, just to show that everything was truly alright between them again, said, "You don't need Farmer Joe—you've got Nikki Langley, right? Now what's all this about your dick falling off?"

. . .

On the drive back to Talbot, Brandon leaned over and turned the volume on the stereo low enough so as to be nothing more than an alien whisper behind the noise of the Jeep's engine and the steady shoosh of the tires against the cold blacktop. This time in the parking lot, the boys *had* shared a joint, and the weed had loosened something inside Brandon until he knew it was finally time to tell Chad about Christmas Eve. That night felt so long ago now—a lifetime ago.

"What's up?" Chad said.

For a moment, Brandon was lost to the vague shapes of tall pine trees rushing past them on either side—as if the trees were moving and the Jeep was standing perfectly still. The trees leaned in to form a tunnel, and the Jeep was inside the tunnel, and very far away—miles and miles away—a round silver orb was beginning to climb over the distant horizon. A glowing thing, a ghostly beacon, sitting there on the cusp of the night sky. Calling. Pulling at some invisible string that connected his very soul to the streaming darkness outside the Jeep.

"Dude, what's up?" Chad said again, and this time Brandon managed to turn away from the window and focus his attention on the idea that had blossomed inside his head despite the hum of the Jeep and all the whooshing darkness.

"How about a little detour on the way home?" he said. "I think I need to show you something."

. . .

Amazingly, Brandon didn't have any trouble finding the location again. Landmarks meant little in the sharp darkness of the northern Minnesota night, and the roads had been covered with snow and plowed clean again ten or fifteen times since Brandon's initial drive in December. But even with his eyes closed and his head against the headrest, he knew almost to the foot when they'd reached the exact spot.

"Stop here," he said—and Chad brought them to a halt and threw the Jeep into park. Brandon reached over and turned the key. "This is it," he said. "Last stop, everybody out."

They stepped out of the Jeep and stood on the frozen road beneath an enormous silver-blue full moon. There was no wind and no sound save for the soft crunch of gravel beneath their shoes and the whisper of their exhaled breath. "It's cold out here," Chad said. He rocked back and forth to get some blood flowing into his feet and shoved his bare hands into the pockets of his ski jacket. He thought about going back to the Jeep for his stocking cap, but then Brandon's voice broke the stillness:

"It was cold out here that night too."

Chad turned and was surprised to see Brandon staring into the distance with a fervor that looked almost religious. Even wrapped in a thick layer of down and thermal insulating fabric, Chad was shivering, but Brandon, wearing only a T-shirt and his ratty leather jacket, almost glowed with a weird internal heat. "What night was that?" Chad asked.

"Christmas Eve," Brandon said. "When I left your house that night, I came out here and saw something amazing. And I think I finally need to tell somebody about it."

Chad shrugged. "Hit me."

Brandon told Chad the story exactly as he remembered it—the road, the realtor's sign, the animal loping up out of the ditch. Chad listened silently, the way he always did, and only when Brandon uttered the word "wolf" did he feel the need to interrupt. "You saw a wolf out here? And it just came up to the car? Dude, that is so cool—do you know how rare something like that is? It must have a been a scout or something—I'd have to check the map back at the Center, but I think the Damarchan Pack was in this area around that time. Was he tagged? Did he have a radio collar? It could have been—"

"There's more," Brandon said.

He told Chad the rest of the story—the wolf's smile, the business of standing up and walking—and watched Chad's enthusiasm wilt like a child's balloon losing its helium. When he was finished, Chad frowned. "Man, you get me all excited for what sounds like a genuine encounter with a wolf in the wild, and instead you're trying to sell me some crazy werewolf story."

"It really happened," Brandon said.

"Dude," Chad said. "You know that bud we smoked earlier? You still feeling it like I am?"

Brandon shrugged. "Yeah. So?"

"Think about the last time you had any of it."

A frown furrowed Brandon's forehead, as if his head knew before he did what was coming next.

"We were smoking the same stuff on Christmas Eve. Up in my room while Mom was frosting your cake, remember? And we came down, and it was all she and I could do to keep you from licking up all the frosting right then and there."

Brandon's frown worked its way down to his mouth. His body finally felt the cold, and he shivered and pulled his jacket tighter around him.

"Listen," Chad continued. "You were pretty toasted that night. And it was your birthday, which is always traumatic for you anyway. And you were freaked out about us giving you the new tires for your car..."

Brandon flushed. He was glad for the cover of the night and the color vagaries produced by the moonlight.

"You tore out of our house, freaked as usual about your birthday and the holiday, you came out here, you had one of the coolest and rarest experiences a person can ever have in the wild, and your crazy stoned mind just added a weird little twist of its own. That's all."

Brandon didn't know whether to laugh or cry. Of *course* that's what had happened. He'd seen a plain old wolf—the same animal he saw every time he went to the Center, the same animal he'd seen three or four times in the wild—and his psychotic, crazed, and, granted, chemically enhanced mind had created an entire story around it. A story that had wound him nearly to the breaking point for weeks. A story that had induced him to wear who knew how many miles off his beautiful new tires as he drove the dark country roads for nights on end throughout January and February.

Chad placed a hand on Brandon's shoulder and gave a gentle squeeze. "You saw a wolf, man," he said.

A *wolf-man*, Brandon thought, and now he did laugh. He could be such an idiot sometimes. Thank God or the Great Spirit or whatever for Chad. And Kate. Without the Bowmans, Brandon knew he would have been irretrievably lost long ago.

"Damn," he said. "A werewolf would have been really cool, though, don't you think?"

Now it was Chad's turn to laugh. "Let's get you home, stoner-boy." He shook Brandon good-naturedly by the shoulder. "Methinks you need some serious church time under your belt before you go straight to Hell."

"One minute," Brandon said. Without another word, they turned to look at the moon. They stood for a long time, silent and together, moonlight flowing over them like a cosmic waterfall. When they had both started to shiver in earnest, they climbed into the Jeep and headed down the dark country roads that would lead them finally, inevitably, wherever the rest of their lives might take them.

Had they known this was the last time they would ever stand together beneath a brilliant full moon, they might, despite the cold, have lingered.

Had they known the kind of changes the moon would soon be bringing to each of their lives, it's nice to believe they might never have gone home at all.

April

Farmer Joe made his move against Brandon toward the middle of April. *Lulled* was the word that came instantly to Brandon's mind, because by that point he'd no longer been imagining any sort of ulterior motives on the part of his employer. He didn't give the matter a second thought when Joe opened the side door of the barn, didn't even look up from the carburetor he was piecing back together on the workbench in the corner. He muttered a soft "Hey" and didn't bother to listen for Joe's greeting in return. A split second later, Joe was on top of him.

Joe Westcott was two inches taller than Brandon and outweighed him by eighty pounds. Despite his lackadaisical approach to work and the case of beer he downed every afternoon, a lifetime of farm work had left his body, even at forty-six, still relatively solid and much stronger than it appeared at first glance. He slammed into Brandon from behind, pinning the younger man against the workbench and sending carburetor parts flying. Brandon felt the air rush out of his lungs in a convulsive heave, and then one of Joe's arms wrapped around his throat while the other snaked around his chest and pulled him back against the farmer's bull-like torso. Joe's beery breath was warm and damp against his right ear. "I know you've been waiting a long time for this," he said.

Joe flipped Brandon around so they stood face to face, his grimy hands clamped tightly over Brandon's wrists. Brandon could feel the sharp edge of the workbench pressing into his spine, and some tool or carburetor part digging into the soft flesh over his kidney. Joe's mouth was all over his face—licking, kissing, biting in tiny nips like an annoying little dog. He could feel Joe's razor stubble strafing like heavy-grit sandpaper, feel Joe's thigh muscles grinding against him. Then he could feel another part of Joe as well, pulsing against his leg, his groin, his hip as Joe attempted to turn him around once again, no doubt in order to bend him more properly over the workbench. That's when Brandon began to fight back in earnest.

He wrenched one hand free, and aimed a wide, swinging roundhouse at Joe's head. The blow glanced ineffectually off Joe's chin, and bought Brandon a resounding, dead-on cuff in return that filled his ear with a hollow ringing and caused tiny lights to dance across his field of vision like a swarm of fireflies.

"Stop pretending you don't want this," Joe said. "You've wanted this exact thing since the first day you came here." He brought one hand down to clamp vise-like on Brandon's testicles. Brandon gave a breathless yelp and tried to pull away, but Joe only squeezed harder and then brought the hand up in another deft blow to the side of Brandon's head. "Knock it off, you little tease," he said, his mouth so close to Brandon's that Brandon thought he could taste the words more than hear them.

A surge of adrenaline—bitter and metallic in his throat—allowed Brandon to kick out with a force he'd never imagined, and luck brought his knee up and forward with enough connecting power against the man's groin to stagger Farmer Joe back a few steps. Brandon reached out blindly and came up with the carburetor he'd been working on. He wailed it at Joe as hard as he could, but fear and anger had messed with his aim, and the metal made only glancing contact with the larger man's forehead. Nevertheless, it opened a small, triangular divot of flesh above Joe's left eye from which spouted a veritable geyser of brilliant red blood. Joe's howl of pain and rage reminded Brandon of the kind of tantrum a five-year-old might throw when denied some particular treat from the store. He backed toward the door of the barn. Farmer Joe, he was pleased to note, appeared disinclined to make any further move in his direction.

"You still owe me for today," Brandon said when he reached the door. His voice came out shaky, but didn't actually break until he added, almost as an afterthought: "Fucking asshole."

This made Joe grin for some reason, his mouth opening like a razor slash and blood seeping in to paint his teeth a rich, velvety red. "You know you want it," he said.

Brandon turned and ran. Farmer Joe's final words followed him out into the warm April afternoon: "If you say one word about this to anyone, I swear I'll kill you where you stand."

. . .

Driving slowly, nursing his aching balls and nearly catatonic with shame and anger and embarrassment, Brandon knew he *wouldn't* ever tell anyone. That was the worst part of the whole experience. To know he would never admit what had happened in the barn that day because somehow, no matter how much he protested, no matter how innocent he truly was, the world that had always despised him would find some way to bring the whole situation back around to reflect badly on him.

Even Chad couldn't be trusted with something as ugly and embarrassing as this—Brandon was certain his friend would never be able to look at him again if he knew what had happened. The only image he'd ever be able to see after that would be Farmer Joe grinding his body against Brandon's body, Farmer Joe forcing his mouth against Brandon's mouth, Farmer

Joe ready, willing, and clearly able to *fuck* Brandon right there in front of the cows and the owl and the small scurrying things that lived deep in the straw. *Right there in front of God or the Great Spirit or whatever*, Brandon thought.

A mile down the road, Brandon felt a warm slither of wetness on his chin and glanced at his reflection in the rearview mirror. He'd bitten a jagged wound in his lower lip and it was bleeding freely, the blood flowing from his mouth and dripping onto the faded Green Day T-shirt he'd borrowed from Chad's closet and hadn't gotten around to returning. *Ruined now*, he thought. *Another thing completely ruined.*

With a snarl, he slammed his fist against anything he could find to make contact with—the steering wheel, the dashboard, some random car parts scattered across the passenger seat—and it was only when he heard the sharp snap of breaking bone and felt the first prick of splintery fire deep inside his hand that he finally calmed and pointed the car in a different direction. Silent and resigned, hand screaming in pain, he drove to the nearest emergency room—fifty miles away in Duncton—and told them he'd had an accident while fixing his car. The on-call physician didn't even try to pretend that he could not have cared less had he tried.

. . .

Brandon tweaked his story just a little on the drive home—"I was working on the Mustang and the hood fell on my hand"—and was pleased in some odd, indefinable way when no one questioned the lie even for a moment. "Dude, that heap's gonna kill you one of these days," Chad said, and Father Holloway placed his hand gently on Brandon's cast and intoned solemnly, "Boy, heal thyself. The lawn needs raking."

Brandon tried not to think about his hand too much, or the circumstances that had brought about the injury, and thankfully there were plenty of other things to keep his mind occupied. Six more weeks of school, six more weeks until graduation, and the need to start studying for final exams would no doubt rear its ugly head any day now. His head felt completely empty, devoid of any information he might ever have learned. Certainly empty of anything his teachers might have tried to push into it this final semester.

Much to his own surprise, however, two different schools had deemed Brandon worthy of acceptance into their fall classes. One was a community college in Ely, the other a combination college and vocational school in Grand Rapids. Not Harvard, by any means, but now that the possibility of post-high-school education was real, he supposed he needed to give some serious thought as to what he might want to go to school *for* and how he might pay for it once he actually got there.

No one bothered to ask about his job at the Westcott farm, and Brandon didn't volunteer any information. He continued to disappear from Saint Ignatius for most of the day every Saturday, and on the couple of Sundays that Joe came into town for church, Brandon made a point of locating him in the pews right away and then never looking in that direction again.

One afternoon while he was fiddling with the Mustang's choke in the Saint Ignatius parking lot, Joe pulled up behind him in a new and almost blindingly shiny half-ton pickup. As Brandon turned to face him, Joe leaned out the window and pointedly stared at Brandon's groin. "If you were still working for me," he said, "you might be able to afford something that actually *runs* once in a while."

Before Brandon could formulate a suitable response, Joe dropped a small fold of bills at his feet and drove away again.

Brandon fought himself for a solid thirty seconds before picking up the money, but what the hell—was he just gonna leave it there to blow away down the hill and across the fields?

The bundle was three fifties paper-clipped together with a small Post-It note stuck to the top one: *Final wages.* And one more fifty with a note of its own: *Bonus for special services.* Brandon felt a sour ooze of bile percolate in the back of his throat, but he pocketed all four bills nonetheless. He'd just make damned sure he spent every last cent of it before the stores in town had closed for the day.

. . .

As April drew toward an unnaturally warm close, a single phrase began to play through Brandon's head randomly, seemingly of its own accord. *I'm gonna make it. I actually think I'm gonna make it.*

What "it" was never clearly defined itself in his mind. Make it through high school? Make it out of Talbot? Brandon couldn't say. He knew only that some switch had flipped inside his brain, and at the oddest of moments he'd tune in and find himself listening to *I'm gonna make it, I actually think I'm gonna make it.*

It helped that he was friends again with Chad. And for whatever reason Nikki was even being nice to him—or at least tolerating him. He'd tagged along on a couple of movie dates with the two of them, and never once felt like Nikki would rather have seen him dead in the street than sitting in the seat next to her. He'd even gotten a genuine laugh or two out of her, helping her tease Chad with embarrassing information from Chad's past that she otherwise would not have been privy to.

Even the other kids at school had mellowed out for the most part. Perhaps all of their fear and loathing was directed at finals and financial aid applications right now, or perhaps Nikki's apparent acceptance of him had changed his status in everyone else's eyes in some weird, high-school-caste-structure sort of way. Brandon knew only that he no longer heard quite so many whispered declarations of hatred in the hallways, no longer came home with quite so many "accidental" bruises. One day he had even looked across the cafeteria at lunch and found himself being looked back at by Theresa Bennett, one of Nikki's inner circle, with something that suspiciously *didn't* look like unadulterated loathing.

On April twenty-second, Brandon came home from school, took care of a few things at the church, showered, changed into clean clothes, and told Mrs. McGowan he would be eating dinner at the Bowman house that night. His car keys jangled a jaunty tune in the front pocket of his jeans as he headed for the parking lot.

Keys, and a jaunty tune—but no car. The Mustang wasn't there.

His first instinct was to think he'd driven it to school that morning and then forgotten and walked back home. But he knew that wasn't the case. He remembered seeing it in its usual spot as he was leaving for school, and thinking to himself that it was too nice a day to drive anyway.

The slightest whisper of doubt wafted through his mind, but he refused to hear it—at least for the time being. The Mustang wasn't worth stealing—anyone with any sense would have seen that the second they took a close look—but he could imagine Chad or even Kate "borrowing" the car, either as some sort of elaborate joke or, more likely, to make yet another improvement on it (like the new tires) that they knew he couldn't afford himself.

Or, of course... his brain tried to cut in, but Brandon shut it down right away. He wouldn't go there. Not yet.

Instead, he shoved his hands into his pockets—mainly to stop the keys from jingling their happy reminder—and started walking down the hill toward Main Street.

He thought he would get to Main Street and be able to hitch a ride to the Bowman house. Or, if he had to, he could find a phone and call Chad to pick him up. Best case, Chad would pull up in the Mustang, laughing and beaming at whatever great joke he'd just managed to pull off, or whatever awesome new improvement he'd just made to Brandon's beloved heap.

Worst case...

But Brandon had only to hit Main Street and walk three blocks to the north to see the worst case with his own eyes. There was his father's garage—Turner's Talbot Auto—and there, outside the front door, was the Mustang.

The whisper in his mind grew louder, but Brandon still didn't want to hear it. Even now, he wanted to imagine other possibilities for as long as he could.

The service bay door was open, and his father was just finishing up an oil change on some beat-up old Cadillac. He wiped grease from his hands onto an even greasier rag and hooked one finger into the breast pocket of his coveralls to snake out a cigarette. Brandon hoped beyond hope that he'd light it and the grease would burst instantly into flame, but no such luck. The cigarette remained unlit, stuck in one corner of his father's mouth, and the gray eyes tracked Brandon's approach without blinking.

"So what's the deal?" Brandon said. "You tuning up my car as a graduation present or something?" He tried to keep his tone light, knowing the slightest misstep would turn the conversation into one holy mother of a fuck-all before he even knew what was happening.

His father stared at him, the cigarette bobbing at the corner of his mouth like some weird paper tumor. "*My* car, I think you mean," he said.

For the first time in his life, Brandon understood what people meant when they said they "saw red." An oil slick of pure crimson cascaded over the world, and he had to clench his hands into tight fists and shove them even deeper into his pockets to keep from taking a swing.

"I paid for that car," he said. "I worked my ass off three summers down at Bridger's Resort and saved every cent I earned to buy that car. That car is mine."

The whisper in the back of his mind finally worked its way up to the forefront. But he'd known the entire time what it was trying to tell him anyway. At some level, he'd known the second he discovered the car missing from the church parking lot.

"The thing is," his father said, "you were too young to buy a car at the time, and I had to put my name on the title too. You may have paid out the actual cash for it, but that's nothing compared to the food and shelter and everything else your stepmom and I laid out for you for ten fucking years. Now her car is broke down and she needs a new one. I already went down and fixed the title this morning. No use bitchin' about it now."

Brandon thought he might vomit. Or, that he might pick up some nearby wrench and pound his father's head into a shapeless pulp.

And then he discovered that he no longer cared.

The Mustang had been his final link to those awful people, to that terrible life. Somewhere, deep in his subconscious, he'd known the title situation was hanging out there waiting for him, unfinished business, and that sooner or later it would come back to bite him on the ass. But ultimately it didn't matter. He was simply done now.

He turned and walked down the rapidly darkening street. When he reached the turnoff that would have taken him to the Bowman house, he hesitated only briefly and then kept right on walking.

. . .

Two hours later, he stood alone beneath a vast blanket of stars on the dark country back road where he'd seen the strange wolf *(alas, just a wolf)* on Christmas Eve. The sky was a deep bluish black, and the stars were so low and bright they looked like something out of a movie. Their brilliance was not remotely dimmed by the perfect round disk of silver just now rising over the tops of the trees.

Brandon couldn't think of any other place in the entire world he might like to be at this moment, car or no car, and he couldn't imagine anyone else feeling the same sort of peace and tranquility and...*completeness*...he was feeling right now. The Bowmans would be worried about him, but they were used to his eccentricities and wouldn't think too much about the fact he hadn't shown up tonight. He'd call and smooth everything over in the morning, maybe get up early and borrow Father Holloway's car to run them out some fresh goodies from the bakery and some "real" coffee from the new café that had just opened on Main Street. Yes, he would do all that, but for now it was enough to just stand by himself on some dark gravel road in the middle of the north woods, watching the moon, remembering the night he'd been so certain, so absolutely convinced, that he'd just encountered an actual, honest-to-goodness creature of darkness.

He laughed at his bizarre conviction and his subsequent obsession and, as if in response, a familiar voice behind him said, "You know, I was wondering just the other day if our paths would ever cross out here again."

. . .

The tiny hairs on the back of Brandon's neck stood on end, and gooseflesh broke out on his arms even under the heavy sleeves of his leather jacket. He hadn't seen a single car since turning off the main road to walk the back roads, and he hadn't heard a snapping twig or crunch of gravel to indicate anyone else was out here walking in the night and approaching him from behind. He closed his eyes—a mere blink or a wish upon the rising moon, he couldn't say—and then opened them again and pivoted to face his unexpected visitor.

"Father Holloway," he said.

In some remote, detached area of his mind, Brandon realized the oddest thing about this encounter should have been the distinct luminescence that flared behind Holloway's eyes, or perhaps the silvery sheen emanating from the priest's skin in the glow of the moonlight. But what Brandon actually found weirdest was the fact that Father Holloway was standing at the side of the road, in the middle of the woods, absolutely, unashamedly, naked. Without even realizing he was doing it, Brandon flicked his eyes in the direction of the priest's groin and then away again. He'd never really thought before about Father Holloway even *having* privates. Yet now...well, here they were—plain as day and big as life right in front of him.

Father Holloway saw the flush of red rising on Brandon's cheeks and laughed. The sound was different from the laugh Brandon was used to. This one sounded somehow distant, as if it were coming from a shadow image of Holloway that was no longer precisely there. "So," the priest said. "To what do I owe this unexpected visit?"

"I...I just went for a walk. I wasn't really..."

"...looking for me?" Holloway offered a thin smile. "Oh, I don't know. You were out here often enough this winter, looking for me. Isn't that true?"

"I don't know what I was looking for," Brandon said.

Holloway laughed again. He cocked his head to one side, weighing some option Brandon couldn't guess at, and then said, simply, "Take off your clothes."

"What?" Brandon felt frozen in place, *tharn*, a rabbit trapped in the luminous headlights of Father Holloway's glowing eyes.

"You'll just get blood on them otherwise," Holloway said.

"I—"

"Your clothes, Brandon. Time is very short here." Holloway's voice deepened as he spoke. The luminous eyes bored into Brandon's own, and the silvery sheen of the priest's bare skin was darkening, flowing, moving somehow under the deceptive light of the moon.

Brandon removed his leather jacket. He folded it carefully and placed it gently, almost reverently, on the gravel beside him. Holloway paced, and his breath began coming in heavy, wet-sounding huffs. Back and forth, back and forth—quieter, louder, quieter, louder. *Doppler effect*, Brandon thought.

Brandon peeled his T-shirt over his head and the night air wrapped around his torso like a thin layer of frost. He shivered as he pulled off his jeans, skinned out of his boxers. Time stopped, as the cliché goes. That solitary moment, standing naked beneath the moon, seemed to stretch into eternity.

Finally, Holloway stopped pacing and moved to stand directly behind Brandon. He placed his hands on Brandon's shoulders and lowered his head to rest on the cold bare flesh between Brandon's shoulder blades. Brandon shivered, and Holloway pressed against him and wrapped his arms around the younger man's chest. The heat rolling off Holloway's body was unbelievable—as if the man had his own built-in blast furnace—and his embrace was not the terrible, rage-fueled awfulness that Brandon had experienced with Farmer Joe. There was something gentle, almost apologetic about it. Even when Father Holloway grew hard and pressed against him, it felt nothing like sex or violence, as he might have expected, but more like a vague, ill-defined remnant of some lesser stop along the evolutionary path.

Brandon felt Holloway's mouth at the back of his neck, and looked down to see the priest's hands begin to change and grow as they moved across his chest. The silvery sheen had grown duller and more tinged with gray, and now soft gray hair was oozing out from every pore of the man's skin. Holloway's fingernails had darkened, solidified, and now were elongating, sharpening, curving right in front of Brandon's eyes. The chest that pressed into his bare back was growing furry as well—he could feel it—and the mouth on the back of his neck stretching, widening, and growing hotter and wetter and somehow...*sharper* with each panted breath. A low growl emanated from deep inside Holloway's chest, but it was something Brandon felt more than he heard.

Much to his own amazement, Brandon felt no real fear. He leaned into the moment, let the moment be whatever it was going to be. And even though his heart was beating a mile a minute and his breath was becoming louder and deeper and faster, he still, at the very center of his being, felt calm and at peace and—

The sudden blossom of fire across his chest was like no pain he'd ever experienced. Like no pain he'd ever *imagined*. He opened his eyes and stared at four deep, gaping slashes across his chest. Blood was rushing up from each slash in a torrent, a veritable eruption, and the cold night air bit into each wound as if a glowing piece of metal was being inserted there. The only possible consolation Brandon could see was that certainly the massive amount of blood flowing down his chest and stomach would kill him quickly and end the mind-splitting pain that pulsed through the wounds like something alive.

Father Holloway was completely transformed now, and he moved out to stand in front of Brandon like something out of God's own nightmares. His broad wolf's chest heaved with the exhausting yet exhilarating effort of the transfiguration; his eyes glittered with red, savage, almost mindless hunger; and Brandon's blood dripped from his dagger-like claws onto the dusty gravel of the road.

Brandon stumbled and nearly fell, but he knew the beast would show no mercy once he was on the ground. So long as he remained standing, he thought he had a chance—although a chance for what, he couldn't imagine. He managed to retain his balance and stood unsteadily in the middle of the road. When Holloway spoke, Brandon was shocked to hear a human voice come out of the animal that stood before him. In those brief few moments, he'd almost forgotten that Holloway, the man, even existed.

"And now you have to decide," Holloway said. "Joe Westcott has conveniently forgotten to put one of his cows back in the barn this evening, just as he does every month when the full moon first rises. And you need to decide if I'm to go down there for my dinner or remain here and finish the job I've started. Life or death, Brandon—but unlike most people, you get to make that choice for yourself. You've wanted this since you first looked into my eyes on Christmas Eve. You've waited for it, thought about it, dreamt of it—and now here it is. But you'll have to ask, either way. I don't want that kind of decision on my head."

Brandon tottered, his mind fuzzy from loss of blood and the sheer overwhelming trauma of the night. "Oh Christ," he said. "Oh God, oh my God, oh Jesus fucking Christ."

"No," Holloway said in his faraway wolf's voice. "Our Lord Jesus Christ has nothing whatsoever to do with this. This is you and you alone. And time is running out very quickly, I'd say, from the look of the red puddle forming at your feet. I'll ask you once again, but this will be the last time, so answer quick and answer well. Life or death, Brandon?"

Brandon's eyes fluttered and the world rolled and floated and dipped like something out of some old psychedelic hippie movie. He thought of all the pain and awfulness of his first eighteen years on earth. Thought of his dreadful father and stepmonster, of Daryl Reisling and the other bastards at school. Thought of the punches and kicks he'd taken on the street, the punches and cigarette burns and worse he'd taken at home. He thought of how exhausted he was, and how much he hated it all, hated every last minute of it sometimes, and how, yes, he could see it all being over once and for all, how nice that might be, how quiet, how *clean*...

Brandon swayed on his feet but managed to raise his head from its drunken loll. He thought of the poem that had been on his mind so often in recent months:

Ah, ye wolves in all your ranging,
I have found you kind and true;
More than man—and now I'm changing,
And will soon be one of you.

For a moment he couldn't get his mouth to work. Then he surprised even himself by offering up a soft, nearly airless, *"Life."*

Father Holloway moved forward, and now the claws on Brandon's skin felt like the softest of caresses, the fur pressing against him like a lover's embrace, and the tongue lapping to close his wounds like nothing so much as love's first, most gentle, kiss.

May, Concluded

In his sleep, Farmer Joe's ancient German shepherd perked up a single ear and then let it relax again. He crinkled his nose and discovered everything he needed to know in a single sniff. Someone was out there, out in the yard, but it was someone he knew, someone who'd been to the farm before and who'd even been nice to him. No need to wake the farmer for someone like that.

Joe was awake anyway. He lay on his back in bed, staring at the patterns of light and shadow that danced across the ceiling of his bedroom. Outside, frogs and peepers and crickets courted prospective mates with annoying croaks and blats and chirrups, driving away any possibility of sleep and making Joe want to rip out his own eardrums. A breeze too warm for May ruffled the curtains and carried the scent of budding trees and the mossy fragrance of good black dirt waiting to be tilled. Joe scowled. Every other farmer in the county already had his crops in the ground, but Joe hadn't even finishing tilling his fields yet.

Not that this was entirely his fault, he reasoned. That little prick Brandon was supposed to be helping him. He'd promised, practically begged Joe to give him a job—and then he'd run off at the busiest time of the year. Plus, the kid was probably blabbing all over town, making up all sorts of stories. Miserable teasing little—

Snap.

Outside, the frogs and crickets fell silent. The sudden absence of sound settled over the night like a damp blanket.

Joe sat up in bed. Now the shadows played over his flimsy white boxers and his broad chest. He leaned over to see if the snap of the twig had disturbed Bo, but the stupid mutt remained sprawled on the floor, sound asleep and snoring softly. Bo's eyes rolled behind closed lids and his paws twitched spasmodically in the throes of some idiotic canine dream.

Regardless, Joe knew what he had heard. Someone was out there, out in his yard. He eased off the bed and crept over to the window, careful to remain in shadow until he could peer out from the side of the curtains.

At first, the yard appeared empty. Then, Joe caught a momentary shimmer of moonlight on skin. Someone was there all right, right there, standing in the heavy shadows at the base of the willow. The willow branches filtered the moonlight and moved the shadows in hypnotic swirling patterns around the yard. Even when the shadows hid the intruder completely, Joe could sense his presence, feel his steely gaze leveled, unblinking, at the front door of the farmhouse.

Joe snagged a pair of dirty jeans from the floor and pulled them on as quietly as he could. He grabbed his shotgun from the rack above the dresser and padded down the hallway toward the stairs.

On the floor beside the bed, Bo slept on, oblivious and content. Dreaming of rabbits.

. . .

The door of the farmhouse opened and Joe stepped out onto the porch. Farmer Joe, everyone in town called him, knowing it drove him crazy. *Farmer Joe*, Brandon thought now, and the absurd nickname made him want to start laughing. He forced himself to remain perfectly still.

Joe came down off the porch and took a few tentative steps toward the willow. "I don't know what you're doing out here, buddy," he said. "But this is private property and this gun is most definitely loaded. You got about five seconds to show yourself before I put a fist-sized hole right through your goddamned heart."

Brandon shifted, but remained in shadow. A spear of moonlight illuminated his face, and Joe stopped in his tracks. "Brandon?" he said.

Brandon did not respond. He hunkered down, burrowing deeper into the darkness.

"I was just thinking about you," Joe said. He moved forward a few steps, squinting to see through the swaying tentacles of the willow. "Do you know what time it is? What are you doing out here anyway?"

Brandon rose and stepped into the light. Soft moonlight shone down, caressing his chest, his back, his arms, his legs— every inch of him. He stood in the glow, free and at one with the night. Naked.

A grin oozed across Joe's face like a slug's trail. "I knew I was right about you," he said. He set the shotgun down in the grass. "I knew exactly what you wanted the second I laid eyes on you. Don't know why you had to make such a fuss about it that day in the barn."

He took another step forward, and Brandon ducked back into the shadows. Joe hesitated. Could this be some sort of a trap? Maybe the kid had a bunch of buddies waiting back there, ready to pound the shit out of Joe as soon as he made his move.

Only the kid had no buddies. Joe had checked before offering Brandon the job. Lonely kids were the best, the easiest. They accepted whatever attention he felt like giving them, and accepted again when he was finished with them. The best of them were long resigned to being used and discarded at the whims of others.

Still, there was no sense walking into a situation he wasn't completely comfortable with. Sometimes even a single freaked-out kid could be more than a handful—no need to add darkness to the mix. Joe backed up a few steps, until he was in a clear spot in the middle of the yard. The full moon hung low in the sky directly overhead, almost impossibly huge, and Joe thought it looked like an enormous unblinking eye floating above him.

Brandon did not budge from the darkness of the willow, and Joe wondered briefly if he'd somehow managed to sneak away. Then a glint of moonlight flared against one of Brandon's eyes. Still watching him, still staring at him with the same sort of lust—the same sort of hunger—he'd seen the very first day they met.

"Come on out now, Brandon," he said. "Let's do this if we're doing it. I know exactly what you want, and I've got it right here."

Brandon smiled. His smile was too large for his face all of a sudden, and he wanted to laugh again, but now even the laughter was gone. He stretched elaborately, his body alive with muscles he'd never known he possessed. His smile continued to widen and expand, his teeth pressing sharply against his lips and his lips stretching outward to accommodate them.

He stared at the farmer in the middle of the moonlit yard. Joe was cupping his crotch and leering toward the willow. "Come and get it," he said. "Now or never."

Now, Brandon thought.

The oozing smile froze on Joe's face as Brandon emerged from the shadows. Joe tried to scream, but his vocal cords were a tight knot in the back of his throat. He tried to run, but shock was already shutting down his nervous system, making his legs ultimately as pointless as the shotgun that now lay some twenty feet away.

Summoning every ounce of his remaining strength, Joe managed a single, choked: *"Brandon?"*

For a moment, the hurtful names of the past swirled once more through Brandon's head: *Freak. Weirdo. Queer.*

He shook them away with a jerk of his new muzzle, a snap of his sharp new teeth.

They'd have to think up other names for him now.

Tourist Season

June

Millie Hayworth had been delivering mail along County Road 6 for as long as anyone could remember. Even Millie wasn't sure if she'd been with the Talbot Post Office for twenty-one years or twenty-two. She knew she wasn't close enough to her pension to get all worked up about it yet, and she wasn't looking forward to retirement all that much anyway. Millie liked knowing things about people—private things, secret things— and once she retired she knew she'd miss all the private, secret things she'd learned from peoples' mail over the course of her long, otherwise dull career.

Millie never gossiped about any of the things she learned. She didn't snoop to share, but simply to fulfill some deep, inner need. *To always have the upper hand*, was how she thought of it. She never used anyone's private information against them—not Eileen Forrester's Home Shopping Network addiction, nor Ray McCormick's secret child in Detroit—but it was nice to know the possibility was there should she ever need it.

Today, Millie tucked a few bills and some junk flyers into the Weaver mailbox and waved a greeting at Lorena Weaver, already making her way across the front yard. An awful lot of bills came to the Weavers, and judging from how quickly Lorena always spirited them out of the mailbox and into her pocket, Millie guessed Lorena's husband Jack didn't know about half of them. Every so often, Millie would sneak a peek at the balance on one or another of Lorena's credit card bills, and *oh*, that woman was walking a mighty fine line for someone whose husband was never more than one or two paychecks away from the poorhouse...

Smiling, Millie trundled toward her next stop. Millie's car was a battered Ford station wagon with a hand-painted MAIL CARRIER sign jutting from the roof rack. Talbot had one regulation U.S. Mail truck, but it was used only for in-town delivery. The rural routes utilized hardier, more disposable vehicles: Millie's wagon, Floyd Janisch's yellow Chrysler, Fred Weisinger's pickup.

The area surrounding Talbot was either farmland, forest, or lake country, and mail stops might be one or even two miles apart. The farms were wide stretches of fertile black soil, each dotted with a single house and a few outbuildings set at the end of a long, unpaved driveway. The farms were bordered by—indeed, had been painstakingly cut from—great expanses of verdant forest, the edge of the Superior National Forest, some of the last virgin woodland in the central part of North America.

Eventually, most of the rural routes curved around to meet one or another of the lakes—remnants of the last glaciers to cut across the lower continent, sparkling clear water still icy much of the year, surrounded now by fishing resorts and private cabins and, just lately, lavishly inappropriate "rustic getaways" (with every modern convenience their owners could imagine) and palatial "second homes" that might get used two or three weekends a year by people who rarely stepped outside for fear of bugs or bears or Bigfoot (each of which posed an equal threat in the minds of some of the "summer folk").

One thing Millie would *not* miss once she retired was the daily reminder she received of how much the area was changing. Family farms being devoured by big corporate operations. Family resorts falling to investment firms up from the Twin

Cities or even farther away. The hunters and outdoorsmen of the Iron Range being replaced by men with cell phones and laptop computers, men who didn't know a fresh walleye from a frozen fishstick, but who came to this open country anyway and tried to turn it into an exact replica of the place they were supposedly trying to escape. Always trying to tame the wild right out of a place, these men, then whining that there were no longer any wild places left in the world.

Deep in her thoughts, Millie nearly missed the next stop on her route—the Westcott place. *Farmer Joe*, Millie thought, and her face blossomed with a thin smile that didn't have a trace of friendliness in it. Joe Westcott—now *there* was a man with some private, secret things in his mail.

Millie clunked the station wagon to a stop a few feet beyond the Westcott mailbox. She threw the car into reverse, but then remembered that she had a package for Joe today. More private, secret things, no doubt—more of his magazines or videos or God only knew *what* that pervert might think to order next. Millie turned the station wagon into the Westcott driveway, sorry she hadn't thought ahead this morning and snuck a look inside the package before heading out.

Millie was halfway up the drive when she saw Farmer Joe's German shepherd pop his head up from the middle of the yard. He stared at her car long enough to process who the car belonged to and what his reaction should be, then dipped back down into the grass and continued whatever he'd been doing. Millie had a standard-issue canister of pepper spray on her belt, but she had no doubt in her mind that she was more likely to need it for Farmer Joe than for stupid old Bo the dog.

Millie pulled her car into the gravel turnaround between the barn and the house and gave her horn a couple of short blats. She got out of the car and went around to the passenger side to bundle the rest of Joe's mail with his package. No sign of the man himself, but that wasn't unusual for any of her farm deliveries. He might be out in the field, or knee-deep in cow shit in the barn, or, knowing Joe Westcott, sleeping off a hangover inside the house. Even with the package, the bundle of mail would easily fit inside the screen door on the front porch, and Millie thought she might even be able to catch a glimpse *inside* the house if she paused a moment beside the front window after putting the bundle inside the door. She shivered at the possibility.

As it turned out, the inside door was open. Millie was able to get more than a glimpse—not that there was anything to see. She could see the entryway and most of the living room and a bit of the kitchen down a dim stretch of hallway. The whole place looked neater than she would have given Joe credit for, and if he *had* been having an orgy any time recently, there wasn't any sign of it now.

Disappointed, Millie placed the bundle of mail on the floor just inside the screen door, called out halfheartedly, "Mail, Joe!" and turned to go back to her car. A hot slick of wetness across the back of her hand made her jump about a foot and nearly scream out loud, but then she realized it was just Bo, padding up behind her with a wet doggie kiss. She reached down to scratch between Bo's ears, and noticed that the smear of saliva he'd left across her knuckles was distinctly bloody.

"Jesus, Bo!" Millie recoiled and, without thinking, wiped her hand across the knee of her uniform pants, leaving a dark smear. The dog's entire muzzle was a bright, wet crimson, the fur there matted into spiky clumps and the bridge of his snout coated with a rust-colored glaze. "What you been into out there, boy? You catch yourself a rabbit or something?"

Bo merely cocked his head and panted at her, so Millie shaded her eyes with one hand and tried to see what Bo might have been eating out in the middle of the yard when she first arrived. Too big for a rabbit, Millie could tell immediately—had Bo somehow brought down a deer? She clumped down the porch steps and started toward the big red blotch in the middle of the yard. Bo padded beside her, happier and more lively than she'd seen him for ages, and when they were halfway across the lawn he broke into a run and soon had his nose buried deep inside the carcass once more.

Millie slowed her pace a little. It had to be a deer. A carcass that big, a splotch of bloody grass that wide. Closer, ever closer, and although the day was quite warm Millie felt gooseflesh break out on her arms. Perhaps wolves had brought down the deer and left the scraps for Bo, she thought. Or perhaps Joe had shot the deer for Bo—there was his shotgun, right there in the grass just a few yards away. The only thing Millie could not quite wrap her mind around was why a deer might be flayed out in the middle of Farmer's Joe's yard with a pair of dirty blue jeans bunched tenuously around its lower half. Or why the single eyeball staring at her from the partially denuded skull wasn't the usual soft amber of a deer's eye, but an icy biting blue. *Almost the blue of Joe Westcott's own eyes*, Millie thought, but her mind quickly thrust that thought aside.

It wasn't until Bo had ripped a juicy chunk of liver out of the carcass and laid it at her feet like a gift—*what a good doggie he is*, Millie thought absently—that Millie finally started to scream.

. . .

Davis Langley stepped out of his cruiser just in time to see his youngest deputy, Benjy Tatum, splatter the remains of his lunch across a freakishly wide swatch of Joe Westcott's lawn. "Damn it, Benjy," Davis hollered. "Can't you at least keep your insides off the crime scene?"

One of Davis's more seasoned deputies, Larry Emory, spun Benjy away from the body and gave him a little shove to set him in motion. Benjy managed to duck-walk a total of three steps before his stomach decided to empty again. "Sorry, Chief," he croaked after the worst of the heaving was over. He collapsed into the grass and lay panting like a dehydrated dog.

"Not sure it *is* a crime scene, Chief," Burt Kowalski said. The county medical examiner was hunkered down in an awkward squat, jabbing a pair of forceps into Joe Westcott's gaping chest cavity and then plucking them back out in a manner that reminded Davis of some predatory water bird—an egret or a heron—spearing at minnows. When Kowalski finally managed to tweezer some fiber samples out of the bloody hole, he sealed them in a small plastic zip bag and handed the bag to Emory. "The body's been pretty well picked-over, so precise cause of death might take a while," he said. "But off-hand my first guess wouldn't be murder."

Davis ran the medical examiner's words through his head a second time. Kowalski's sentences always had too many points for Davis to process all at once. Finally, he settled on: "Picked over?"

"Yeah, poor bastard's been out here for two days or better, I'd guess." Kowalski rose and each of his knees offered an audible, painful-sounding *pop*. "You've had skunks and badgers and raccoons out here, maybe a coyote or a lynx. Then of course there was the dog."

Davis groaned. "Jesus, Burt—you don't think it was the dog, do you?"

Kowalski squinted into the sun as if giving the matter real thought for the first time. Finally he turned back with his decision. "Nah. At first I thought it was suicide—his gun's right over there, and we all know Joe Westcott wasn't exactly the poster boy for mental health. But the gun hasn't been fired, and Joe seems more like the basement or attic type anyway."

Davis nodded. He and Kowalski had long ago determined there were two types of suicides here on the Range—those who pulled the trigger right out in front of God and everybody, looking for a show; and those who found some hidey-hole to crawl into to do the deed—some dark, secret place in which their remains might stay hidden for weeks or even months.

"And no," Kowalski continued. "I don't think a dog like Bo ever would have gotten up the nerve to cross a master like Joe Westcott aggressively enough to bring him down."

"Didn't have any qualms about eating him after the fact, though," Emory said. In the grass behind them, Benjy Tatum's stomach tried in vain to empty itself one more time.

"Well, after a couple days without, a dog's gonna eat," Kowalski said. "We should just consider ourselves lucky that a bear or pack of wolves didn't stumble on the remains. We'd be looking at nothing more than some bloody grass and a few bits of ripped denim."

"What about one of those?" Davis said. "Bear or wolf—that a possibility? Killed him but then got scared away from the..." He searched in vain for the proper word. *Remains? Carcass?*

"Buffet?" Emory offered. Davis shot him a look.

"Hell, anything's possible at this point," Kowalski said. "Maybe some angry boy or some angry boy's daddy clocked him and he's too chewed up to show immediate evidence of that. Maybe he ran into a bear or a wolf or even a cougar, although I haven't heard tell of one of those this far north for twenty years or better. Even some old bull moose could have done one hell of a number on him before he even knew what was happening, although I don't see any tracks nearby to support that. Maybe he just came out here to look at that big full moon the other night and his ticker decided enough was enough. That's pretty much how his old man went, you know."

"You can figure that out back in the lab, though, right?"

"Could if I still had the heart."

Benjy offered a thin groan and pressed his face into the grass. Even Davis felt his stomach shift a little at that one.

"Heart, tongue, one eye, both kidneys, most of the liver," Kowalski said. "All gone."

"Privates too," Emory said.

Davis chose to ignore that entire catalog for the moment. Instead he said, "So why would he bring a gun to look at the moon?"

Kowalski offered up another thoughtful squint, this one directed right at Davis. "Go ahead and put up your yellow tape, if it'll make you feel better. But I still don't think it'll end up murder once we get him down to the lab."

"What makes you so sure?"

"Let's just call it my gut."

Behind them on the grass, Benjy rose shakily to his knees. "Please don't say gut, Mr. Kowalski." He caught another glimpse of the corpse and decided his stomach still wasn't quite empty.

"Rookies," Emory said under his breath.

. . .

Just as Kowalski predicted, the lab results proved inconclusive for murder—and pretty much everything else. "No sign of heart attack in the preliminary blood work," he told

Davis over the phone that evening. "No gunpowder residue in the body, no obvious knife wounds..."

Davis rolled his eyes and offered a distinctive one-handed whack-off gesture to the phone. From her seat on the other side of his desk, Kate Bowman stifled a laugh. Knowing how late he'd be working, she'd stopped at the Dairy Queen on her way back into town from the Center. Unfortunately, she'd chosen sloppy joes. Normally they were one of Davis's favorites, but tonight he managed only a single bite before thinking about the name and pushing his sandwich aside.

Despite the fact that it wasn't strictly procedure, Davis had Kowalski on speaker phone, and Kate offered a commiserating look as the medical examiner pointed out all of the ways in which Joe Westcott *hadn't* died. Finally, his unhelpful litany came to an end. "So, I see what you don't know," Davis said. "Is there anything you *do* know at this point?"

"Well, I know the guy died," Kowalski said.

"Very helpful."

Kate stifled another laugh and Davis raised one finger to his lips. Kowalski probably wouldn't have cared that a civilian was listening in, but it was nearly eleven o'clock at night, and Davis and Kate were alone in his office, and Talbot was still a very small town, no matter how much it liked to think otherwise.

"All right, here's what I'm thinking for the paperwork," Kowalski said. "Exsanguination. Massive blood loss due to traumatic injury."

"Yes, but traumatic injury caused by what?" Davis said.

The speaker phone hummed and buzzed as if trying to come up with the answer on its own, and finally Kowalski said, "My best guess is that his throat was torn out first. Now again, that's just a guess because of the massive tissue loss after the fact, but I don't think we're going to come up with anything better. So, let's just say traumatic injury caused by...oh, what the hell—bear attack."

Davis shot a preemptive placating look at Kate. "Bear and not wolf?"

Kowalski chuckled. "Considering who else is listening in on this conversation, we'd no doubt be here all night if I said wolf, wouldn't we?"

Kate blushed but Davis only offered a chuckle of his own. "Can't keep anything from you, Burt. Must be why they pay you the big bucks."

"Yeah, right," Kowalski said. "So that sound about right to you, Kate? Bear a more likely candidate than wolf?"

Kate knew he was baiting her—Kowalski ran a sheep ranch south of Talbot when he wasn't carving up dead bodies, and they'd been on opposite sides of the wolf debate for years—but she refused to start anything this late at night, especially when Davis clearly needed to get home and get this day behind him. "Wolves don't kill people, Burt," was all she said.

"Bear it is," Kowalski said. They could hear him shuffling papers, preparing to call it a night, and then he said, in a voice smaller than normal for him, "You know, I've gotta be perfectly honest here. I'm not all that broken up that Joe Westcott has left this earthly plane, and I guess I don't really care what helped that process along."

"Sad to say, I feel pretty much the same," Davis said. "I'll check with the game warden about unusual bear activity in the area, and I'll send a couple guys into the woods for a day or two. Hopefully this was just some freak event we can put behind us before the real summer craziness begins."

"Take me off speaker for a minute, would ya?" Kowalski said.

Davis offered Kate a shrug and picked up the receiver. "What else you got?"

"Well, I don't want to start some big brouhaha with Kate because, again, this could all be after the fact," Kowalski said. "But the fibers I pulled off Westcott's rib cage looked pretty damned wolf-like to me. Just thought you should know."

Davis looked across the desk, but Kate was pointedly examining a calendar on the opposite wall, as if by not looking at him she could give him some extra bit of privacy.

"Pleasant dreams to you too, Burt," Davis said, and gently placed the handset back in its cradle.

. . .

Talbot buzzed with the grisly news about Farmer Joe, and his funeral was a hot ticket for a populace that had either ignored or openly despised the man while he was alive. No one really bought the medical examiner's marauding bear theory, but no one questioned it too openly either. If it *had* been one of their own, fed up with Joe Westcott's perversions, no one really wanted to know about it—at least not yet.

For Brandon, the night of the full moon had offered a true epiphany in the deepest, most spiritual sense of the word. The awakening of the creature inside him had been like a divine visitation, the sudden validation of a long-suspected but previously unseen alternate reality. In this new world he was nearly a god—strong, judgmental, frightened of nothing. The knowledge of a deeper identity hidden inside him colored everything. Even his wretched past became something different viewed through the new, sharper eyes that had borne witness to Joe Westcott's last moments on earth.

Memories of that night cycled through Brandon's mind like an old-time movie. He remembered the clearing, and Nikki's kiss, and running through the forest, and then the farmhouse looming up like destiny itself. And later he remembered swimming in a warm red pool, nearly bottomless, salty like he imagined an ocean must be. He remembered the death of Farmer Joe, how that had felt and how it had tasted, individual moments coming back in tiny bites both thrilling and terrifying, and then he remembered even further back, to a lonely walk on a dark country road. He remembered Father Holloway, and blood pooling at his bare feet, and a warm tongue lapping to close his wounds. Finally he remembered waking in his bed at the rectory, some new bit of knowledge germinating like a seed inside him.

Round and round the images cycled as he stood shirtless beneath the blazing June sun and applied a fresh coat of paint to the trim around the windows of the rectory. *The moon the kiss the lake of blood. The moon the kiss the lake of blood.* He dipped the brush into the bucket of paint. *The road the moon the hands like claws. The road the moon the hands like claws—*

He thought about the party Kate had thrown a few days earlier to celebrate Chad's graduation. She'd claimed the party was for both Chad *and* Brandon, and that was nice, but of course everyone had known the truth. He thought of the way Kate had kept finding excuses to touch Chad, to hug him, and how her eyes had appeared shiny and ready to overflow at the slightest provocation. Chad's eyes had misted up at several points as well.

Brandon wondered what that must feel like—the connection between a parent and child who not only loved but genuinely *liked* one another. Kate rarely spoke of Chad's father, and Chad had never met the man, but Brandon knew Chad didn't perceive this as a loss or a hole in his life. Kate had always been enough, and she and Chad—despite the usual minor squabbles between any parent and child—had always been thick as thieves.

Had Brandon had that kind of relationship with his own mother? He couldn't remember. In his memories his mother was always in motion—coming from or going to one of her three jobs, hurrying to change clothes so she could get to the bar before last-call, shuffling him from the small bedroom they shared to the sofa in the living room because she'd brought home a "friend" for the evening. And then she was simply gone.

At some point during the graduation party, someone had asked Chad the inevitable—what did he plan to do with his life? "Yeah, Chad," piped up one of Kate's assistants. "Are you still planning to come back after school and take over your mom's job?"

"It's in his blood," one of the gift-shop volunteers said. "He's been plotting his takeover of the Center since he was three. Our little wolf-man."

"Woof-man," Kate said, and they all laughed.

Brandon had heard the story a hundred times, but now it pulsed inside his head with a new energy and importance.

One day when Chad was very little and his daycare provider was down with the flu, Kate had brought him to work with her. Midway through the morning the toddler had gone missing. It was early enough that the Center wasn't open for visitors yet, so Kate knew the boy couldn't have gotten far, but where he *had* gotten was so mysterious and unlikely that it had remained one of the central stories of Chad's life to this day.

They'd finally discovered him—Kate and a girl named Amanda, their sole grad school intern at the time—somehow, inexplicably, *inside* the wolf enclosure. The tanned and towheaded three-year-old was laughing merrily and trying to climb onto a boulder while Tiaga, the alpha female of the Center pack at the time, patiently grasped the back of his shirt in her teeth, preventing him from getting more than a few inches off the ground. This barrier to his efforts only made Chad laugh all the harder, and Kate could have sworn the look in Tiaga's eyes was something very close to human exasperation. When she finally got her wits about her enough to get to the gate and open the enclosure, Tiaga had padded over with Chad's shirt still gripped gingerly in her teeth and dropped the giggling boy at his mother's feet with a look that clearly said, *That was amusing once...but try to watch him a little closer in the future, would you?*

To this day, they'd never figured out how Chad had found his way into the fenced enclosure—even at the time, he hadn't had any answer beyond his infectious little laugh—but after the incident, whenever some adult would ask him what he wanted to be when he grew up, Chad would always answer, "A wolf-man!" Or, as he'd said until he was five or six, "Woof-man!"

Considering recent events, and the blur of red thoughts cycling through his head as he stood painting the same spot over and over, Brandon wondered if anyone had ever questioned Chad's true meaning. Had he really known at such an early age that someday he wanted to be a man who, like his mother, studied wolves for a living? Or had he meant literally that he wanted to become a wolf-man, laughing and frolicking with the rest of the pack as he'd done on that one storied day of his distant childhood? It bore thinking about. Brandon liked the idea of running through the moonlit forest with his best friend at his side. Or perhaps, someday, even a mate.

As if in response to such thoughts, a big late-model SUV pulled into the parking lot of the church, packed to the brim and towing a U-Haul trailer. Because the lot was empty, the vehicle was able to make a wide, smooth arc and pull right up parallel to the sidewalk. The driver-side window buzzed down, and a voice from inside said, "Help, we're lost."

Brandon walked over to the vehicle. The driver's seat held a sweating, middle-aged man who looked like an accountant; the passenger side, a thin unhappy woman who could only be his wife. Brandon gave them each a glance, but then his focus shifted to the singular vision of perfection sitting in the back seat. Her hair was a shade of red so deep it bordered on maroon, and her eyes were as green as Brandon imagined emeralds must be. She was lithe and tanned just enough to accentuate a spatter of freckles across the bridge of her nose, and her smile was directed at Brandon like some deeply personal gift. A word floated up from the depths of his childhood: *twitterpated*.

"Whoa there, boy," the man in the front seat said. "At least let us get settled in before you carry off our daughter."

"Daddy!" said the vision in the back seat, but there was no real anger in her voice. She offered Brandon the tiniest roll of her emerald eyes.

"Bob Henning," the man in the front seat said. He stuck his hand through the open window and Brandon gave it a cursory shake. The man nodded to the woman beside him. "My wife, Christine. And there in the back is our daughter Melissa, who's going off to college in a few months and who is *not* going to be marrying any local boys from Talbot, Minnesota, just so you know."

"All right, Daddy, that's enough."

This time there *was* a little fire in the vision's voice, and Brandon smiled when the fat idiot accountant wilted right in front of him. *Stupid slab of meat*, he thought, and that made his smile even toothier. "So, you were saying something about being lost?"

"Yes," Henning said. "Although not in any spiritual way or anything." He nodded toward the church and offered up a sickly chuckle. "You're not the priest here, I take it?"

Brandon laughed. "No, I'm not the priest." But in his mind he thought: *Am I the priest? I'm like the priest now, only different. How am I different? Why do I think that? It's true, though, I know it.*

"We're from Chicago," Henning said. "We bought the Whispering Pines—you know, the bed and breakfast? But now I...um, can't seem to figure out where it actually *is.*"

"You bought the place without seeing it?" Brandon said. The wife in the passenger seat offered up a sharp laugh.

"No, we—*I*—was up here once," Henning said. "And we saw lots of pictures—you know...on the Internet."

"Oh yeah, the Internet," Brandon said. "I've heard about that. Some newfangled type-a-writer thingee, right?"

Melissa giggled from the back seat, and Brandon felt his heart actually stop for a moment. Then he noticed Henning's face coloring, and he backpedaled a little. "I'm sorry," he said. "I was just giving you some grief. Trying to impress your daughter." He surprised himself by smiling directly at the vision and almost offering her a wink. Then he gave the slab of meat simple directions to the Whispering Pines and offered his hand one more time to make sure there were no hard feelings.

"So, you know this place?" Henning said. "It's not a total dump, is it?"

"No, not at all," Brandon said. "The Weickerts—they're the ones who owned it before—they would have taken real good care of the place."

"See, Christine?" Henning said.

"Kinda getting a late start, though," Brandon said. "You planning to open this season still?"

"See, Bob?" Christine said.

Henning wilted again, and Brandon knew it was time to extricate himself from the conversation. "Well, I guess I'll see you around," he said, primarily to the vision.

"You're dripping, you know," she said with one last breathtaking smile.

"Sorry," Brandon said. "It's pretty hot out here and I've been working—"

"She means the paint, Gomer," Henning said. He laughed and moved the SUV forward.

Melissa waved at Brandon until they'd pulled out of the parking lot, and only then did Brandon look down and notice that he was, in fact, covered with splotches of paint from his sneakers to his navel. He didn't care in the slightest. He had the oddest desire to tilt his head toward the sky and howl a song of pure animal joy. It was going to be one hell of a summer here in Talbot, he could tell already.

. . .

Inside the rectory, Father Holloway sat at the big, burnished dining room table and watched the brief exchange out in the parking lot. Even from here, he could see the changes taking place inside Brandon. Burgeoning confidence, energy like a wire vibrating with current, boy turning into man right in front of him.

Holloway had a number of week-old newspapers spread across the table. Talbot...Duluth...Minneapolis. The story was front page on all of them. And why not? A bear attack was big news. Especially here in tourist country, right at the start of the summer season.

Of course, how much bigger would the story have been if anyone knew the truth? Did Holloway even know? Could he say, beyond a shadow of a doubt, that he knew what had really happened out on the Westcott farm the night of the last full moon? Could he even say definitively that *he* hadn't been the one who'd visited Farmer Joe that night?

No—now he was being ridiculous. Paranoid. He would have known, he would have remembered. And he *did* remember visiting the cow Joe had left out for him in the lower field that night—the stalk, the attack, the subsequent feast. He would have had no reason to go up to the farm, no reason to turn on one of the few individuals who'd helped him maintain his secret all these years.

Of course, reason didn't always play much of a part when he was...like that. Even after twenty-odd years of monthly forays into the moonlight, his memories still came jagged and piecemeal. A cow's staring eye, white around the edges with terror. A panting reflection in a pool of still water. And running, always running. With all the running he did through moonlit nights, Holloway couldn't believe he still carried an extra forty pounds around his waist during the rest of the month.

Actually, he *could* believe it—Mrs. McGowan was, at that very moment, bringing him fresh coffee and a plate of homemade cookies from the kitchen. Holloway smiled despite the dark questions cycling through his mind. Mrs. McGowan glanced at the newspapers spread across the table and tutted under her breath. Holloway wasn't sure how to read that. Before he could pursue the matter, Brandon came in from outside, flushed and covered in paint.

"So dearie," Mrs. McGowan said. "Are you painting the windows or are the windows painting you?"

Brandon laughed and stole a cookie from the plate on the table.

"Who was that?" the priest asked. He casually folded the newspapers and set them aside.

"Just some new people asking directions," Brandon said. His grin betrayed his excitement and he knew it. "The guy was a total tool—just a big useless slab of meat. And the wife seemed pretty pointless as well. But oh, you should have seen the daughter..."

He snatched another cookie and wandered down the hall toward a shower and some clean clothes. Holloway watched the boy's new swagger with a distinct sense of foreboding and regret. When he looked away again, he was startled by the piercing dark gaze Mrs. McGowan was leveling at him. "I'm afraid I've done something very stupid," he said.

"You're just realizing that now?" The old woman turned back toward the kitchen. "Gorry, you can be a slow bastard sometimes."

As the dining room door snicked shut behind her, Holloway realized a truer assessment of his personality had probably never been uttered.

. . .

Obviously, it would have been easier to ask the vision out if he'd still had his car, but even that obstacle didn't seem insurmountable. Chad was always pestering him to ask someone out, double with him and Nikki, and Brandon thought the presence of another couple might even help smooth over his own awkwardness a bit. He'd need a new vehicle before he left for school in the fall anyway; until he found one, he and Melissa could bum rides off Chad. The real problem was going to be making the initial phone call, getting the invitation to come out of his mouth, figuring out where to take her...

The telephone on his nightstand blatted its odd, atonal ring. "A Catholic ring if I've ever heard one," Chad had said once, when Kate called while he was visiting. Brandon smiled at the memory and waited for the phone to bleat a second time. It pretty much had to be either Chad or Kate—who else would be calling him?—but still his mind insisted upon whispering, way off in some hidden corner, *What if it's her, what if it's her, what if it's her?*

It wasn't her. Father Holloway's voice on the other end of the line was flat and slightly electronic, as if he were calling from the other side of the world instead of just down the hall. "I was wondering if I could see you in my office for a moment," he said.

Man, he's lazy, Brandon thought. *Calling instead of walking ten steps down the hallway.* But into the phone he said only, "Be there in a sec."

He hung up and pulled on a T-shirt. He noticed how his shirts fit differently now, gliding down over new muscles like another layer of skin. A new layer of skin over a new layer of skin. And underneath that...

Brandon smiled at his reflection in the mirror above the dresser. His smile was sharp and white and his dark eyes flared from somewhere deep inside. He made a halfhearted attempt to tame the thatch of unruly black hair that fell over his forehead, but decided it was a losing battle. *Better get used to being hairy, I guess.* He laughed and padded down the hallway toward Father Holloway's office.

. . .

"You can't ever let this happen again," Holloway said. "You know that, don't you?"

Brandon sat in one of the overstuffed guest chairs in the corner of Holloway's office and wondered for a moment what the priest was talking about. A jumble of thoughts flashed into his head—

(the moon the kiss the lake of blood)

—and then departed just as abruptly. He frowned.

His brain was moving too fast to focus properly, and the priest seemed to be speaking a foreign language. He'd felt like this once before, that night by the lake, but certainly this had to be something different. Daylight streamed through the windows of Holloway's office. The moon wouldn't rise for hours yet and even when it did it wouldn't be—

"Farmer Joe, Brandon," Holloway said. "You can't let what happened to Farmer Joe happen to anyone else—ever. Do you understand?"

Brandon's thoughts ratcheted down a notch and the memory chunked into place fully-formed, blossoming like a flower out of the darkness. *Farmer Joe in the middle of the yard, Farmer Joe gutted like a fish at the edge of a salty red ocean.* The memory made Brandon surprisingly happy. "Why not?" he said.

"Because you just can't, damn it! Don't you know how much you've complicated life—for both of us? Joe Westcott was the one who kept me *fed*, Brandon. Every month for twenty years, he'd leave a cow out in the field for me. I would have shown you, I would have shared with you. I thought we had months to cover those things. I didn't think it was possible for anyone to actually transform their first month out."

"Why? How long does it usually take?"

Holloway rose from his chair and moved to stare out the window. When he turned to face Brandon, the flare of sunlight behind him turned him into a faceless silhouette, a shadow figure with luminescent pinpoints where his eyes should have been. "I don't know how long it usually takes," he said. "With me it took nearly a year, but I fought it every step of the way."

Fought it? Brandon thought. *Why would anyone fight it? I was never so sure of anything in my entire—*

"In any case, there's nothing we can do about it now," Holloway said. "Joe Westcott was useful in his time, but there are other farmers and other cows, and I'll find us another situation eventually. In the meantime, we're going to have to control your nocturnal activities for those several nights each month that might present a temptation—at least until you gain a better understanding of what you are now."

"What are you gonna do?" Brandon said with a grin. "Lock me in the basement?"

The silhouette at the window stepped forward and became Father Holloway again. His expression was deathly serious. "Yes," he said.

Brandon was instantly on his feet and backing toward the door. *"No!"* His shout was nearly a scream, his terror almost a living thing. Holloway might have been brandishing white-hot tongs and threatening to peel Brandon's flesh strip-by-strip that very moment.

"Calm down," Holloway said. "We're only talking a couple of months. Two or three nights for the first—"

"I'll die down there! I swear I'll chew off my own hands—"

Brandon knew that the basement of the church was pleasant and well-lit and perfectly safe. He could picture the exact room Holloway would put him in. Could see the shelves lined with books and the nice TV/DVD combo unit, smell the fragrant warmth of Mrs. McGowan's cooking that would waft over from the rectory...

(Mrs. McGowan's chili, Mrs. McGowan's cookies—that's what I want. Not the salty red pool.)

But behind the image of the Saint Ignatius basement, underneath that image, was another basement. Pipes dripping condensation onto his wrists, wooden beam groaning and nylon digging into his flesh as he tried to snap the rope, bite through the rope, anything, *anything*, to get away before—

The belt.

The belt, the belt, always the big leather belt with the fraying edges. Cement floor cold against his bare flesh as he slid down as far as he could, arms taut above him, shoulder blades stretched almost to the snapping point, thin strips of flesh peeling when he finally managed to stand again, because the blood from the belt lashes had congealed and glued his skin to the wall.

"Forget to put my tools away again," his father had said, "and next time I'll take the tin snips to your fingers."

Brandon had been twelve years old at the time, but he heard that line quite distinctly again now—still his father's voice, only now coming from Father Holloway's mouth. A noise escaped his own mouth that sounded like someone deliberately stepping on the hindquarters of a puppy.

"Brandon, calm down. We'll figure something out." The priest was speaking in his own voice again, although it sounded like it was coming from very far away. "I would never hurt you, Brandon. You know that, don't you?"

Pain blossomed across Brandon's chest, four distinct rows of buried fire, and then his eyes rolled in his skull and he crumpled to the floor.

Holloway knelt and gently pushed unruly hair away from the boy's forehead. He caught a glint from the top of his desk: the sterling silver letter opener the parish had given him for one anniversary or another. He couldn't actually use it for its everyday purpose—his hand blistered after the slightest touch—

but he kept it around so visitors to his office would know how much he'd appreciated the gift. He considered picking up the blade and plunging it deep into Brandon's heart. He'd have to ice his hand for days, no doubt, but the alternative...

He's done so much damage already, Holloway thought. *But he's just a boy and it's your own damned fault for making him what he is.* The priest imagined a tiny angel on one shoulder, a tiny demon on the other, each whispering in an ear. He tried to smile but didn't quite manage it. The boy stirred beneath his hand and opened those bottomless brown eyes. The eyes that had caused all this damage in the first place—captivating him instantly last Christmas Eve.

"Please—" the boy croaked. "Please don't put me in the basement. I promise I won't do it again."

"It's not that easy to control," Holloway said. "Especially at first."

"I can do it. I know I can. You can teach me."

"In less than three weeks?"

"Look how fast I managed to transform."

"That's true," Holloway said. He helped Brandon into a chair. "You didn't fight it, even for a moment."

"Nope," Brandon said. He was fairly beaming now. "I didn't fight it at all. I liked it."

That's just what scares the living hell out of me, Holloway thought.

He glanced at the calendar on his desk and noticed the symbol for the full moon a mere eighteen days away. Then his eyes fell once more on the silver letter opener, gleaming from within its felt-lined display box. He was surprised at the amount of effort it took to make himself look away again.

. . .

After a week of worrying about it almost continuously, Brandon finally got up the nerve to ask Melissa out. Bullets of sweat peppered his forehead; his throat threatened to close at any moment; one nerve in his left temple twitched spasmodically as if bombarded by tiny jolts of electricity. He forced himself to dial the Whispering Pines number. He offered a silent prayer of thanks when Melissa herself picked up the phone, another when she remembered him, and one more when he actually managed to force the question out of his mouth.

"Be warned," Melissa told him. "I'll order the most expensive thing on the menu and I'll talk all during the movie."

"Well, I just got paid and I've already seen the movie," Brandon replied. "So I think we're okay."

He couldn't believe how suave he sounded. The old Brandon never would have pulled off an exchange like that. *Stupid mewling whiner*, he thought. *I can't believe how long I was stuck inside that pathetic loser.*

Chad sounded even more excited than Brandon when he heard the news. "Are you kidding me, man? It's about time!"

Brandon heard a whisper of cloth against plastic as Chad held the phone to his chest to holler at Nikki: "Hey, we're going to the movies tomorrow night, and you won't *believe* who's got a date for once!"

Brandon couldn't hear Nikki's response, but he wasn't sure if that was a byproduct of Chad's lousy cell phone or his own heart going *thump-thump, thump-thump* loud enough to drown out everything else in the world.

They decided to stay in Talbot, which meant dinner at either Wally's Steak House or the Dairy Queen, and then the choice of exactly one movie screen, two shows nightly. The movie this week was a comedy and Wally's ran a two-for-one special on

Wednesdays, so the night looked to be relatively painless and easy on the wallet besides.

Melissa knew nothing of Brandon's former slot on the lowest rung of the Talbot social ladder, and now that high school was finally, blessedly over, the old ranking didn't seem to matter quite so much anyway. Already, Brandon had received several nods of greeting from former classmates on the street and even a casual "What's up?" from a girl who, a month earlier, wouldn't have deigned to look at him in the hallways of the school.

The only wild card of the evening, Brandon thought, was Nikki. She could be ferociously territorial around other girls— even her best friends—and she was sometimes particularly ill at ease around people who came from somewhere other than Talbot, especially if that somewhere was an actual city like Chicago. Whether it was some weird self-esteem issue or just a small-town girl's innate distrust of "summer people" (the term many in Talbot used year-round for anyone from out of town), Brandon hoped that putting Nikki and Melissa together wouldn't throw off the otherwise smooth trajectory he was hoping the evening would follow.

As it turned out, his fears were ungrounded. Nikki and Melissa began chattering away like long-lost friends before Chad's Jeep was even out of the Whispering Pines driveway, and by the time Chad had parked in front of the restaurant their easy, free-flowing conversation had already encompassed the clothes each of them was wearing, the earrings Melissa had found at an antique store on the drive from Chicago, the bands that appeared most frequently on each of their playlists, and the fact that yes, Brandon's hair *did* look like a squirrel's nest from this angle of the backseat.

Riding shotgun, Brandon blushed to the core of his soul, but Chad only rolled his eyes and mouthed a quiet, "Chicks, man."

Then they were climbing out of the Jeep and Melissa was taking Brandon's hand for the short walk to the Steak House door. Chad flashed Brandon a grin and kept Nikki back so that Brandon would be sure to open the door for Melissa. Then the four of them were inside, seated around a candlelit table, and the evening had begun.

I made it, Brandon thought. *I'm actually here, sitting next to this beautiful girl, out on the town with my very best friend in the world. I must be just about the luckiest son of a bitch in all of Talbot right now...*

And Fate, of course—God, the Great Spirit, or whatever—heard Brandon's arrogant thoughts, and immediately adjusted the evening accordingly.

. . .

The first tremor in the perfection of the evening came when the waitress set Brandon's steak in front of him. He was listening intently as Melissa described the school she'd gone to in Chicago—nearly as many students as Talbot had year-round residents—and all at once the smell of cooked meat was overpowering, right under his nose. He literally blanched.

"Are you all right?" Melissa said.

"Man, you just went white as a sheet," Chad said. He wondered if his friend was having a heart attack or something.

Brandon leaned back in his chair and gasped in several gulps of slightly fresher air. In the meat-infused haze of the Steak House, air quality was relative, but at least the general atmosphere wasn't quite as overwhelming as the stench emanating from the plate three feet from his nose.

"That was weird," Brandon said. "Thought I was gonna pass out there for a minute."

Melissa leaned over and placed one soft hand on his forearm. "Are you feeling better now?"

Her unexpected touch sent tiny spiders of electricity skittering up and down his arm. Now he didn't know *what* he was feeling.

"I think so," he said, but the second he leaned forward far enough to get another whiff of the meat, he nearly swooned. "Whoa," he said, and this time he pushed his chair several feet back from the table. People at tables adjacent to them paused mid-bite or mid-sentence to stare at him.

Waste, waste, what a complete waste, he thought. In his mind he saw mounds of succulent flesh, rivers of glistening fat, gleaming bones still gripped tight by sinew and tendon. He heard the splinter of bones between sharp teeth, tasted the slow, sensuous suck of marrow over his tongue and down his throat, felt the ooze of warm blood down his chin and chest as he moved on to the engorged flesh. Then he once again smelled the charred remains on his plate and nearly gagged. *What a complete and total waste.*

"Dude, what's up?" Chad said. "What's going on?"

Brandon shut his eyes and willed himself not to smell the incinerated slab before him. He opened his eyes and concentrated on the pinkish juices oozing onto the plate. *Almost right,* he thought. *Almost red, almost right.* Slowly, almost gingerly, he pulled his chair back to the table. "Sorry," he said. "We eat strictly vegan at the rectory, and I guess my body forgot what meat smelled like. I'm not gonna be able to eat this, if anybody wants it."

"Don't have to ask me twice," Chad said. He leaned across the table and forked Brandon's steak over to his own plate. The meat left dribbles of pinkish-gray ooze across the tablecloth and Brandon made sure he didn't look at them too closely. Nikki stared at Chad and appeared to be deciding something definitively all at once. Melissa offered a sympathetic smile and moved her own plate a little farther away from Brandon.

"You're going to starve," she said. "Order something else, at least."

"Nah, I'll be fine," Brandon said. "The salad filled me up pretty good, and I've still got my baked potato and these onion rings. Eat up, everybody. Don't mind me at all."

Almost hesitantly, Melissa began to nibble at her own dinner. Brandon made a show of digging into his baked potato with gusto, slathering it with butter and sour cream, but his stomach kept trying to roll over from the general meat smell permeating the restaurant. He grew quieter and more withdrawn as the dinner progressed, his focus narrowing away from his date and toward keeping himself from vomiting right there at the table. He was so intent on his own situation, he barely registered the change when Chad started talking more and more, and Melissa's attention made a slight but very noticeable shift toward the other side of the table.

. . .

Later, Brandon would place nearly all of the blame squarely on himself. By losing focus, by pulling into himself, he'd almost *forced* Chad to fill the conversational gap to keep Melissa entertained. *Ask a girl out, then freak out on her thirty minutes into the date. Smooth.*

What Brandon didn't take into account—at least at first—was how active a role Nikki had played in how the evening eventually turned out.

Nikki's feelings for Chad had been on the wane for some time. When she saw Chad step up to cover for Brandon's sudden weirdness, when she noticed Melissa's burgeoning interest in Chad, some part of her mind had looked on it as a pass, a Get-Out-Of-Jail-Free card.

Her break-ups were almost always unpleasant, tedious affairs. The boys would become angry, sometimes violent; then morose and despairing; finally whiny and pleading to a degree Nikki found almost comical. Here was the perfect opportunity to transition herself away from Chad with no muss, no fuss, and, presumably, no hard feelings.

She *would* have to sacrifice Brandon, she realized, and this prompted a twinge of guilt; she'd almost come to like Brandon over the past couple of months. But, realistically, what sort of chance did he have with a hot summer girl like Melissa anyway? Especially one who would soon be leaving Talbot forever?

In a way, I'm doing him a favor, Nikki thought. *The first one's always the hardest, and this one was way out of his league to begin with. Better to call in the dogs now, before he gets in too deep, than to have to watch him cut out his own heart when Melissa goes off to school in the fall.*

She made one last canvass of her feelings for Chad to make sure she wasn't giving him up before she was ready, and then she let herself fall further and further away from the thread of conversation around the table. By the time they left the restaurant, she was already thinking about who else she might want to hang out with this summer.

"You should tell Melissa about the Wolf Research Center," she told Chad, knowing the subject would make him light up like a pinball machine. "There's an hour yet before the movie starts. Brandon and I will go buy the tickets, and you can tell Melissa about the wild animals you hang out with every day."

Brandon looked into the night sky and let Nikki tug him down the sidewalk. Melissa had become the least of his concerns, barely a blip on his internal radar. He heard her laughing somewhere back there with Chad, heard Chad telling her his famous wolf evolution theory.

"See, early *Homo sapiens* saw the way wolves hunted in packs, how closely they cooperated, and adapted the same style to wipe poor *Neanderthal* right off the map. At the same time, wolves discovered human garbage dumps. Such easy pickings made them lazy, started them down the evolutionary pathway to becoming dogs."

"Doesn't sound like a very fair trade," Melissa said.

Brandon stopped listening. The sky was too big, the breeze too full of intriguing scents, the new muscles beneath his old muscles too taut and full of...*anticipation*.

The next full moon was still nine days away, but already Brandon could hear its call, faint and far in the distance. He could feel its tug, stronger and more basic than gravity, and he could feel his bones and muscles straining against their humdrum, everyday confines. *How long 'til this stupid night is over and I can run toward the moon?* he thought.

At his side, tugging him toward the theater, Nikki caught an echo of his thought—*how long 'til this night is over?*—and in her mind she saw the summer now stretching before her like verdant, uncharted wilderness. Free of high school, free of Chad: anything was possible. *My last summer in Talbot*, she thought. *My last summer ever in this pissant little burg...*

Overhead, a melon-colored half-moon appeared on the horizon like the birth of a sworn promise. When Brandon tilted his head to offer up a joyous, ragged howl, Nikki surprised even herself by laughing and joining in.

. . .

Father Holloway hadn't said another word about locking Brandon in the church basement during the full moon, but Brandon knew the idea was still on the priest's mind. Holloway watched him all the time now. Showing up unexpectedly while Brandon was doing yard work; finding excuses to keep Brandon at the dining room table long past dinner each night. Watching, always watching—not even pretending he wasn't. Trying to gauge the effects on Brandon as the moon grew fatter in the sky.

Even when he managed to avoid Holloway for an hour or two, Brandon felt constantly under observation these days. Invisible eyes always watching, invisible fingers reaching out to caress his skin. He could hear the moon calling, calling almost constantly now, until sometimes it felt like all he could do not to answer its siren song then and there. Actual transformation was impossible without the moon—*The Darker Heart* was adamant on that point—but this intractability only made the moon's call louder and more plaintive. The moon wanted him as much as he wanted it.

For the entire week leading up to the full moon, he was twitchy and anxious, horny beyond belief, and he didn't sleep for more than two or three hours at a stretch. His reflection in the mirror looked darker somehow, swarthier, and his mouth and eyes were very dry. Every so often his vision would blur, or veer into black and white for a moment, and he was able to hear and smell things almost unimaginable distances away. The wait for the full moon was endless, interminable, and sometimes he caught himself staring into space, scratching at some unreachable itch inside his hands until his palms literally bled.

No way in hell was he going to let Holloway put him down in that basement. Farmer Joe had been an isolated incident, a mistake of the moment. He'd been carried away by the thrill of his first shocking transformation, and Joe had simply gotten in the way—that was all. He felt no guilt over what had happened, but that didn't mean he was going to let it happen again. He simply wouldn't let himself go around people at all. He had no desire to be around people anyway. He wanted only to run through the forest, run with the moon. His heart ached for a run in the moonlight, a run like that first run, only this time he wouldn't let himself leave the trees to lap at the red pool. He'd simply continue on, deeper into the forest, farther and farther away from people and town and the strange unknowable boy he'd once thought of as himself.

Fortunately, he had miles of forest in which to try to lose that former self. He could disappear for days within just a few miles of town and never encounter another living soul. Even if there *were* people in the woods closer in, the forest sprawled across more than a million acres between Talbot and the Canadian border. A person—Brandon smiled at the inadequacy of the word—could hide in those trees forever.

On the morning before the full moon, Holloway finally broached the subject again. "You won't actually transform until tomorrow night," he said over breakfast. "But you'll definitely be feeling the effects of the moon already tonight. You'll feel quite unsettled and perhaps even violent, so I think it's best if we start you downstairs tonight, and keep you down there on the night *after* the full moon as well."

"I don't think—"

"I know you have strong reservations about being locked-in down there, but there's simply no way I can allow you to roam the countryside until you learn to control yourself."

"Control myself like you do?" Brandon said. "Like you did with me in April?"

This stopped Holloway cold. He looked at his plate as if hoping to find a suitable response hidden among the toast crumbs. A flush of embarrassment spread across his forehead and turned his ears a bright, painful-looking red. His voice was soft and somewhat hoarse when he finally spoke. "That was...an anomaly," he said. "A simple moment of weakness."

Brandon raised an eyebrow. "So you're telling me I'm the only—"

"No," Holloway said. "I won't lie about that." He wondered how much he should tell Brandon. Certainly not everything. Some things he didn't even allow *himself* to think about. "There were three others, very early on," he said. "Three moments I would give anything in the world to take back."

He thought three sounded like a reasonable number, and the three he had in mind still had specific faces he could recall. Two of the faces were blurred and indistinct now, two anonymous boys who'd meant little at the time and faded a bit more each time he thought of them, which wasn't often. The third face, however, remained startling and distinct even today. This was the one face that truly haunted him.

Of course, he'd actually *known* Dean Sommers—that made all the difference. He'd known Dean's dark eyes, his shaggy hair; known the dark smile that flashed from the other side of the small room they'd shared at the seminary. Holloway realized with a start how much Brandon reminded him of Dean, and the question he'd been asking himself for weeks found its answer.

Was I really so naïve to think I could atone for what I did to Dean by offering the same choice to this lonely outcast of a boy? Dean, who ran screaming at the first hint of my transformation. Dean, who died *screaming.*

That's exactly what had flashed into the strange spiral of his transformed mind when he first saw the boy out on the dark country roads on Christmas Eve. *Dean's come back to me. He's changed his mind after all these years and come back looking for me in the night...*

Never mind that the few measly scraps of Dean he hadn't devoured were now long-buried in a swamp nearly a thousand miles away. Never mind all the intervening years, or all the transformations since. His memory of Dean was still so fresh he could taste it.

Brandon's voice teetered between rage and anguish: "So would you take back what you did to *me* if you could?"

Holloway wasn't sure how to answer. Not because he wanted to spare Brandon's feelings, nor because he felt the need to justify his actions at this late date. He honestly didn't know how he felt—or perhaps he had too many conflicting emotions battling inside to pick just one.

Brandon's attack on Farmer Joe had been horrific—but ultimately no worse than anything he'd ever done during his transformed life. And he certainly understood how a man like Joe Westcott might have incited such a particular rage in Brandon. Holloway found it difficult to imagine Brandon releasing similar savagery on a purely anonymous or blameless victim.

Of course, he'd also found it hard to imagine, once upon a time, that a human being could turn into an animal in the first place. Even after he'd been bitten, even once he'd started to feel the beast inside him working its way to the surface, he'd grasped at every other possible answer first. Some sort of fever virus, delusional paranoia, outright insanity—any of these had seemed more likely and even more appealing than the freak-show truth of what he'd finally been forced to accept.

True, Brandon was different from him in many ways. For one thing, Brandon had actively sought the bite. At least that's what Holloway told himself when he was feeling guilty about what he'd done. And even if the boy hadn't actively been looking for the bite, he'd *accepted* the bite when the time came. The bite and its consequences had been entirely his own choice. Or so Holloway tried to convince himself.

Then there was the apparent ease and speed of Brandon's first transformation. Holloway had fought against the beast for ten agonizing months after he'd been bitten, desperate not to lose his humanity, desperate not to follow the call of the moon. But Brandon hadn't given the matter a second thought. He'd *liked* it, he said. He'd taken Joe Westcott down and fed upon him with no more hesitation or remorse than he would have felt in ordering a couple of burgers, rare, from the Dairy Queen.

Still, Holloway couldn't help but remember the quiet, solemn boy who'd shown up on his doorstep on Christmas morning. The boy so uncertain of his place in the world that he would sometimes go days without saying a word if someone else didn't speak to him first. The boy so painfully shy that for the first month he was at the rectory he couldn't even bring himself to ask for seconds at dinner if he was still hungry.

That boy—now a ruthless, cold-blooded killer, ready to prey on any innocent victim who might accidentally cross his path?

"No," Holloway said. "I wouldn't take back what I did to you. You asked for something you wanted, and I complied with your request. I'm just afraid it's all too new for you to truly understand what the rest of your life is going to be like. I want to keep you close for the next few nights as much for your own safety as anyone else's."

"Keep me close?" Brandon said. "Chain me up, you mean."

Holloway thought about this. "We probably wouldn't need to use chains tonight yet," he said. "Tomorrow night, during the actual full moon, they certainly wouldn't hurt."

"Wouldn't hurt you, maybe. I'm telling you, I won't be able to handle it. I'll freak out. I'll—"

"Would it help if I stayed down there with you?"

"Oh yeah, that's much better," Brandon said. "Chain me up helpless next to a goddamned werewolf."

Holloway flinched, although it was hard to say at which word in particular. The flinch amused Brandon, and Holloway noted the distinctive luminescent flare that played momentarily behind the boy's dark pupils. A single word, a concept more than an actual thought, flashed deep inside his brain—

(alpha)

—and then dissipated again like smoke. The human side of his mind grasped just enough of the moment to reaffirm, yet again, what a terrible mistake he'd let himself make. The weakness was still there, always there, even all these many years later. Dean should have been lesson enough. But that was yet another aspect of the weakness: the heart wants what it wants, and it steadfastly refuses to learn.

"Will you please just do it for me?" he said. "I know I can't actually force you, it's entirely up to you, but it would mean a lot to me, Brandon. Just this first month."

"Second month," Brandon said. He heaved a great sigh and tossed his napkin onto the table.

Giving in, Holloway thought. The relief he felt was palpable. Brandon would no doubt do it more to get Holloway off his back than because of any real sympathy for his concerns—but ultimately the reason didn't matter.

"I appreciate this, Brandon," Holloway said. "I really do."

"I've got a bunch of stuff to do today. I assume I'm still allowed outside until dark?"

"Of course. And you'll see—it won't be nearly as bad as you think."

Brandon rose from the table and disappeared down the hallway toward his bedroom. A few minutes later, Holloway noticed him outside the dining room window, moving across the parking lot as if planning to walk down the hill into town. Holloway was wondering if he should run out and offer the use of his car—a peace offering—when Brandon took a sharp turn and cut down into the grassy scrub on the other side of the hill, down a ragged path that would lead away from town and into the forest. He was carrying a bulging duffel bag slung haphazardly over one shoulder.

Even then, it took several seconds before Holloway realized what was happening. He almost smiled, but quickly bit the smile back. If he ever saw Brandon again, he'd have to tell him what a good joke that had been, how completely he'd been taken in by such a simple and obvious ploy.

In the meantime, perhaps he'd go tell Mrs. McGowan to take the rest of the summer off, go visit one of her sons in another part of the country. Mrs. McGowan, not nearly as slow or easily fooled as he, would no doubt have her bags packed and be out the door before dinner-time.

The rest of the town, Holloway knew, wasn't going to be nearly so lucky.

. . .

Friday night, the night of the full moon, Holloway retreated into the basement shortly before sunset. Mrs. McGowan had refused his offer of an extended vacation—"I'll decide when it's time to head for the hills, thank you very much," she said—and instead had spent the day thawing several large slabs of beef and venison to leave with him when she locked him in. Despite what he'd told Brandon, Holloway knew being locked inside during a transformation wouldn't be easy. He'd already resigned himself to going without a live cow this month (and perhaps for many months to come), but the thought of going without meat entirely was unbearable.

He'd briefly considered venturing into the forest himself. He was reasonably certain he could control his own impulses if he encountered any people—he had for years, after all—and being outside would have allowed him a chance to hunt, to perhaps bring down a small deer or at least a rabbit. How long had it been since he'd actually hunted? Not some slow, stupid, half-dead cow from Joe Westcott's farm, but a wild, living creature intent on avoiding his jaws? The thought of a real chase, a real kill, both thrilled and terrified him.

He'd also wondered if he might somehow be able to find Brandon. Find him—but then what? Lead him deep into the forest, away from civilization? Convince him to return to the church? Perhaps even...challenge him for dominance? The thought of encountering the new Brandon under the baleful eye of the moon finally tipped the scale. Holloway could live with a little claustrophobia and discomfort for one night. And venison was still venison, whether it arrived wrapped in butcher paper or in soft, eminently chewable hide. And so he'd slunk away into the basement—he'd even felt something approaching relief when he heard Mrs. McGowan slide the heavy deadbolt shut behind him.

Truthfully, the night had gone better than he'd expected. He'd been anxious and fidgety prior to moonrise, and for a short time after he transformed the wolf in him became panicky and terrified, frantic to get out of the room. Then he'd found the raw meat and settled down to feed. Once his belly was full, he calmed and resigned himself to his fate.

Eventually he slept, and woke to the sound of Mrs. McGowan releasing the deadbolt. He gathered the clothes he'd scattered during his transformation, checked the room for damage—there was none—and made his way upstairs to breakfast. He felt a bit hung-over, but otherwise none the worse for his ordeal. He wondered if Brandon had fared anywhere near as well.

. . .

Brandon spent the night before the June full moon on a hillock of soft grass in what had once been a small vegetable garden behind the Hackamore shack. The shack—or what was left of it—huddled deep in the forest about five miles northeast of Talbot. The narrow dirt path that had once led to it was now overgrown with brush and nearly indistinguishable from the landscape around it, and the cabin itself was little more than a vague rectangle of spongy wood sinking slowly into the earth.

The Hackamore shack was the stuff of local legend. For nearly a century, each new generation of Talbot teenagers had thrilled and terrified one another with stories of how the owner of the shack, George Hackamore, had taken an axe to his wife and children one snowbound night, then spent the remainder of that long-ago winter first sewing their remains back together in new and interesting ways and finally devouring their bodies bit by succulent bit.

In truth, Brandon knew, the cabin had belonged to a man named Henry Froehlich, a shell-shocked World War I veteran who had disappeared into the woods to live out the remainder of his life in solitude. His death had been even more lonely than his life: one day he simply left the tiny shack, walked into the forest, and was never heard from again.

As always, the truth had been helpless in the face of a good story. Some enterprising soul had discovered the abandoned shack several years later—already falling apart in the harsh extremes of the Minnesota climate—and spun the tale of the infamous George Hackamore. Sometimes, people claimed, you could still see a lamp burning at the Hackamore place late at night, as George stalked the forest in search of new victims. Brandon knew that any light in the vicinity more likely came from a campfire, around which a group of teenagers drank beer, made out, and told their own versions of the Hackamore legend in an effort to entice reluctant dates to sit closer.

In the last few years, even teenagers had mostly stopped coming to the shack. Once the last structural planks had collapsed in upon themselves, once the land had begun to recycle the boards into rich, musty-smelling loam, the site had lost much of its appeal. Now it was just another clearing in the forest. Difficult to reach, full of poison ivy and thorns, protected just enough from the wind to be a haven for mosquitoes and biting flies.

Even as he was walking away from Saint Ignatius, Brandon had known the Hackamore shack was his destination. He made the trek through the thick brush and tangling undergrowth in just over two hours. He flattened a patch of grass and rolled out his sleeping bag, then slathered himself with bug repellant and waited to see what the night would bring.

He'd never had a great fear of the woods to begin with, and he had even less now. Now the woods were a part of him; now some part of him was a creature made to run through the woods without hesitation. He lay on top of the sleeping bag, smelling the mossy dirt and the fragrant greenery all around him, and watched as the light slowly bled from the sky. Stars appeared, and a fat glowing orb inched over the tops of the trees on the other side of the clearing. Close, so close to full—and yet out here, away from town, the moon's call did not feel nearly so frantic and overwhelming as it had before. *Patience*, it whispered. *You're in the forest now, where time means nothing, and tomorrow night will come soon enough. Rest now, rest for tomorrow, rest for the time when you'll finally be able to run just as you were always meant to run.*

On the soft grass, beneath the not-quite-full moon, Brandon slept. The insomnia and twitchiness of the past few days finally caught up with him—or perhaps left him for different reasons altogether—and he sank into the soft warmth of the sleeping bag, sank into himself, and finally sank beyond himself into a series of startlingly vivid dreams.

In the first, he was on his belly, very low to the ground, staring through stalks of tall grass and clusters of tiny leaves at a fat brown rabbit nibbling wild clover a few paces away. Some stray weed tickled his belly, or perhaps an ant crawled there, and he desperately wanted to move, to scratch the itch, but he also knew the slightest motion would startle the rabbit, and this would make his belly itch in a different way. Then he was out of the grass and the rabbit was wriggling in his hands; he was gnawing at its throat.

As sometimes happens in dreams, Brandon experienced the moment and watched it from somewhere else at the same time. The watching Brandon smiled, horrified and amused in equal measure. Dreams were so strange. He'd once had a pet rabbit—Fluffy—that his father had killed and cooked for Sunday dinner for reasons Brandon still to this day could not imagine. He'd told Brandon they were eating chicken, but Brandon had put two and two together quickly enough as soon as he'd discovered Fluffy's empty hutch. He remembered running behind the garage and vomiting until he thought his stomach would come up in little shreds, and it was inconceivable he would ever again eat rabbit after that. Yet the dream Brandon continued to gnaw at the bunny with his inadequate human teeth until even the watching Brandon could feel little tufts of fur sticking in the back of his throat, feel tiny lice fleeing the carcass to swarm across his hands and down his arms.

Later, the dream changed. Brandon was still in the clearing, still eating the rabbit, but now his teeth and fingernails were much better equipped to rip through the fur and skin and sinew, and his bunny meal was infinitely more satisfying. Even so, something was missing. Some part of the event was vaguely unsatisfying, incomplete, and the dream Brandon and the watching Brandon looked up at the same moment to see, across the clearing, a pack of wolves bringing down a terrified deer. The chase had evidently gone on for a while, and the deer was exhausted. Three of the wolves circled in front of it while a fourth darted around and bit through a tendon in one of the deer's hind legs. The deer overcompensated, tumbling forward in an awkward somersault, and a fifth wolf—a huge black female—leapt onto its belly and bit through its jugular in a single clean snap.

The dream Brandon and the watching Brandon settled down to watch the wolves feed, and after a time the dream Brandon grew disappointed with his own meager bunny meal in light of the feast just a few yards away. The wolves sensed his disappointment, his new hunger, and eventually the entire pack turned away from the deer and stared at him across the clearing. They looked at the ragged, bloody rabbit carcass in his hands, and appeared to be smirking at his weakness, his pathetic snack. The dream Brandon shrugged and tossed the bunny aside, and the black wolf ripped a hunk from the deer's juicy hindquarters and padded over to drop it at Brandon's feet.

Later still, the dream changed once more, and Brandon found himself alone in the clearing with the deer carcass, experiencing the dream but no longer seeming to watch from the sidelines at the same time. The wolves had departed, but the deer carcass was still full of meat, and the dream Brandon wished the watching Brandon was still there to share such a bounty. Then he became distracted by the clean, sharp *snap!* each of the deer's ribs made as he cracked it away from the central cage, and then he was lost inside the rib cage, and the splintery texture of bone in his mouth, and the warm, yeasty paste of marrow mixed with saliva.

Brandon woke to sharp sunlight and the insistent buzz of a bumblebee that apparently thought his ear was some new sort of flower. He brushed the bee away and sat up. He was surprised to discover he was naked—he'd been wearing boxers and a T-shirt when he first lay down on top of the sleeping bag—but he assumed he'd simply gotten too warm during the night and slipped them off in his sleep. He used to do that with his pajamas all the time as a kid. The discarded garments weren't immediately visible, but Brandon assumed he'd find them somewhere in the general vicinity.

Blinking sleep out of his eyes, Brandon noticed his shadow stretching out away from him. His hair was standing up in crazy spikes and tangles, and he smiled at the comical image he knew he must present. Naked, grinning, a crazy briar patch of hair going every which way. Anyone wandering into the clearing would think they'd stumbled upon some hippie refugee from the sixties, or perhaps George Hackamore's long-lost great-grandson, now gone feral. Brandon laughed, and a chipmunk that had been hiding nearby bolted for the safety of a fallen tree.

Brandon pawed around in his duffel bag until he found a pair of shorts and a different T-shirt. He pulled them on and then found his wristwatch underneath a small zip bag of granola he'd smuggled out of Mrs. McGowan's pantry. He started to slide the watch over his wrist, amused at how late he'd slept—it was nearly one in the afternoon—but then noticed the number in the little date window. June 22. According to the watch, Brandon had not only slept through the night before the full moon, but through the full moon and into the following day as well. Sixty hours. Was it even possible for a human being to sleep that long in a single stretch?

Human being, Brandon thought. He smiled.

Somewhat befuddled now—was his watch broken? was this some sort of unfathomable trick?—Brandon shook out his sleeping bag and rolled it into a tight bundle. He shoved it into the duffel bag and slung the bag over one shoulder, then headed down the vague trail that led away from the Hackamore shack and back toward civilization. If his watch was correct and the full moon was truly past, there was no longer any threat of the basement back at the church. He could ask Father Holloway's forgiveness, point out his successful, kill-free transformation. Holloway wouldn't have to worry about any subsequent full moons. Brandon moved through the brush with animal-like ease, and by the time he reached the edge of the forest he'd almost forgotten about waking up naked, and about the clothing that had never appeared like he'd thought it would.

A lost pair of skivvies and some grungy old T-shirt didn't matter anyway. What mattered was that he'd gone through a full moon without a kill. He was sure of that. For one thing, he'd woken up hungry as...well, a wolf. And he'd also woken up almost pristinely clean. No blood, no scrapes, no indication he'd even moved from his sleeping bag in that unbelievable stretch of hours. He was smiling as he left the forest, and by the time he approached the church he was humming one of Mrs. McGowan's dishwashing songs.

Had he taken a moment to really look around before he left the clearing, he might have noticed one thing that would have given him pause. He might have noticed the trampled-down grass just over the hill from where he'd been sleeping, and inside it the now almost completely denuded skeleton of a large deer, too stripped of flesh to even be of interest to crows.

Having noticed this, Brandon might have moved a little closer, and discovered a strange and terrible anomaly inside the deer's splintered rib cage. This anomaly was the skeletal hand and forearm of a fisherman who'd heard the wolves bringing down the deer and who'd come up from the nearby river to investigate. The wolves, wary of humans, had startled at the fisherman's approach and prepared to bolt, but Brandon had no such innate fear. He was already full from his share of the deer, so he ended up dumping most of the fisherman's body into the river when he went to clean himself, and the fisherman was already several miles downstream, his bloated corpse bobbing in a gentle current.

Brandon had held on to the hand and forearm, delicately nibbling flesh from bone as he left the river, because the taste was so strikingly different from the taste of the deer, and it had triggered a puzzle deep within him. He'd obsessed about it for hours under the moonlight, until finally he understood. Only then was he able to discard the bones in amongst the deer's rib cage.

Human is to deer as deer is to rabbit. Bunny was perfectly fine, sweet and succulent, but also vaguely unsatisfying. Deer was better, with its solid heft, its gamey wildness that tasted of oak and maple. But human—there was the true delicacy. The buttery flesh, the sinewy muscle. Marbled fat seasoned in the last moments of the person's life by adrenaline and the pungent tang of sheer terror.

Back in his sleeping bag, Brandon ran the different flavors over and over through his mind as his eyes grew heavy and his full belly drew him down toward sleep. *Rabbit, deer, fisherman. Rabbit, deer, fisherman.* There were lots of fisherman around Talbot this time of year—and other delicacies as well.

Chad, his mind whispered. *Kate. Melissa.*

A single sharp canine tooth glinted over Brandon's lip as he smiled and burrowed deeper into sleep. His final waking thought was of the old Ojibwe story, the tale of the forsaken boy. *I am a wolf!* he thought, and even in sleep he reared his head and offered up a laughing howl.

When he left the forest a day and a half later, his memory was as clean and blank as a freshly laundered sheet, the only thought in his mind what amazing vegan delicacy Mrs. McGowan might prepare that night to celebrate his triumphant return to civilization.

July

Brandon wasn't all that surprised to find he still had a room and a job waiting for him at Saint Ignatius. What *did* surprise him was that he also had a message waiting upon his return.

"Melissa Henning called?" he said. "For me?"

"Well, she wasn't calling for religious instruction," Father Holloway said. "Or the secret to Mrs. McGowan's oatmeal cookies." He smiled until he remembered he was still trying to be angry. Some part of him *was* angry—a large part—but mostly he was just relieved Brandon had returned home safe and there'd been no word of any new Farmer Joe-type incidents during the full moon. At least so far.

"Did she say what she wanted?" Brandon asked.

"I would imagine she wanted to know when you were going to ask her out again," Mrs. McGowan said. "Gorry, is every one of you men slower than the next?"

. . .

Melissa *was* calling about the prospect of another night on the town, but Brandon didn't think his own involvement mattered all that much. "I assume a town like this makes a big deal over the Fourth of July," she said when he called her back. "If you guys are going to see fireworks, I thought maybe I could tag along."

"Us guys?"

"You and Chad," Melissa said. "And Nikki, of course."

"Chad and Nikki broke up," Brandon said. He doubted this information was entirely new to Melissa.

"Oh," she said. "That's too bad. They seemed like a nice couple."

"Did they?" He had no idea why he was acting snarky, or why the next words out of his mouth were a blatant lie: "Besides, Chad has to work that night." He listened to the momentary silence on the other end of the line and wondered if Melissa was trying to think up some way to wriggle back out of the evening.

"I guess it's just you and me then," she said. "I mean, if you're interested."

"Sure. Sounds like fun."

"I also hear there's some big arts and crafts festival in town that day. Maybe we could wander around there a bit before the fireworks start."

"It's mostly just tourist junk and overpriced jewelry," Brandon said. "Although there *is* a stand that serves some mean fry-bread and kettle-corn."

"Overpriced jewelry and empty carbs," Melissa said. "Now you're talkin' my language."

. . .

They met at the entrance to Ferris Park, on the western edge of Talbot. The park was only a couple of blocks square, little more than swing sets and a jungle gym for the kiddies, but the Chamber of Commerce had put in paved walking paths that led from the park all the way down to Deadfall Lake, where fireworks would be set off at dusk from the large, well-maintained public access area.

As part of Talbot's Fourth of July celebration, Ferris Park hosted an arts and crafts festival every year, and the selection was quite a bit more eclectic than Brandon had led Melissa to believe. They wandered through several avenues of booths and tents containing everything from intricate leatherwork to wood carving to painting and hand-made jewelry. Fancy camping equipment was on display, as well as Native American artwork and even several stands featuring sled dog equipment and guide services.

"This is amazing," Melissa said, casually taking Brandon's hand and leading him around a logjam outside a booth of wildlife photography. "And look at this crowd! Where do they all come from?"

"Every resort and campground for miles," Brandon said. "And every little town between here and Grand Rapids. Just something for people to do."

"It must be weird to live in a place where there's not always something to do."

"Well, I guess there's always stuff to do," Brandon said. "It just usually isn't very entertaining."

She squeezed his hand and he smiled. He was surprised at how well the evening was going so far. He was feeling more relaxed than he would have expected, and Melissa didn't even seem disappointed that Chad hadn't joined them.

Chad had laughed when Brandon confessed his lie. "Betrayed over a chick," he'd said. "Guess I'll stay home with Mom this year, watch the fireworks from the other side of the lake so I don't cramp your style."

"Appreciate it," Brandon said. And now that he was here on his own with Melissa, he was both surprised and pleased to discover he was doing just fine without his friend along as a safety net.

As they reached the end of one lane of exhibits and prepared to move on to the next, Melissa stopped and squeezed Brandon's hand a little harder. "Look," she said. She bounced on the balls of her feet like a four-year-old seeing Santa for the first time, and began dragging him toward a small, shabby tent in the farthest corner of the park. Its placement at the very edge of the festivities—*bastard cousin at a family reunion*, Brandon thought—made it seem even sadder and more dilapidated than it otherwise would have.

"This is new," Brandon said. "The last time I saw a fortuneteller in town was at a school carnival, and that was just the principal dressed up in his wife's housecoat and a clown wig."

"We have to go in," Melissa said. "I went to a palm reader once when we were on vacation in California, and everything she told me came true."

"Spooky," Brandon said.

They reached the tent and had just enough time to read a hand-painted sign insisting *"Madame Irglova Knows YOUR Future!"* before the tent flap folded back and Madame Irglova herself emerged from the incense-scented darkness within. "Welcome, welcome!" The old woman bowed theatrically and only managed to right herself with obvious effort. She didn't seem dressed so much as draped in what looked to be about twenty layers of gauzy, diaphanous silk of varying colors, and she wobbled in place as if about one rum-and-Coke away from passing out at their feet. Still, her dark eyes were sharp and smiling, and her voice was strong and cheery as she told them, "You see? Even with the flap closed, I saw you coming just as clear as I see your futures."

Brandon noticed the small hole in the side of the tent through which Madame Irglova had undoubtedly seen them coming—in more ways than one—but Melissa was nearly bursting with happy excitement, so all he said was, "How much?"

"Twenty dollars each," Madame Irglova said. "Plus a tip, if you're so inclined."

. . .

The inside of the tent was dark, lit only by flickering candles, and so overwhelmingly filled with scent Brandon felt his sinuses clench shut in protest the second the flap closed behind them. Madame Irglova guided them to two wobbly camp chairs beside a small round table, and eased herself into a slightly more substantial armchair on the other side. The table was bare save for a stubby candle in the center. *No crystal ball?* Brandon thought.

"You two are not actually together, I think," Madame Irglova said. She appeared to be aiming for some sort of vague eastern European syntax, but her voice was strictly cornfed Midwest. She leaned back in her armchair and examined them carefully, her eyes glittering in the candlelight like beetle wings.

"No," Melissa said. "We haven't really known each other very long."

"But that's not the reason," Madame Irglova said. "There's another boy, I think, hovering nearby."

Chad, Brandon thought. *Chad's the one who should be here with Melissa.*

Madame Irglova freed one hand from several layers of silk and waggled her fingers to the left of Brandon's shoulder. "No, it's not the boy you're thinking of," she said.

Brandon raised an eyebrow, but remained silent.

"Not the boy you're *both* thinking of," Madame Irglova said, and Brandon saw Melissa's shoulders jump a little.

"It's not the blond boy," Madame Irglova continued. "Not the boy who somehow connects the two of you, but another boy I can't see clearly. A dark boy, a shadow boy, hovering just...*here*."

She once more waggled her fingers to Brandon's left, and Brandon thought of a dozen old black-and-white movies on late-night TV. *Here's where she calls me out, here's where she finds the mark of the beast, here's where the villagers come with their torches and their pitchforks and their silver bullets...*

But Madame Irglova merely shrugged and brushed the shadow boy away with a flick of her hand. "So tell me," she said. "What would you like to ask Madame Irglova this evening?"

"I guess I'd like to know if I'm going to like college," Melissa said. "Will I like my dorm? Will I get good grades? Will I gain the 'freshman fifteen'?"

"Hold out your right hand," Madame Irglova said. She once again extricated her own hands from several layers of silk, but rather than examining Melissa's palm, as Brandon expected, she took Melissa's hand in both of hers and looked piercingly into Melissa's eyes. She appeared to ponder something puzzling for a long time before releasing Melissa's hand and settling back in her armchair. "No," she said. "It's too early to tell if you will even *go* to school, I think."

"Of course I'm going to school," Melissa said. "Do you think I'm going to hang out here in the sticks and—"

"Yes, yes, duckling. You have plans, you hear the city calling. I'm only saying sometimes the world doesn't cooperate with the plans of young girls."

Melissa sat back with a huff. Brandon wondered if they should cut the reading short and head back out into the park, but Madame Irglova reached out and took his left hand between hers. Her hands were dry but firm. Not the dusty, wrinkled grandma-claws he expected, but solid and strong and slightly cool to the touch. "Now you," she said.

As with Melissa, Madame Irglova looked deep into Brandon's eyes for what felt like several minutes. Then, to Brandon's surprise, she bent to closely examine his palm in the flickering candlelight. *Here's where she finds the mark. A pentagram—like in the old movies.* It was all he could do to keep from wrenching his hand away and bolting from the tent.

After a moment, the fortuneteller released Brandon's hand and settled back once more. "You also have plans for school that might be interrupted," she said. "And somehow these things are connected, but—"

"What do you think?" Melissa said. "We're gonna run off and get married or something?" Brandon blushed, unsure if Melissa's anger was at the thought of delayed college plans or the idea of marrying him.

"No," Madame Irglova said. "There's no marriage in store for either of you—not anytime soon. I just see that your plans are not as set as you think they are, and again I see that shadow boy hovering somewhere very close. He's the key to what will ultimately happen. And his heart's more unknowable than any I've ever encountered."

Melissa snorted and folded her arms across her chest. Brandon pulled his wallet out of the pocket of his jeans, but Madame Irglova held up both hands and shook her head. "No, young man, no. Your girl was not so happy with Madame Irglova, so let's call this a free sample and part ways here."

"What about me?" Brandon said. "Do you think I liked what I heard?"

Madame Irglova eyed him shrewdly, and Brandon wondered if he was going to regret his question. "Oh, you already knew your plans were likely to change, I think, and I get the feeling you won't be upset if they do. Unlike the girl, you like it here in the sticks. The sticks, the trees, the lonely woods."

Brandon stared at her. *Do you know or don't you? If I come back later, alone, will you tell my real future or run screaming down the sidewalk? What if I come see you the next time the moon is full?*

Then Melissa was on her feet, grasping his hand, dragging him out into the warm July evening. Even without looking back, Brandon knew Madame Irglova was busy blowing out candles and packing up her tent. Not a profitable night for fortunetelling in Talbot, she was no doubt telling herself. Time to move on to the county fairs that would begin popping up across the state over the next few weeks. Or perhaps time to head south, out of the state altogether. How many days did she have, she was perhaps wondering, before that next full moonrise, and just how far away could she get?

. . .

"Sorry about that," Melissa said as they wandered back toward the center of the park. "I thought it would be fun."

Brandon knew he would become distant and tongue-tied if he let himself brood too much on the fortuneteller's words, so he manufactured a smile and tried to compel his energy level to rise by sheer force of will. "Yeah, that was weird, wasn't it?" he said. "I think the principal did a way better job."

Melissa laughed and together they began to weave their way through the crowd. There was a Sno-Cone stand right before the start of the lake path, and Brandon excused himself and went over to buy them each a big mound of flavored ice for the walk. He'd just finished paying and was lifting the overflowing paper cones out of the holder on the counter when he realized he'd made a huge tactical error by leaving Melissa alone. Behind him, he heard a familiar voice say, "You must be new, cuz I sure the hell would have noticed an ass like that if I'd seen it before." He turned to see Daryl Reisling sidle up beside Melissa while several of his friends hung back and smirked.

"I'm actually with someone," Melissa said, more ice in her voice than in the two Sno-Cones combined. She nodded toward Brandon, and Daryl turned to size up his competition. His expression when he saw who it was made Brandon's stomach turn—as if a hyena was hiding just beneath the surface of Daryl's smooth, blemish-free skin.

"Hey, rez rat," Daryl said. "When did you start liking girls?"

Daryl's cronies laughed, but there wasn't the slightest trace of humor in the sound. *Hyenas*, Brandon thought again. *A whole pack of them, and not a single teacher to keep them from tearing me apart this time.*

Daryl turned back toward Melissa. "So tell me," he said. "Did you know this boyfriend of yours is a big ol' queer?"

"That's funny," Melissa said. "He seems pretty straight whenever we're in bed."

Daryl barked out a laugh. "You must be pretty easily pleased. Or just pretty easy, if you're sleeping with him."

Melissa's right hand twitched as if she were about to slap Daryl, and Brandon immediately threw the Sno-Cones onto the ground and stepped in front of her.

This made Daryl laugh again. "You gotta be fucking kidding me. What do you think *you're* gonna do here?"

"You might be surprised what I can do now," Brandon said.

He stepped forward, hands automatically forming fists, and was pleased to see a look of genuine surprise on Daryl's face. Maybe even a little fear.

Then another voice cut through the tension between them like a big, blunt knife—"Trouble here, boys?"—and Davis Langley was standing next to Melissa as if he'd been there the entire time.

Brandon thought he could see Daryl's mouth re-forming words even as they were coming out: "Nope, no trouble here, Chief. Just saying howdy to an old school bud."

"Yeah, looks like the two of you were real close," Davis said. "How about you reconnect with your old friend some other time, and right now get your ass back to your own date. Last I checked, you were with *my* daughter tonight, and I don't see her anywhere in your general vicinity."

"Yes, sir," Daryl said, and behind him his friends sniggered. "Nikki's just over at one of the jewelry tables, and I thought—"

"I doubt you thought much at all," Davis said. "Brandon, this goes for you too. You boys steer clear of one another the rest of the night, understand? And Brandon, clean up those Sno-Cones or I'm gonna cite you for littering."

This brought another humorless laugh from the hyenas, and then they slunk away. Davis raised his eyebrows at Brandon in something between a question and a warning and then he, too, left the scene.

. . .

"I take it there's some history there," Melissa said as they made their way down the path toward the lake.

"With Daryl?" Brandon said. "Yeah, I guess that would be one way to put it. Let's just say he's not my number one fan."

"Why?"

Brandon had asked himself the same question hundreds of times. Thousands. Not just about Daryl, but all of them. Why had they taken one look at him back in second grade and decided he was going to be the one they'd all hate?

He thought of the threadbare clothes he'd been wearing, scrounged from a church rummage sale. He thought of the hole in his shirt and the patches on his jeans; the clean Levi's and printed t-shirts his classmates had worn. He thought of their sturdy backpacks, their full lunchboxes, their stickers and trading cards—the secret code of their shared history.

He remembered the bruised banana he'd brought for snack time, and how he'd practically salivated over the Oreos and graham crackers and Little Debbie cakes the other kids had carried. He remembered how, one day, their teacher had surreptitiously slipped him a Snickers before class—the look of pity in her eyes, the kindness that somehow felt like punishment. The candy bar had burned like molten lava going down his throat, and to this day that specific combination of chocolate and caramel and nougat could still make him gag. The taste of shame, still sharp after more than ten years.

"Hey, you still with me?" Melissa asked.

"I remember once, right after I came here," Brandon said. "Everyone was playing cowboys and Indians at recess and Daryl wouldn't even let me be the Indian—that's how much he hated me."

Melissa wasn't sure what to say. She'd certainly seen enough bigotry and bias growing up in Chicago, but for some reason she'd always assumed small towns would be nicer. "After you came here?" she said.

"I moved here when I was eight." Brandon hesitated. He rarely talked about his mother with anyone, not even Chad, but Melissa was gripping his hand again, looking at him with her amazing emerald eyes, so he took a deep breath and made himself continue. "I was living with my mom on the reservation in Mille Lacs, but then she died and some social worker managed to track down my dad here in Talbot. I can't believe she put that asshole's name on the birth certificate. Knowing my mom, I'm surprised she even *knew* his name."

Melissa remained very still. Brandon turned away from her and stared at some distant, unknowable horizon. She was afraid he might be checking out on her again, like he'd done that night at the Steak House. She gently waggled his hand in hers. "What happened to her?" she said.

Brandon shrugged. "She drank too much and passed out in some dude's pickup. He thought she was dead and he panicked. Threw her body into a dumpster and later that night she puked and choked on her own vomit." He cleared his throat. "And I got to move to Talbot."

They continued on, moving through the crowd, and Brandon grew silent for a long stretch. Lost in memory, churning through muck he could never quite push all the way under the surface. *I don't know why I even try*, he thought. *I'm never going to be someone who can be with someone like Melissa.*

"Sorry," he said. "I'm not a very good date."

"You're fine," Melissa said, but they both knew she was lying. They watched the fireworks in near silence, walked back up the path overly absorbed in the banal conversations going on around them, and then parted at the edge of the park as if the night had never happened.

"Good luck at school this fall," Brandon said, his gaze locked on a spot just beyond her right ear.

"Hey, you're stuck with me for another month and a half yet," Melissa said. "I'll call you tomorrow."

But Brandon only smiled and stared beyond her, and finally she turned and disappeared into the departing crowd.

. . .

He knew he didn't want to go back to the rectory, but he didn't know where else to go, either. The next full moon was more than two weeks away, and Brandon felt nothing of its siren song yet except a dull, unreachable itch in the palms of his hands and the soles of his feet. He thought about calling Chad, but didn't want to talk about his latest failure with Melissa just yet. He thought about hiking out to the Westcott farm to sit in the quiet darkness of the abandoned barn, but worried someone might see him along the road and wonder what he was up to. For a long time he simply sat beneath a towering oak tree in the darkest corner of Ferris Park, letting his mind go utterly blank. When he finally came back up out of himself, the park was empty and the entire town eerily silent.

Brandon didn't have his watch with him, but he knew it must be very late. Even Talbot, small as it was, had a nightlife, but there were no cars driving down any of the streets, no music or laughter emanating from any of the bars a few blocks away. Last-call was long past, closing time had come and gone, and even the two overnight police cruisers had apparently decided the town was buttoned up tight for the night and headed back to the station.

Brandon imagined himself the only person left alive, and he remembered how Talbot had felt like a ghost town as he drove its empty streets on Christmas morning. How nice that had been, how peaceful and welcoming. Then, far in the distance, somewhere on the other side of Deadfall Lake, a few leftover fireworks popped and whistled halfheartedly. His heart sank as he realized there were still other people alive and awake in the night. There would always be other people.

Soon enough, the night offered even more proof of life continuing on around him. Brandon heard the footsteps long before he saw the person responsible for them, and instinctively he ducked back into the shadows to hide from whoever it might turn out to be.

It turned out to be Nikki Langley, and Brandon had a flash of memory of watching her walk alone down another dark path. She emerged from the shadows of the Deadfall Lake pathway and began a ragged diagonal through Ferris Park, her footsteps instantly silenced as she left the pavement to cut across the grass. Brandon inched around the tree for a better view, but he probably could have leapt right out in front of her and still not received so much as a nod.

Nikki was very drunk, and she was either crying or had only recently stopped. When she passed beneath one of the streetlights at the edge of the park, Brandon could see that her blouse was torn and hanging funny off one shoulder, and she had a smudge across one cheek that looked very much like the type of bruise his mother had come home with every once in a while.

He thought about going to Nikki, helping her home, but then remembered who she was dating now, who she'd been with earlier, and Nikki slipped from Brandon's mind as easily as she slipped into one of the dark yards across the street from the park and began making her way home. Brandon pivoted and followed Nikki's diagonal in its opposite direction. He hit the pathway to Deadfall Lake and disappeared into the darkness.

. . .

Daryl Reisling was sitting on one of the benches the city had placed near the public access area, drinking a beer and staring blearily at the dome of sky over the mirror-like lake. Periodically, a straggler bottle rocket would whistle up from one side of the lake and then be answered a minute or two later by a small burst of color arcing up from another area entirely. Daryl met each of these tiny volleys with a loud whoop and a toast with his beer can. He met these lame homemade displays with the same enthusiasm the crowd earlier had expressed for the professional, city-sponsored event.

Brandon paused just out of Daryl's sightline. Daryl was shirtless and the top two buttons of his Levi's were unbuttoned to reveal a thin line of dark hair disappearing into his groin. There was enough light from the sky—or perhaps Brandon's eyes just handled the darkness better now—to see what looked like a flush of color across the knuckles of Daryl's right hand. *No doubt the same general shape as Nikki's bruise*, Brandon thought. A jumble of scents hung over the night—adrenaline, sweat, semen, blood—and Brandon's nostrils flared with understanding. Instantly he was bounding toward Daryl, and Daryl was on his feet turning toward the sound, and then, in Brandon's head at least, the night turned red.

"What the—?" Daryl began, but Brandon slammed into him and sent him sprawling onto the damp sand of the public access. Daryl scrabbled backward toward the water's edge like an oversized crab, and when he finally found his feet, he realized his pants were falling down and he quickly buttoned the sagging fly. Brandon laughed, and Daryl paused and cocked his head as if realizing for the first time who was facing him on the deserted beach. "You are so fucking dead, faggot," he said.

Brandon slammed into him again, planting a fist against Daryl's jaw, another into Daryl's rib cage. Daryl stumbled back, trying to get his head around this previously unimaginable situation.

"Did you hurt her?" Brandon snarled. "Did you rape her, you piece of shit?"

Daryl's body finally found its rhythm and he managed to shove Brandon far enough away to allow room for his own punches. His fists connected with Brandon's ribs, his chin, his nose, his forehead. Still Brandon kept coming at him and coming at him. The freak had never shown this kind of sack before—or *any* kind of sack—and Daryl wondered if he'd had some secret thing for Nikki all these years. Why else would he be so pissed at something that clearly did not concern him in any way, shape, or—

Sprawled at Daryl's feet, Brandon began moaning and shaking, blood pouring from his shattered nose. Daryl wondered if he was going into convulsions, or simply choking on the blood leaking into his throat. He was coughing out thick, guttural sounds that weren't quite words but seemed to want to be. Daryl thought he heard "How?" and "No" and then even something that sounded like "Run, you stupid fuck!"

And then the writhing thing on the ground truly *was* a freak, something no longer human, something monstrous and changing and growing. Daryl backed away but couldn't stop watching. Running didn't even enter his mind. The thing on the ground contorted and screamed as bones cracked and shifted, a muzzle extended and fangs pierced raw flesh, clothing ripped and fell away, and finally the animal expelled the remaining blood from its throat in a single, explosive howl.

Color and sound burst over the lake like a true Fourth of July finale, the amateur fronts on every shore combining the rest of their illicit skyrockets and streamers into a true crescendo. Daryl finally turned to run, but shock had messed with his bearings and he found himself running entirely the wrong direction—toward the lake, toward the beautiful streamers of color—as the animal leapt upon him and tore his spine from his body like a poorly sewn zipper.

When the night was silent once more—fireworks over, the town asleep over the crest of the trees—Brandon settled down to feed. He knew something was different in his world, but his wolf mind couldn't conceive of what that difference was. He thought about it and thought about it—as much as he *could* think in that state—and it wasn't until he'd cached part of Daryl's body in the woods for later, and washed himself in the lake, and transformed back into Brandon—that he realized how far away the moon was from full right now, and how wonderful and satisfying that new bit of knowledge felt.

. . .

The Talbot Public Library was the first place that popped into Brandon's head the following morning, and he resolved to go there as soon as he'd finished the most pressing chores on the day's list.

The moon had been nowhere near full the night before, and yet his transformation had been effortless, virtually spontaneous. He remembered watching Melissa leave the park, remembered sitting beneath the oak tree, remembered seeing Nikki stumbling home, drunk and crying.

Then, it felt like only seconds later, he was back at the salty red pool, calm and at peace, and it wasn't the full moon but it was like the full moon. *The Darker Heart* had nothing helpful to say on the subject, but some book or website surely must be able to tell him how and why he'd transformed without the moon. He had the distinct impression this wasn't the sort of question he should be Googling into Father Holloway's computer, however.

. . .

Nola Fenster watched Brandon approach up the sidewalk and her heart quickened. She remembered him as a bruised and shabby little boy, always hovering in the children's section, checking out one book after another or just reading quietly for hours on end at one of the private carrels over near the windows. He had always been polite and quiet, never disrespectful of her or the books, and he'd never done anything that would have allowed her to send him packing. For some reason, this had made Nola dislike him even more.

As he grew older, as he became a bruised and shabby teenager and moved away from the children's section and into the library proper, Nola had grown impatient. She'd waited for him to develop that snotty, belligerent attitude they all developed; waited for the moment when he would finally mouth off to her or damage some book he shouldn't have been reading in the first place; waited—after she'd finally buckled and allowed public computers into the library—for him to access some inappropriate website that would allow her to bar him from the library permanently.

But Brandon had continued to disappoint. He'd remained unfailingly polite and almost monk-like in his silence; he'd continued to offer Nola no reason whatsoever to challenge his presence in her domain—until now.

"No, no, absolutely not," she said as soon as he walked in the door. "You are not allowed back in this library until you've settled your account."

Brandon stopped in his tracks, completely at a loss. "What the hell are you talking about?"

Nola was so pleased at finally having something to hold over the head of this horrible young man that she didn't even acknowledge his rudeness. "You have a book from this library that is now *six months* overdue. We've sent umpteen notices to your house and haven't heard a single word back."

The Darker Heart. Returning it had never crossed his mind. He didn't think he'd ever even been *late* with a book before, but this book he'd accepted as his own personal property the second he'd taken it from the library. He laughed. "Oh, yeah, sorry about that. I forgot all about it. And I don't live at home anymore, so I never got the notices."

He turned as if to continue into the library but Nola came around the desk with a speed that belied her years. "Be that as it may," she said. "You are barred from this library until that book is back in my possession and your fines have been paid."

Brandon stared at her, and Nola was shocked to see his eyes flick appraisingly up and down her body. *Sizing her up.* No one had looked at her with that kind of blatant hunger in years, and she actually felt a blossom of warmth deep in her belly. *Dear God*, she thought. *What kind of man has that horrible little boy grown into?*

Brandon took out his wallet and thumbed through bills. "Here is...eighty-seven bucks," he said. "It's all I have on me. I'll buy that book from you. You didn't want it in your library anyway, remember?" When Nola didn't accept the cash, he let the bills flutter to the floor and walked around her as if she had no say in the matter whatsoever.

Nola felt something shift inside her and made a beeline for the ladies' room. Her one consolation was that she made it into a stall and got her skirt hiked and her undergarments out of the way before her bladder let go in a single convulsive burst like a water balloon exploding.

. . .

When she'd finally managed to calm herself, Nola re-entered the library with a fresh resolve to rid her domain of Brandon Turner once and for all. He'd just *see* who was in charge here at Talbot Public.

She expected to find him over by the shelf that housed the library's tiny collection of books on the supernatural, or perhaps at one of his usual reading carrels. Instead, he was sitting at one of the library's Internet-access computers, concentrating intently on whatever was on the screen.

"You need to sign in if you're going to use the computers," she said from the relative safety of the checkout desk. "We need to maintain strict time limits so everyone gets a chance."

Brandon lifted his gaze from the monitor and took a languid survey of the rest of the library. There were three other people in the building—most everyone in Talbot spent their summer Saturdays on one of the lakes, not in some dusty, airless building in town—and none of the other patrons appeared to have the slightest interest in using one of the computers at the moment.

"I signed your stupid sheet while you were...*otherwise occupied*," he said. His nostrils flared as if he was scenting something in the air, and a hint of smile hovered at the edges of his mouth.

Mocking her—he was openly mocking her. As if he knew exactly what had happened to her in the ladies' room, and was feeling oh-so-smugly happy about it.

Nola glanced at the sign-in sheet and noted with dismay that Brandon had indeed filled out his name and the time he'd started on the computer. She allowed each patron exactly thirty minutes on the computers per visit, no exceptions, so she would let him have his remaining twenty-two minutes and then he'd damned well better be ready to leave. Hopefully, he'd never darken her door again.

At the end of twenty-two minutes, however, Brandon showed no sign of leaving the computer on his own. Nola decided to give him another eight minutes, the full half-hour from when she'd first *witnessed* him using the computer, and that would simply have to be the end. Her sudden timidity surprised her, but she wasn't really feeling herself today. Perhaps her age was starting to catch up with her, or maybe she was coming down with a summer flu bug. That would explain the incident in the ladies' room, as well as the clammy knot of headache at the back of her skull. She watched the second hand of the clock above the desk sweep around the dial eight full rotations.

At the end of eight minutes, Brandon still showed no signs of budging. Worse, all three of the other patrons had checked out their books and left, and no one else had come in. She was alone with him now, alone with the shabby boy who'd somehow grown into a swaggering, mocking man clearly unafraid of her. A man who wouldn't leave, who wouldn't turn off the computer at the end of his allotted time, who watched her without watching her and smiled a secret smile while she squirmed in obvious distress.

This was the final tipping point for Nola. The smug little bastard openly flaunting her rules and then enjoying her discomfort. She marched over to the computer table and yanked the power cord out of the back of Brandon's PC. Instantly the monitor went dark, but Brandon continued to stare at the screen as if he could still read some secret message displayed there.

"You've had quite enough time here today," Nola said. "I want you to leave the library now, and I would appreciate it very much if you never came back. You...you can keep the book."

Brandon continued to stare into the darkened monitor, and the smirk that had so antagonized Nola slowly grew into a full-on grin. His smile was sharp, almost predatory. He leaned back and unfolded from his chair. He stood face-to-face with her, and although he was not much taller, he appeared so much more solid than Nola, infinitely more substantial. Nola wondered briefly if she really existed at all.

"People have fucked with me all my life," Brandon said. "Trust me when I say you really don't want to fuck with me anymore."

Nola was surprised to find her voice on the very first try. "Don't you threaten me in my own library, young man."

"I'm not threatening," Brandon said. "I'm just stating a new fact of life for you and everyone else here in Talbot. You just really don't want to cross me anymore."

They stood, eyes locked, and Nola was amazed her legs would even continue to support her. She had the oddest sense that if she showed any sign of weakness, it would trigger something within Brandon he wouldn't be able to control even if he wanted to. *I really do need to think about retiring one of these days*, she thought. *Old age is just creeping up and creeping up.*

As if in direct contradiction to such thoughts, a wet trickle slithered down the inside of her thighs and she realized with a desolate, nearly forgotten ache in the pit of her stomach that it wasn't merely urine this time but blood; she was inexplicably having her period. For the first time in perhaps thirty years, Nola Fenster found herself bleeding down there like a common little bitch in heat.

To make matters worse, Brandon was laughing at her again, his nostrils flaring as if he could actually *smell* the blood. His eyes danced with an odd, anticipatory merriment, and his body almost quivered with some unknowable excitement. Nola had once owned a beagle that wagged the entire rear half of its body whenever it was happy, and for some reason Brandon reminded her precisely of her beloved Li'l Snoopy. But there was nothing lovely about the young man staring at her with the grin too wide for his face, and certainly nothing lovely about the way he padded to the door of the library, clicked the deadbolt, and turned the CLOSED sign outward to face the street.

Nola finally found her bearings again. "Now see here—" she began, but the creature that turned and began walking toward her—a creature no longer quite man *or* beast—held one dagger-clawed finger to its lips and said, "Shhh, no talking in the library."

But it took many minutes before the library was silent once more.

. . .

Officially, the Talbot Wolf Research Center sprawled across twelve acres of land several miles northeast of Talbot, but in reality the Center buildings and even the sizeable pack enclosure occupied a much smaller area. The visitor center, lab facility, and various outbuildings took up an acre; the pack had the run of three additional acres; and the rest of the land remained more or less indistinguishable from any of the forest around it: trees and more trees, rough granite outcroppings, and whatever flora and fauna naturally existed there. Kate Bowman and the rest of the Center staff considered the unused acres a buffer zone between the Center wolves and the outside world. Too often lately, the outside world thought of those unused acres as prime real estate simply going to waste under the dubious guidance of the Center.

"So it's sort of a constant struggle," Chad said. He offered Melissa a hand-up as they skirted a rotting log along the far edge of the enclosure fence. "My mom fields two or three offers a month from out-of-town schmucks who want to know when she's going to let them *do* something with the extra land."

"Like build houses?" Melissa said.

"Only they never call them houses," Chad said. "They're always 'luxury estates' or 'vacation villas' or something lame like that."

Melissa laughed. "I think my dad used that phrase in one of his brochures. 'Whispering Pines—your vacation villa in the middle of nowhere.'"

"Middle of Nowhere, Minnesota," Chad said. "I like it."

"I'm not sure I'd want my luxury estate butting up against a pack of hungry wolves, though," Melissa said.

"That's because you haven't met them yet."

They stopped beside an enormous flat-topped slab of granite pushing up out of the forest floor like a giant's coffee table, and Chad brushed away some stray leaves and offered Melissa a seat. He shrugged off his backpack and brought out two bottles of water, then smiled as Melissa twisted the cap off one of them and took a big glugging swig. Despite the heat of the day, despite their lengthy trek over rough terrain, she was barely sweating. Not bad for a summer girl.

Melissa screwed the cap back on her water bottle and smiled at him smiling at her. "Where are we?" she said.

"We're almost exactly opposite the visitor center. You could actually see it if the ground was level and there weren't any trees."

"So we've basically walked halfway around the enclosure perimeter, and we've pretty much been following the fence the entire time, right?"

Chad nodded.

"It's weird," Melissa said. "I don't think I really even noticed the fence."

"That's the idea," Chad said. "Try to be as unobtrusive as possible."

"But the pack still knows the fence is there, right?"

Chad didn't want to give Melissa the same stock answer they gave groups at the visitor center: *The wolves don't really understand the concept of a fence. They've never known anything else, so the fence is just another part of the forest to them. This is their territory, and they're perfectly happy and content with it.*

Chad didn't believe that for a minute. Lame platitudes to fool the masses.

"They know it's there," he said. "And I think they know it's somehow related to us—to people. We mark the fence with scent from another pack to make it seem more like a natural territorial boundary, but at some level our wolves have to wonder why the other pack never appears for a friendly rumble, or why they can't just wander off somewhere else if the notion strikes them. They must resent the hell out of us sometimes."

"You don't sound very scientifically detached," Melissa said. "You're about one step away from anthropomorphizing them right into our slightly furrier cousins."

Chad laughed. "Big words from the city girl. Methinks I'm out of my league already."

"No," Melissa said. "I'll let you know."

Chad paused to consider the ramifications of that statement. *What am I doing out here with this girl—with Brandon's girl?* "Yeah, no, you're right," he said. "My mom says that's gonna be my downfall as a biologist. I never just want to observe. I always want to be right down in the thick of things, rolling around in the dirt with them."

Movement on the other side of the fence caught Melissa's eye. She turned to see a large black wolf emerge silently from behind a stand of jack pine. "Oh," she whispered.

"There you go," Chad said.

Without turning away from the wolf, Melissa could feel an immediate relaxation in Chad's posture, a sense of calm enveloping his body. Simple, pure happiness radiated off him like waves of clean white light.

"That's Dojo," Chad said. He reached over and touched the top of her hand. "Wait here a minute. I'm gonna go over and say hi, and then I'll introduce you."

He walked to the fence and knelt down next to it. Dojo continued to stare at Melissa for a moment, then turned his sharp amber gaze toward Chad and padded closer. Even from a distance, Melissa was surprised at the distinct sense of intelligence she could see in the wolf's eyes. *They're not dogs at all*, she thought. *They're something completely unique. And old— old souls, old memories.*

Chad stuck his fingers through the chain link and waggled them in a goofy wave. Dojo feigned indifference for as long as he could, but ultimately Chad's taunting proved irresistible. Dojo lunged at the chain link and begin gnawing on Chad's exposed fingers as if they were rubber chew toys, his enormous canines flashing in the sunlight.

"Oh my god!" Melissa was instantly off the rock and trying to pull Chad away from the fence. Dojo leapt backwards with a terrifying snarl, and in a flash he was back behind the jack pine, teeth bared and fur bristling.

"Now you've done it," Chad said. He held up his fingers and wriggled them in front of Melissa to prove they were still intact, albeit slimed now with wolf spit. He turned to Dojo and said, "Oh, knock it off, you big baby. She's no threat to you."

Dojo stopped growling, and the tension in his stance slowly seeped away. Eventually, he turned to stare in another direction and yawned a little too extravagantly for either of them to take seriously.

"I could've had a coronary," Melissa said. "I could've peed myself."

"I'm sorry," Chad said. He pulled gently on one of her arms until she relented and sat down next to him. "I was just showing off, I guess."

Melissa heard a faint echo of that phrase in the back of her mind—*just showing off for your daughter*—but quickly thrust it aside. From the safety of the jack pine, Dojo gave her a dismissive glance and settled down on a bed of dried leaves and matted scrub grass.

"My mom would have about seventeen different kinds of hissy fit if she knew how much interaction I've been having with the pack," Chad said. "There's this thing called 'observer effect' that I have totally messed up beyond all measure here, so please don't—"

"It's a little early in our relationship to be asking me to lie to your mother, isn't it?"

Her cheeks colored as soon as the words were out of her mouth, and she quickly looked away. When Chad's silence forced her to look back, she noticed he was blushing too. His mouth was slightly open, as if he'd started to say something but then thought better of it. Finally, the silence between them stretched beyond the breaking point—at least for Melissa.

"We learned about 'observer effect' in anthropology," she said. "But I think actually *playing* with the wolves is stretching anybody's def—"

"You see, the thing is," Chad said. "Brandon's my best friend."

Another long moment stretched taut between them, uncomfortable silence broken only by the power-line buzz of a lone cicada in some tree nearby. This time it was Chad who felt the need to speak first.

"I know Brandon kinda freaked out on you that first night," he said. "And I can only imagine he was even more awkward on his own at the fireworks. But the thing you need to understand about Brandon—"

"Why'd you bring me out here if Brandon's such a stumbling block for you?"

Now there was a million-dollar question. Chad's initial surprise over Melissa's unexpected appearance at the Center carried only so much weight. He'd known exactly what he was doing when he decided to take her on a private tour, and Brandon's feelings—fragile on the best of days—had never crossed his mind.

"Listen," Melissa said. "Brandon seems like a really nice guy, but I only went out with him because I was bored out of my skull and didn't know anyone else in town. I'm leaving in less than two months, and I was never going to have a relationship with him in the first place."

"Still..."

"I'm not going to have a relationship with *you*, either, if that's what you're thinking. When I said the 'r' word, it was just a slip of the tongue. It didn't mean anything. We can be friends and everything, but that's as far as I'm looking to go this summer. So why don't we just forget the last ten minutes ever happened, and go back to your completely arbitrary re-definition of 'observer effect' and—"

Another scientific term—*biological imperative*—popped into Chad's head, and then he was leaning forward and stopping her diatribe with a kiss.

This time, when the silence stretched out, it didn't feel uncomfortable at all. When it had gone on long enough for the sun to begin its slow slide down the backside of the day, Dojo trotted over to the fence and watched the couple on the other side. One by one, the rest of the Center pack joined their alpha, and five pairs of amber-colored eyes, slightly luminescent in the fading light, watched until Kate Bowman blew a silent whistle back at the visitor center.

Nothing that was happening on the other side of the fence could ever compare with feeding time, and the pack slipped away as silently as it had arrived. Even the cicada in the tree gave up its relentless commentary on the events unfolding below. As afternoon crawled into evening, Chad and Melissa lost all but one of their observers.

Their sole remaining witness watched with luminescent eyes much like those of the wolves in the Center pack, but with a strange constriction of the chest that, presumably, no mere animal could ever feel. When Chad and Melissa finally rose, quiet and fumbling, their observer took a step back into the shadows to make sure they wouldn't see him, and shuddered a bit when the neon sign inside his head began blinking *Now, now, now...*

. . .

Tuesdays and Fridays were always the liveliest nights of the week at the Center. Each of those nights, the Center scheduled two events that outshone everything else in both popularity and profitability.

The first was a wolf feeding. One of the staffers would present a short lecture on wolf predation habits; the audience would watch video of a wild pack taking down a full-grown moose

(Chad could practically narrate the video in his sleep); then the lights in the viewing gallery would dim and the staff would give the Center pack an entire deer carcass—usually road-kill donated by the Highway Department—right in front of the gallery's panoramic viewing windows.

Chad loved to watch the audience's reaction. Even the most matronly grandmother-types lit right up when the wolves ripped into the deer's flesh, pulling off bloody strips of hide, fighting over the most tender and succulent morsels, hauling away bits of bone and meat to cache for later.

"The crowd ate it up—no pun intended," he always told Kate when he arrived home after a feeding. "One of these days we're gonna have to throw a live deer in there and see how the city folk feel about *that.*"

The other event that always drew lots of attention was the Center's late-night howling. One of the staffers—more often than not Chad or his mom just because they liked it so much—would drive a van-load of "civilians" deep into the forest and, literally, howl at one of the wild packs in the area. Nine times out of ten, they managed to get the pack to respond with howls of its own, and the attendees would return to civilization with a truly hair-raising memory of their time on the edges of the wild. A successful howling all but guaranteed return business from the participants, and new visits from that group's family and friends and neighbors back home.

This particular Tuesday, Chad was leading the tour. "If we're really lucky, we might even get a scout wolf to check us out," he said. He piloted the Center van down a dark and narrow corridor of gravel deep in the forest. "Does anyone know what a scout wolf is?"

"One who's trying to earn all his merit badges?" Melissa said from the passenger seat to his right. Laughter rippled through the van.

Chad flashed her a grin—*think you're pretty smart, dontcha, city girl?*—and then raised his voice to carry over the rumble of the van's engine and the noise of the road. "A scout wolf *is* sort of like a Boy Scout—always prepared. He—or she—is always on the lookout for a new food source entering the region, or strange wolves threatening the pack's territory, or whatever. The scout spends a lot of time and expends a lot of energy just assessing the general conditions of the pack's domain."

"Dojo was scouting today when we first saw him, wasn't he?" Melissa said. "But didn't you tell me he was the alpha male?"

Chad offered Melissa another smile—couldn't seem to *stop* smiling—but he directed his comments to the entire van.

"Melissa and I were observing the Center pack earlier this afternoon, and Dojo—the alpha—*was* acting as a scout. Basically checking out this strange new girl before he'd let any of the rest of the pack come out into the open. But Dojo's kind of a special case because, obviously, the Center wolves have made some modifications to their behavior based on their specific circumstances. In the wild, a scout might be an alpha or some other rank entirely. In that case, he or she would ultimately report back to the alpha on what was happening around the territory."

"Report back how?" The question came from a lumpy, balding businessman in the second row who'd already been grumbling because Chad had given Melissa the shotgun seat instead of him. "You make it sound like they talk or something. They're just stupid animals."

I'd like to smear you with chicken guts and throw you in amongst them, Chad thought. Aloud he said only, "You'd be surprised. Not only do they manage a wide range of messages or emotions through howling—which hopefully we'll get to hear tonight—they also communicate through posture, touch, scent, and a veritable plethora of vocalizations: barks, growls, yips, sighs, groans..."

"Plethora?" the jerk in the second row said.

"It means an abundance," Melissa said. "In other words, they communicate a whole bunch of ways."

Chad bit the inside of his cheek to keep from laughing and made sure he continued to stare straight ahead.

"I know what it *means*—" the jerk began, but then Chad brought the van to a stop and flicked off the engine and lights all at once.

"We're here," he said. "Now, when we get out of the van, I want everyone to be as quiet as they can, and to gather right over in the little sandy area in front of the van."

"I can't see a sandy area or anything else out there," said a small, timid voice from the back. Chad remembered a mousy-looking woman back at the Center, obviously coerced by more adventurous family members into an outing that held no appeal for her. The type who would either be in hysterics before the end of the night, or hooked on wolves forever. Chad knew from experience it could go either way.

"It's going to seem really dark outside at first, and much quieter than you're used to," Chad said. "But I promise, you have nothing to worry about, and if we're lucky you'll even have one of the most—"

"What about the killer bear that was all over the news a while back?"

The jerk in the second row again—who else? Chad narrowed his eyes and forced himself to take a deep calming breath. *I'd like*

*to coat you with peanut butter and stake you to the ground outside
a grizzly den.*

"Bear?" This time the voice was a young boy in the third row.
Probably eight or nine, eyes like saucers, voice shaking a little
although he was clearly trying not to let it.

Turning in his seat, Chad smiled his most reassuring smile
right at the boy and said, "Bear? We ain't afraid of no stinkin'
bear." Beside him, Melissa laughed. More importantly, so did the
boy. *Take that, Mr. Plethora Sweating Jerk*, he thought. To the rest
of the van he said, "Okay, everybody out, nice and quiet now."

When the group was gathered in front of the van, Chad
waited a full minute to let them settle, let their eyes adjust to the
dark. The woods at night were rarely ever as dark as a person's
imagination made them seem. The sky overhead almost always
offered at least some sort of glow, and the human eye was
amazingly adaptable to even the lowest input levels if you just
gave it a chance.

When Chad sensed that the group's initial wave of
nervousness had passed, he knelt down and put one hand on the
shoulder of the saucer-eyed boy. "What's your name?"

"Danny."

"Cool, Danny." He kept his voice low, so that it barely carried
beyond the boy. "My name's Chad, and I'm wondering if you'll
do a favor for me."

The boy nodded, his big eyes already completely adjusted to
the dark. Chad knew most of the adults would still be struggling.

"Okay, Danny," Chad said. "When I give the signal, I want
you to cup your hands around your mouth and point your head
to the sky. Then I want you to give the loudest, very best howl
you can possibly give. Just like the ones we heard on the tape
back at the Center." He stood to address the group. "After Danny
howls, we'll all need to be really quiet for a minute, to give the

other pack in the area a chance to decide whether or not they're going to respond."

"I thought we were all gonna get to howl," the second-row jerk said. "I distinctly remember from your brochure—"

"We will," Chad said. So calm, so quiet. "But first Danny. Danny's our alpha male tonight, and he's going to be the one to howl first."

Danny puffed up like a little owl as soon as Chad called him the night's alpha male. *Works every time*, Chad thought.

The jerk thought about saying something more, but his eyes had apparently adjusted enough to read something in Chad's expression that made him keep quiet. Chad kept his eyes locked on Mr. Second Row a few seconds longer, then turned once more toward Danny. "Ready?" he said.

"I think so."

"Nice and loud now," Chad said. "Straight up into the sky, like you're inviting all your neighbor wolves to come right on out and say howdy."

"Oh Lord," came a whisper from the back—the mousy woman, Chad supposed.

Danny cupped his hands and let forth a high-pitched, wavering howl that was really pretty good for a first try and, more importantly, carried easily across the warm July night.

"Shh, everybody quiet now," Chad whispered.

They waited, their anticipation almost visible, a pale glow vibrating around them. Chad knew it was highly unlikely that an initial howl would get a response, but sometimes using a kid loosened up the wolves a little faster. He thought maybe they interpreted the kid as a lost pup or something, and reacted with less natural reluctance.

Unfortunately, not tonight. Chad smiled another big smile at Danny. "Great job, but I guess we have to make them think a whole pack's invaded their territory." He turned to the others. "Okay, now we're going to howl as a group. I'll start us off, and you can all join in one or two at a time. Try to match my pitch as closely as you can, and when I stop, taper off gently. Again, not all at once, but just whatever feels natural. And then wait another minute or two."

He raised his own expertly-honed howl into the night, and the group followed a little raggedly behind him. Some groups were just naturally great, some never got it at all, and this group was somewhere in-between. He did notice a perfect sweet counterpoint in Melissa's voice raised next to his, and offered her a goofy grin out of the side of his mouth.

When the howl was finished, the group huddled silently once more. Chad frowned. The night seemed inordinately quiet for some reason. Not oppressively still like in the moments before a big storm, but simply absent of even the usual noises of the forest. He was just getting ready to have them try one more time—and then perhaps move on to another spot entirely if need be—when a single, ethereal response cry rose far in the distance.

The ripple that went through the group was instantaneous and exhilarating and Chad felt the very same way, even though he'd experienced the same thing a thousand times. Each group made it new all over again—another reason why he loved going on the howlings so much.

"There you go," he said quietly. "Sounds pretty far away, but now maybe we can scare up a few of his buddies a little—"

Before he could finish, a series of tiny yips and wavering little howls filled the darkness. Not close, but certainly closer than the first solitary cry.

"Wow," Chad said. "Somewhere, right over there, there's a den of new pups trying out their lungs for us. And just listen to them sing!"

A loud and decidedly stern growling bark sounded from another direction, and the pups instantly fell silent.

"In case you couldn't tell," Chad said with a chuckle, "that was big daddy alpha telling the pups to shut up and stay hidden. And did you notice how fast they listened? How's *that* for a wolf's ability to communicate? Even us stupid humans could understand it right away." He shot a malicious grin at the jerk from the second row, but the man was looking elsewhere and his focus was sharper and more intense than Chad would have expected out of him.

"There's something out there," the man said. "Right over there behind that big clump of sumac. See the branches moving?"

Chad *did* see the branches move, but only briefly. The motion stopped the second the man mentioned it.

Toward the back of the group, the mousy woman moaned a little—a sound that would work itself up into an all-out scream if Chad didn't get a handle on the situation pretty quickly.

"I smell something too," a different woman said. "Does anybody else smell that?"

Ah, of course, Chad thought.

"Okay, everybody, calm down," he said. "That shadow over there in the bushes, that musky smell you're smelling—that's the scout wolf, checking us out. Now that he's seen we're not another wolf pack, he'll trot off again soon enough. I've got a little flashlight in my pocket here. Let's see if maybe—"

All around them, one howl after another rose into the night. The night filled with a symphony of eerie, mournful, and absolutely terrifying songs, all coming from very close to the huddled group, virtually encircling them. Melissa grabbed one of Chad's hands, and the boy Danny grabbed the other. It would have been almost comical if Chad hadn't been so completely flummoxed by the situation.

Jesus, they're all around us, he thought. *Right here, probably not more than twenty yards away. No wonder the musky smell is so strong. But why is the entire pack here if the scout's right over there to tell them it's just a bunch of idiot people? Do they think we're a threat to the pups? How do I get these people back into the van and—*

As quickly as the howling began, it cut off again. Chad could hear the smooth, loping gaits of the wolves departing through the scrub and brush, and then the scout wolf bounded out of the sumac and passed by so close that Chad could have touched him if he'd wanted. The mousy woman screamed—one quick little blurt—and several others in the group laughed nervously. After a moment, the night shuddered down into a perfectly ordinary silence once again.

"Well, that was a little weird," Chad said, trying to sound more calm than he felt. "Clearly, we made an impact on the pack, and it's probably best if we climb back into the van now and—"

A loud, snarling frenzy burst out of the darkness directly behind the van, and the van started to rock as if someone—or some *thing*—was trying to push it over. Several people in the group screamed this time, women and men alike, and this only enraged whatever was out there in the darkness. They could hear the piercing fingernails-on-a-chalkboard sound of something very sharp being dragged across metal, and then a series of metal-buckling jolts as whatever was out there pummeled the van in a frenzied rage. One blow hit the rear window and the sound of glass shattering was followed instantly by a sharp yelp and then the noise of angry, chaotic crashing through the deep brush of the forest. The group could hear breaking branches and crunching footfalls for what felt like a very long time, but thankfully they grew fainter and farther away with each passing second.

Chad finally got his head back around the situation and dug the flashlight out of his pocket. *What an idiot*, he thought. *I've had it right here the entire time.* The group, subdued and shaking in the pale glow of the little light, quickly made its way back to the van. Chad took a moment to brush shards of glass off the back seat, but the group didn't seem to care about the possibility of cutting themselves so much as they simply wanted to be back inside somewhere.

Once everyone was safely in the van and buckled back into their seats, Chad and Melissa made a quick survey of the damage at the back of the vehicle. Chad's flashlight revealed a number of deep dents in the back door, and several long gashes of gleaming silver where the paint had been stripped away and deep ridges carved into the base metal itself. *By claws*, Chad thought. *Something came out of the forest and clawed the hell out of the van like it was no more than balsa wood.*

Melissa reached out a shaky finger to trace the razor-path of one of the marks. "What *was* that?" she said.

"I don't have a clue," Chad said. "But I think it's time to call this tour well and truly over and get the hell out of these woods."

He raised the flashlight beam to the jagged broken window, where a startling splash of glistening crimson was already beginning to dry.

. . .

Sound carried easily through the forest. No cars, no airplanes, nothing man-made to crowd the airwaves and distort the natural noises of the warm July night. At the sound of Danny's first test howl back at the van, Roger Lincoln raised his head and listened.

His fiancée, Stacey Caldwell, was frozen beneath him, her heart beating like a hummingbird's and a gasping near-scream strangling in her throat.

"They're miles from here," he told her. "And it's just some idiots from that wolf place I was telling you about. If the wolves are going to attack anyone, it's them."

He tried to pick up his previous rhythm, but the future Mrs. Lincoln was having no part of it. She pushed him away but then pressed back against him, forcing a spoon, until finally he relented and snuggled deeper into the sleeping bag with her to listen for more of the distant howling.

They listened to the group howl, the lone response, and then the thin, quivering voices of the pups. They heard the frightening howls of the entire pack, much louder and more intense than what had come before, and then what sounded like someone beating the hell out of a piece of sheet metal, accompanied by angry snarling and growling like something out of a horror movie. The distant sounds ended with several short, sharp screams.

"What was *that*?" Stacey said.

"That's just something they do," Roger said. "Give the tourists a good scare before they send them on their way."

"We are *not* going on that tour while we're up here," Stacey said.

Roger laughed and burrowed his face into her neck, snuffling and growling and making her laugh too.

They'd chosen a small campsite near one of the more remote portage entries into the Boundary Waters Canoe Area. Roger didn't tell Stacey he'd been tipped to the little-known clearing by a former girlfriend. It had been hard enough to get her into the woods in the first place. No way would she have come voluntarily to the location of one of his previous "conquests," as she called them. She could be a real prude that way sometimes.

She wasn't being a prude now, Roger was glad to see. Now that the night was quiet again, she shifted to make space in the sleeping bag and pulled him close. He was leaning in to kiss her when a cacophony of snapping twigs and crashing footfalls came bounding toward them out of the forest.

"What the hell is that!" Stacey bolted up into as near a sitting position as the sleeping bag would allow, kneeing his groin and whacking him on the chin with her forehead.

"God damn it!" Roger said. A wave of nausea rolled from his wracked balls to the center of his gut. He freed one arm from the sleeping bag and prepared to bring it down in a good, solid whack right across her stupid face.

Then the light from their flickering campfire sparked a reflection in the pupils of Stacey's wide and terrified eyes— something huge and snarling leaping toward them out of the forest—and the arm that Roger had raised to strike his fiancée flopped onto the grass several yards away, severed from his body at the shoulder as neatly as if someone had brought down a butcher's cleaver.

Neither of them even had time to scream after that. Brandon did his work cleanly and efficiently, and through the great gouts of blood and gore he finally felt his rage abate. The salty red ocean calmed him, and he lapped at it, waded in it, and finally settled down beside it to feed.

Sheer random coincidence had landed the two heads side-by-side on a small patch of sand, planted on the stubs of their necks as if their bodies had merely been buried in the sand for fun—a child's amusement at the beach. The expressions frozen on their faces appeared almost bemused as their sightless eyes watched Brandon poke his muzzle deep inside the cavities of their former bodies for the sweetmeats he craved constantly now.

Brandon fed. Between bites he lapped at a jagged wound in the center pad of his left front paw, but already the skin was knitting back together, the cut becoming a shadowy memory.

Brandon started in on the woman's rib cage, and all other thought was lost to the delightful splinter of bone and the lovely rush of sweet marrow, still warm, over his lolling, blood-engorged tongue.

Overhead, the moon floated, not even half full, aloof and untouched by the devastation below.

. . .

Davis Langley was at the Center, examining the damage to the tour van from the night before, when the call came in over his portable radio. A couple of hikers had found a torn-up campsite out near one of the lesser-used BWCA entry points, about twenty miles north of town. Blood everywhere, two bodies. Or at least they thought there were only two—it was hard to tell with all the pieces.

Benjy Tatum was on Dispatch, filling in while Gwen Krazmacek was on vacation, and from the quiver in his voice Davis could tell the rookie was about one more bloody corpse away from bolting the force for good to become an accountant. Tough first summer for the kid.

"Take it easy, Benjy," Davis said. "You know civilians always make things sound worse than they actually are." Davis himself knew no such thing, but right now he just wanted to calm Benjy down a bit.

"They said...oh, god. They said..."

"What'd they say, Benjy?"

There was a weird gurgling noise in the signal and Davis wondered if Benjy had just thrown up all over the Dispatch desk. When Benjy's voice returned, he sounded even shakier than before. "Chief—they...they said the bodies were missing...their *heads*."

"Jesus H. Christ," Davis said. He thumbed off the radio and exchanged a flabbergasted stare with Kate Bowman. Chad and his new girlfriend—Melinda? Miranda?—were standing a few feet away, visibly pale, and Davis winced. He keyed the radio. "Don't think we needed to hear that on an open transmission line, Benjy."

"Sorry, Chief. I didn't mean—"

"Never mind," Davis said. "I need you to get ahold of the medical examiner for me. Tell him to meet me at the Wolf Research Center and we can drive up together from here."

"Mr. Kowalski's already on his way with Larry," Benjy said. "They should be there any minute."

"Are the hikers still at the site?"

"Yeah, Chief. They called in on some sort of fancy satellite phone or something—that's how they got coverage way out there."

"Okay, Benjy. You call them back and tell them to find a place well away from the scene and just sit there. Tell them not to touch anything. You copy that?"

"Larry already gave 'em the drill. He told them to check each body for a pulse, in case they were still alive, but that's when they said that about—"

"Alright, Benjy, I get the picture. You just hang in there now, okay?"

"Okay, Chief, I'll try."

Davis slid the radio back into the holder on his belt. Twenty-five years of police work altogether, nine years as Chief in Talbot, and he didn't have the first clue how to proceed on this one. The death of one problematic local was one thing, but two more bodies in the woods? Mangled and dismembered? And sure as hell they'd turn out to be tourists this time—summer people dead on his watch and the season barely started.

To make matters worse, Daryl Reisling's mother had called the station that morning to say her son had been missing since the night of the Fourth. She'd thought he'd gone off fishing with some of his football buddies, but it turned out they hadn't seen him since the night of the fireworks either.

And old Nola Fenster hadn't shown up to open the library Monday morning, and wasn't at her house or apparently anywhere else in town. What the hell was going on in Talbot all of a sudden?

Davis knew he couldn't think about any of that right now. Right now, he just had to put one foot in front of the other. Retrieve the bodies, work the scene, gather the evidence. If this was another bear attack, they'd track the bear and kill it. If it wasn't a bear, if it wasn't any animal at all, there were bigger issues. Perhaps they'd even need to look at Farmer Joe's death again. And of course that would open another whole can of worms, but that couldn't be helped. *Just do the job. The politics will come later regardless, so for now just take a deep breath and do the job.*

"You okay?"

Kate had moved closer to him and placed one hand on the small of his back. He hated to show weakness in front of anyone, much less civilians, but his relief at her simple touch was unmistakable. He drew in a deep breath and then blew it out in a head-clearing sigh. "I am," he said. "I just don't know what's going on around here this summer."

"Neither do I," Kate said. "Obviously it's hard not to think this has some connection with what happened to Farmer Joe. But do you think there could be a connection between this new business and what happened out on the howling last night?"

Smart Kate, very smart, Davis thought. *Get my mind back on something concrete, something I can focus on until Emory and Kowalski get here. Why the hell didn't I ever marry you?*

"That's a good question," he said. He turned his attention toward Chad and the new girl. "I'm sorry, miss, I've already forgotten your name."

"Melissa. Melissa Henning. My folks bought the Whispering Pines."

"Of course. Think I'm getting that old person's disease—what do they call it?"

"CRS," Kate said.

Davis laughed and Chad leaned close to Melissa's ear to whisper, "CRS—can't remember shit."

"Melissa was on the howling last night," Kate said. "Chad asked her to stop by today to help with anything he might be fuzzy about."

"I appreciate it," Davis said. "And I assume we have the trip sheets if we need to contact anyone else from last night?"

"We do," Chad said. "But they were all summer people."

Kate had mentioned a number of times that summer people sometimes indicated which resort they were staying at, but almost never listed their home addresses or phone numbers. Afraid the Center would hit them up for donations later on.

"Well, I guess that makes you our girl then," Davis told Melissa.

"I don't know what I can tell you that Chad can't," Melissa said. "It was very dark and very scary, and I don't really have a clue what even happened."

"What about the noise?" Kate said. "You said the animal was snarling and growling when it attacked the van. Did it sound like a bear to you?"

"I don't think I've ever heard a bear in my life," Melissa said. "Except maybe on TV." She thought for a moment. "But offhand, just a gut response, I'd have to say no."

"It didn't really sound like anything I've ever heard," Chad said. "It wasn't like a bear and it wasn't really like a wolf. It seemed to be full of all this *rage*—"

"What do you mean, it wasn't *really* like a wolf?" Davis said. "Was it sort of like a wolf?"

Chad shot a brief, sheepish look at his mother, and then offered a small shrug. "Actually, the first thing that came to my mind was a wolf," he said. "A really big, really pissed-off wolf in full attack mode. But then it started wailing on the back of the van with what sounded like fists, and I figured it pretty much had to be standing on two legs. Wolves just don't do that."

"It did yelp like a wolf when the glass broke," Melissa said. "Or like a dog anyway. I guess I've never actually heard a wolf yelp."

"Well, they do," Chad said. "So that part is certainly possible. I guess a wolf could have been ramming its head repeatedly into the van, and then jumped up high enough to hit the window, but it sure seems like it would have had one hell of a headache afterward."

Davis considered this, then turned decisively and strode to the back of the van. "Have you taken any samples of the blood yet?"

"Not yet," Kate said. "I thought you might want to get a look at the damage before we touched anything."

"Good thinking. I'll have Kowalski grab some blood here before we head out. He can check those scrapes in the paint too. Never know what might turn up."

"We're canceling the howlings until further notice," Kate said. "So the van's yours as long as you need it."

"Appreciate it," Davis said. "And I'd also appreciate it if you'd come out and take a look at this campsite with us. Probably won't be real pleasant, but—"

"You want me at a crime scene?" she said.

"Well, first, we're not sure it *is* a crime scene," Davis said. "And if we're talking animal attack, I'd much sooner trust your opinion than Kowalski's."

Kate smiled, but she recognized the political current running underneath Davis's compliment as well. Given half a chance, Burt Kowalski would label the culprit a wolf whether it was a wolf or not. He'd given them the bear verdict in the death of Farmer Joe because he didn't really care one way or another. This time, he'd no doubt be much more inclined to be picky, and as a rancher he wasn't a fan of wolves even on a good day.

"I'd be happy to ride along," Kate said. "But just so you know, I might throw up."

"If this is as bad as Farmer Joe," Davis said, "I might join you."

. . .

It wasn't as bad as Farmer Joe; it was much worse. Davis thought Benjy might not be the only cop fleeing the Talbot force after this summer.

Unlike the dry scrub grass at the Westcott farm, the campsite had nice clay-rich soil tapering down to a sandy beach. Davis didn't need Kate to tell him the tracks around the bodies didn't belong to a bear.

"So much for wolves not killing people," Kowalski said, although Kate was grateful to hear that his statement carried none of the "I-told-you-so" element she might have expected.

"Jesus, look at the size of those tracks," Deputy Emory said. "Those are some big-ass wolves."

"Wolf, singular, I think," Kate said. "I can't be sure until I take some plaster casts, but off-hand I'd say there was only one wolf here."

"A rogue?" Davis asked. Kate had explained to him once that wolves sometimes drove out one member of the pack for reasons no one really understood. The rogue either needed to find a new pack or live out the remainder of its life alone. Roaming alone, hunting alone. For a social animal like the wolf, this must have been torture.

In 1926, a rogue wolf nicknamed "Lobo" had begun a reign of terror in the forests just east of Talbot. An average pack of wolves might kill eighteen deer in a given year, scouring virtually every scrap of meat and hide from each carcass. Lobo took a deer approximately every three days all by himself, and rarely ate more than the sweetest, juiciest morsels. When he was finally killed by a hunter in 1938, Lobo had weighed one hundred and forty pounds—nearly half again as large as any normal wolf from the region.

"I can't say anything definitive until I've checked bite marks and paw impressions," Kate said. "But if a whole pack had been here, I think we'd see a more obvious variety in the sizes of the paw prints, and we'd also find scuffed-up areas where they'd jostled for position to feed."

"Jesus, Kate," Davis said.

"Well, that's what they do," she said. "That's what this one did. It killed and it fed." She glanced at Kowalski and shrugged. "I've never heard of anything even remotely like this."

"Neither have I," Kowalski said, and again Kate was surprised by the lack of smugness in his voice. "You know I don't believe wolves can be trusted for a second around sheep or cattle, but this is so far beyond the pale I don't know what to think."

"How big would you say this wolf is?" Davis asked.

"Just going by the paw prints, I'd say maybe a hundred and eighty pounds," Kate said. "But that's ridiculously out of range, so we must be getting some weird sort of soil distortion or something."

"Proportional erosion all around the site?" Kowalski raised one caterpillar-like eyebrow.

"If not, Larry's right and we have one big wolf on our hands."

Emory hummed a little under his breath—*Who's afraid of the big bad wolf?*—but quickly busied himself at the site perimeter when Davis shot him a look.

Davis turned his attention back toward Kate. "How far out of range are we talking?"

"You know Dojo, our alpha back at the Center?"

Davis nodded.

"He's a big wolf in his own right, and he's all of ninety pounds."

"So you're saying the animal that did this is *twice* Dojo's size?"

"Either that, or he's just got freakishly large paws."

Emory couldn't let that one pass. "You know what they say about wolves with big paws..."

Even Davis had to smile. "Great," he said. "Find me a wolf with paws the size of ping-pong paddles and junk hanging down to the ground and I guess we're set."

. . .

Back at the Center, Melissa couldn't stop shivering. Even after they'd moved into the sun, her shoulders continued to quake slightly and every once in a while her teeth chattered together seemingly of their own accord. Chad brought her a steaming mug of tea and a sweater he'd borrowed from Kate's office. They stood close together in a sheltered patch of sunlight outside the visitor gallery, near the gate the Center staff used on feeding nights to give the wolves their deer carcasses.

"I can't stop thinking about it," she said. "Out there in the dark with...whatever that thing was. And those poor people at the campsite—that could have been us. The whole van."

Chad smiled reassuringly and put one arm around her shoulders. "We don't even know if the two things are related. We'll figure out what that was at the back of the van, and what it was doing, and the explanation will turn out to be totally logical and probably a little obvious. Nature's just like that."

"Well, let me tell you...nature sucks."

Chad laughed and gave her shoulders a jostle. "Nah," he said. "Nature's great. Predictable, reliable, totally structured—"

"Give me a break, Tarzan." She shrugged out of his embrace and pulled the sweater more tightly around her.

"Think about it," Chad said. "Animals eat when they're hungry, sleep when they're tired, and procreate when their environment is healthy enough to support a larger population. They don't kill one another for sport, they don't spew out a bunch of pollution, and they live totally in the moment, without expectation or regret. They're like...completely *Zen*."

Melissa raised one eyebrow. "*Zen*?"

"No concept of 'self,' no—"

"You are totally anthropomorphizing again," she said. "And you also sound like you're about one bead short of Mardi Gras."

"Got you to stop thinking about last night, though, didn't I?"

Melissa found herself smiling despite the traumatic events of the previous night and the even more disturbing news they'd heard this morning. "You jerk," she said, but they both knew there was no real bite behind her words.

"Listen, I know last night was really scary and weird, but that's just part of the package with nature, part of what makes it so interesting and exciting."

"If that's the case, I'll stick with city life from here on out. No offense, but I can't wait to be away from this place and back to Chicago for school."

Not knowing how he was supposed to respond, Chad offered up a shrug. Melissa responded with one of her own. Each of them had a nearly identical thought—*city mouse, country mouse*—and then they turned to watch the Center pack lazing away the afternoon in the central courtyard of the enclosure.

From their vantage point behind the feeding gate, Chad and Melissa could see the vague shadows of a few visitors over in the viewing gallery, taking photos of the wolves and now and again banging discreetly on the gallery glass, trying to draw the wolves over. This was a losing battle, because the glass was one-way and the animals had long ago acclimated themselves to sporadic noises issuing from the tall, shiny wall at one end of their territory.

If anything had been interesting enough to draw their attention, it would have been the presence of Chad in the feeding area. But the warm breeze carried no scent that might be remotely construed as dinner, and no one had blown the silent whistle that signaled a feeding, so even Chad was but a minor distraction in the lazy stillness of the afternoon.

"They do seem pretty contented," Melissa said. "Or, if I'm going to be all un-scientific about it, like others who shall remain nameless, I guess I'd even say they seem happy. Certainly less stressed-out than anyone I know back in the city."

Chad laughed. "Well, to be fair, the pack has it pretty good here. They'd be quite a bit more stressed if they were out in the wild. Nature's great, but it's never easy."

Now Melissa laughed, and something that had been out of alignment between them adjusted itself back to true. Melissa reached over and let her right hand find his left. Chad sidled one step closer to her, and their fingers entwined as if they'd been molded specifically for that function.

"I still don't know how I feel about this whole pack structure business, though," Melissa said. "I mean, it must kind of suck being anything other than one of the alpha pair."

"Not really," Chad said. "You can have a real nice life as a beta, and every member of the pack has a very distinct and important role to play. Even the omega, the very bottom of the wolf totem pole, rarely goes hungry."

"True," said a familiar voice behind them. "But sometimes he *does* lose the pretty female to someone higher in the ranks."

They turned, and there was Brandon, standing in the doorway that led out from the Center into the feeding gallery. He was smiling—smirking almost, Chad thought—and he looked like he'd been standing there a while. Chad and Melissa didn't notice their fingers untangling, but Brandon did. His laugh sounded genuinely amused, and Chad wasn't sure how to interpret that.

"Don't worry," Brandon said, mostly to Melissa. "I wasn't picking out china patterns or anything. Hell, we're in such different leagues we might as well be different species."

This idea made Brandon laugh again, and Chad didn't think he liked his friend's new laugh one little bit. "Come on, bud," he said. "This sorta just...happened. I was gonna talk to you about it."

"Well, now you don't need to," Brandon said. He took a step toward them and Chad had an almost overwhelming urge to step in front of Melissa to protect her. Instead of taking another step, however, Brandon shrugged and said, "I heard you had some trouble out on the howling last night. Thought I'd stop by and see if you needed any help with the van or anything."

"No, but thanks," Chad said. "We're gonna leave it so the police can do some—"

"Where did you hear there was trouble on the howling last night?" Melissa said.

Brandon hesitated before offering up another of his new, unreadable smiles. "A town the size of Talbot?" he said. "You'd be surprised how fast word gets around."

Melissa's abrupt question had triggered a couple more that Chad wanted to ask, but before he could formulate them, Brandon was striding over to the feeding gate. "Hey, check this out," he said.

Chad and Melissa turned and looked at the wolves beyond the fencing. All five of them had gathered just inside the gate, and they were staring at Brandon with an intensity Chad had never seen in them before. They began snarling and fidgeting—as if a new pack had shown up to challenge their territory. Chad watched in disbelief as all five of the wolves leapt toward the fence, throwing themselves toward Brandon as if they might chew their way right through solid steel to get at him.

Brandon watched their frantic efforts with his new unreadable smirk, and finally broke the spell with a sharp little bark of a laugh. "I guess your wolves don't like me very much," he said.

He turned from the fence and the wolves slowly quieted and slunk away. The sun caught Brandon's dark pupils and they flared preternaturally for a moment. "But there's a lot of that going around these days, isn't there?"

In three quick strides he was gone, and Chad and Melissa were alone in the feeding area once more. Appropriately enough, considering the location, each of them had the strangest sensation of feeling almost like food themselves.

. . .

Brandon knew every inch of the church and its grounds—the chapel, the rectory, the offices, the outbuildings—but he was especially familiar with the basement. He was always hauling something either up or down the steep, narrow stairs—books or files for Father Holloway, groceries or cleaning supplies for Mrs. McGowan, decorations or folding chairs for one committee or another. Yet in all the time he'd spent in the basement, he'd never before seen the box currently sitting on the desk in Father Holloway's private study.

The box contained a large number of VHS cartridges, relics of another time. Brandon was surprised the church even *owned* a VCR anymore, but sure enough, the small TV on the bookshelf had a built-in player. Brandon scanned the labels on the top layer of tapes—*Christmas Pageant 1995, Planning Meeting 2002, Choir Trip DC*. Not exactly the latest blockbusters. He assumed Father Holloway had found the box buried in some storage closet and wanted him to haul it away.

The box was starting to come apart at the seams and sagging in several directions. Brandon lifted it to check its weight and stability, and the top layer of tapes shifted to reveal several of the spines directly underneath. These labels were more ambiguous—*Tom (1), Kevin, Robbie/Ronnie?, Marcus, David (3)*—but still not particularly compelling. It wasn't until Brandon noticed his own name on one of the tapes that he paused.

Brandon as in me? he wondered. The tape and label did look fairly new, but Brandon couldn't imagine where or when Father Holloway might have videotaped him. In his room? In the shower? Some pervy priest thing like Kate had warned him about? He couldn't picture it. Holloway had never been anything but straight with him—*no pun intended*, Brandon thought—and certainly he would have tried something by now if he *was* a perv; Brandon had been living at Saint Ignatius for more than six months.

Of course, Brandon knew of at least three *other* Brandons in the Saint Ignatius congregation, and he supposed there could be more. Why Father Holloway might be videotaping any of them—choir auditions? some unknown confirmation ritual?— he had no idea. He took the tape with his name on it and popped it into the VCR.

. . .

It was obvious right from the start that the congregation wasn't really with him this morning. All throughout mass, Father Holloway could sense their distraction, a vague buzz hovering over the pews like a swarm of nervous bees. Their fidgeting finally got the better of him, and he cut a good portion of his sermon altogether, then rushed through the end of the mass as if he'd noticed a small fire smoldering at the back of the church.

Out on the sidewalk, conversation burst from the congregation all at once, as if the balloon of their distraction had reached critical mass and could no longer be contained. Everyone was talking about the mutilated campers. And the missing football player. And the crusty old librarian. And Farmer Joe.

Holloway wasn't sure how he felt about hearing such things. Surely this had to be something besides what he was thinking. There were six days yet to the July full moon; there was no way Brandon could have been responsible this time. Holloway shook hands and offered up innocuous chatter until the congregation had cleared out of the parking lot, but his mind was elsewhere the entire time.

Brandon, he kept thinking. But each time, just as quickly, his mind would thrust the thought aside. There's absolutely no way it could have been Brandon. It simply didn't work like that.

In the early days of his own double life, he'd researched all the legends, read every text he could get his hands on (no matter how ridiculous), and methodically charted his own changes. Some of the older European stories talked of individuals able to transform back and forth at will, but viewed through the fisheye lens of history and logic, most of these tales were surely nothing more than accounts of crazed mental cases and delusional hysterics. And certainly American Indian shape-shifter legends rarely if ever linked transformation with the full moon, but nothing in his own history suggested the change was possible without it.

Each moon cycle, he made exactly one complete transformation. This occurred during the full moon itself, and never lasted more than a single night. The night before and the night after, when the moon was close to full, his mind raced and he felt a strangling constriction in his chest, but always the beast was limited to a single night each cycle, a night both wonderful and terrible in almost equal degree.

Of course, Brandon was different from him in a lot of ways. He supposed it possible Brandon was different enough to have a found a way to transform without the moon—hell, *anything* was possible at this point—but deep down, he couldn't bring himself to believe it.

Yes, Brandon walked with a new swagger. Yes, he had a burgeoning sense of confidence, a more highly attuned sense of self and entitlement. And yes, he'd most certainly torn Farmer Joe to shreds without a moment's hesitation. Still—

"Father?"

Holloway jolted out of his reverie and realized he was still standing on the sidewalk outside the church, although every car had long since left the parking lot. Brandon was standing framed in the propped-open main door of the church, leaning out slightly, his hands grasping the molding at the top of the door. He was looking at Holloway with a moony, wide-open expression that showed no sign of the animal within, but merely the lonely outsider who'd finally found a home here at Saint Ignatius, for better or worse.

"You okay, Father?" he said.

Holloway stared at Brandon—his lanky frame, his unruly hair, his accepting smile—and nearly sighed in relief. This boy was no raging killer.

"Just lollygagging," Holloway said. He walked up the sidewalk to join Brandon. "Sometimes I lose track of what I'm doing, you know?"

Brandon laughed and moved out of the way to let Father Holloway pass. He released the door from its catch and it whisked shut behind them as they turned down the side hallway that led to the door closest to the rectory. Mrs. McGowan was off for a couple of weeks, doing a round-robin tour of her sons' homes in various parts of the country, but she'd left what looked like enough microwaveable meals to see Brandon and Father Holloway through a veritable nuclear winter.

Halfway down the long hallway, Brandon abruptly posed a question that stopped Holloway cold: "So you and Farmer Joe were kinda buddies, huh?"

Holloway didn't turn. He was standing in front of the garish stained-glass window his predecessor had installed along this side hall. The three panels of the window showed the church's namesake, Saint Ignatius of Antioch, first on trial for heresy, then writing his famous letters of martyrdom, and finally being devoured alive in the Roman Coliseum by a trio of gruesomely distorted animals probably meant to represent lions.

"I found the box of videotapes in your office this morning," Brandon said. There was no anger in his voice, but a calm matter-of-factness that Holloway found somehow more chilling.

"At first I couldn't understand what I was seeing," Brandon said. "I watched my own tape, and it was like someone had stuck a camera right inside my head. I couldn't...I literally couldn't understand how something like that could even exist."

"Brandon—" Holloway began, but then wondered what he could possibly say.

"So then I popped in another tape," Brandon said. "Some boy named either Robbie or Ronnie—you pricks didn't even have the courtesy to remember his real name. Again in the barn, every tape in the barn. He had that whole place wired up for your sick shit, didn't he? Do you know how many tapes are in that box?"

"Brandon," Holloway said again, still without turning. "He kept me from killing people. He kept me *fed*."

"And you fed boys to him—boys like me. Did you kill them all afterwards so they wouldn't tell? Is that how Joe *really* kept you fed?"

Holloway didn't answer. *Couldn't* answer—because of course the truth was too terrible to contemplate.

Brandon gave a cry of pain and betrayal and revulsion. Underneath the sound, a distinct growl rumbled within his chest.

All at once, Holloway knew for certain. But still he didn't turn. "Just out of curiosity," he said, "Do you know anything about the missing Reisling boy? Or Nola Fenster?"

Brandon laughed, but there was no humor in the sound. Had Holloway turned, he would have seen Brandon's mouth begin to stretch and widen, Brandon's eyes flare and dance in the cascade of colored light from the stained glass. A series of sinewy ripples quivered through Brandon's body as hidden muscles began to assert themselves over a bone structure that was flexing and changing all by itself, as if such transformation was the most natural thing in the world.

But Holloway didn't turn. He remained focused on the garish images in the glass—the overly vibrant colors, the grotesque distortion of the creatures with their gaping jaws and their jagged, dripping fangs. Even when he heard Brandon's breathing change—when it became a wet chuffing sound as hot as a blast furnace behind him—he didn't turn. He did, however, feel compelled to repeat his original question.

"Seriously, Brandon," he said. "I need to know. I need to hear it out loud. Last weekend, when the Reisling boy and the librarian disappeared. And then those campers..."

"I guess I *have* been eating out a lot lately," Brandon said. His voice was deep and distorted. "Why is eating out always so much better than eating at home, do you suppose?"

Holloway felt every hair on his body stand straight up on end. He heard cloth splitting and bones cracking and the sharp jerk of Brandon's muzzle as his reconfigured jaw snapped definitively into place.

Right here in the middle of an ordinary Sunday afternoon, Holloway thought. *Nearly a week away from the full moon, and in broad daylight.*

"You should really turn around for the rest of this," said the nearly unrecognizable voice from just inches behind him. The breath on his neck was steamy and fetid, ripe with the smell of rotting meat. It called up an image from his past he'd nearly forgotten: bone-crushing jaws clamping down on his femur. The first time he'd been bitten. Now, apparently it was going to happen again.

"I don't think I will turn around, Brandon," he said. "I think I'll just keep looking at the glass, if you don't mind."

"Suit yourself," Brandon said.

For the first time in his tenure at the church, Father Holloway noted the intricate detail work that had gone into the center panel of the Saint Ignatius triptych. It must have cost the church a fortune. Someone had actually taken the time to etch the wording of one of the Saint's most famous letters into the segment of glass.

"*Let me be the food of wild beasts...*" Father Holloway read aloud.

A moment later, he was.

To Rage with Wondrous Ferocity

July, Concluded

An unbroken line of betrayals, stretching back as far as he could remember. The mother who didn't care enough to keep herself alive, the father who couldn't stand the sight of him. Then the kids of Talbot, the whole damned town of Talbot, and now even the two people he'd thought were different—now even Chad and Father Holloway. The betrayals would never end, because deep down *all* people were evil and unknowable. Hyenas. Jackals.

And now, of course, they would come for him. He'd cached the remains of Father Holloway's carcass deep in one of the basement storage areas of the church, but he hadn't even attempted to clean the blood from the walls and floor of the upstairs hallway. So much blood—too much to mistake for anything but raw, violent death.

Plus, he'd packed his few possessions into his duffel bag and left the rectory, a move more suspicious than if he'd stayed and simply reported the blood in the church himself. Now Talbot would turn out with rifles and traps and hunt him down like the animal he had become.

He wasn't going to wait around for that. He had nothing holding him to Talbot now, and he'd never liked the town in the first place. It was time to enter the larger world, to leave behind all the betrayals of the past and see if he might find a life—any sort of life—somewhere else. He didn't know if any other life was possible for a creature such as himself, but he knew Talbot held nothing but pain and eventual death.

The first step to putting some miles behind him was finding a car. But he already *had* a car, and the pure red anger he'd felt that day at his father's garage flashed through his body like a brushfire once again. Had anyone been watching, they would have seen his rage made manifest—a flash of luminescence behind his eyes, the quick protraction and immediate retraction of claws from beneath his fingernails. But, as he had for so much of his life, Brandon walked alone and unnoticed. When he reached the bottom of the hill he flared his nostrils as if scenting out prey, then turned and walked in a rough line toward his father's house.

. . .

Davis Langley discovered the blood at Saint Ignatius less than two hours after Father Holloway's death. One of the part-timers at the library, working on Sunday to catch up on the shelving that wasn't getting done in Nola's absence, finally noticed Brandon's name on the Internet sign-up sheet from the previous Saturday—the last person in the library, apparently (or at least possibly), before Nola had vanished off the face of the earth. Davis didn't give the matter much thought until he mentioned it to Nikki over lunch, and she frowned and said, "You know, Daryl tangled with Brandon right before *he* disappeared."

"I never said Nola *tangled* with Brandon—" Davis began, but then it hit him: "Jesus, Brandon worked for Farmer Joe too."

He drove to Saint Ignatius to talk to the boy, just talk, for surely such a boy—bruised and silent and seemingly afraid of his own shadow—couldn't have murdered three people in cold blood. Davis didn't even try to connect Brandon to the man and woman slaughtered at the campsite. That had clearly been an animal attack, whereas it was at least possible that animals had gotten to Joe Westcott only *after* he was already dead.

Leaving his vehicle and walking toward the church, Davis knew immediately that something was wrong inside the building. It wasn't the absence of other cars in the lot—he hadn't expected any parishioners to still be around—but there was a stillness to the air that felt particularly heavy for such a beautiful July day, and a silence that almost vibrated with the echo of some inconceivable recent event. He walked to the main door, expecting to find it locked. When it wasn't, he felt his uneasiness squirm and grow, a spidery tickle that creepy-crawled from the base of his spine to the base of his skull and made him brush his fingertips across the gun at his belt to make sure it was there.

As soon as he stepped inside the church, he knew someone else was dead. Blood painted the walls and floor—even the ceiling in several spots—and a large central pool halfway down the hallway had already coagulated enough to form an opaque skin. He thought of the boiled chocolate pudding his mother used to make when he was a boy, its own skin rubbery and disgusting, and how he and his brothers had fought over it anyway. He felt the contents of his stomach roll until he thought he was going to pull a Benjy Tatum right there against the gaudy stained-glass window.

He took a deep breath and counted backwards from ten, then radioed for backup. He told Gwen to track down the medical examiner, even though he knew Kowalski would most likely be out on one of the lakes on a Sunday afternoon like this, and wouldn't want to come in when Davis didn't even have a body yet. But there was almost certainly going to *be* a body, so Davis steeled his nerves and moved deeper into the building to see if he could make Kowalski's trip worthwhile.

Now that he'd found the blood and moved past the initial moment of shock and queasiness, his earlier creepy-crawlies dissipated. He realized it was possible that some deranged killer was still inside the building, lying in wait, but somehow it didn't feel that way. The strangeness of the air had cleared a bit with his discovery of the scene inside the church, or perhaps he'd just forced his emotions down into the autopilot focus his daughter liked to call "cop mode." Besides, it was conceivable—unlikely, but conceivable—that whoever had lost all that blood might still be clinging to life somewhere, and if they were he desperately needed to find them.

As he waited for Kowalski and his deputies, Davis moved through the main floor of the church, growing more convinced by the second that he was the sole living being inside the building. He wondered if he should check the rectory before continuing, but instinct told him the rectory could wait. *Stay at the scene, stay with the blood,* he thought. *Do the job in front of you and let the bigger picture fall into place on its own.*

He made his way cautiously down the stairs, but found the basement no more threatening—or lively—than the first floor. Other than a box of old videotapes in what he assumed was Father Holloway's private study, nothing appeared unusual or out of place. He noticed that the TV in the study was on but lacked a signal—a dot of green glowed on the control panel and the words VIDEO 1 blinked in one corner of the screen. He hesitated—*is this really important when someone might be dying down here?*—and then pressed the PLAY button on the built-in VCR.

. . .

Brandon hadn't been inside his father's house since Christmas morning of the previous year. Nearly seven months, and not a single thing had changed. Same bent screen door, same grimy linoleum floor in the kitchen, same haze of yellowish cigarette smoke hanging near the ceiling like a cancerous thundercloud. His stepmonster was sitting at the table in almost exactly the same position she'd been in the last time he'd seen her, and his father was snoring on the sofa in the living room.

Brandon stood just inside the door, looking at his stepmonster and trying to determine exactly how he felt now that he was here. *You can't go home again*, the saying went, and yet here he was, and here *they* were, and he wondered if he was simply coming out of some long, incredibly involved dream. *The wolf, the moon, the feastings in the night—all a dream. And would that be a relief or the latest devastating letdown in a lifetime full of them?*

His stepmonster lifted her owly gaze from the glass in front of her and glared at him through the rising smoke of her cigarette. "If you came back for money, we ain't got any," she said. "If you came back for your car, we sold it for parts a month ago."

His car, his beautiful shitheap of a Mustang—trashed and stripped of its pieces in some junkyard somewhere. Three summers of his life, now rusting scrap metal. They hadn't even offered him the chance to buy it back from them. Just another thing for them to discard once they were finished with it.

Brandon furrowed his brow, as if finalizing some decision he'd previously remained ambivalent about. "No, I'm not here for money or the car," he said. "I just came home to change."

Then, while his stepmonster roused herself enough to scream and his father bolted awake and stumbled into the kitchen...*change* he did.

. . .

"Jesus," Kowalski said. He'd just finished watching the tape of Farmer Joe's attack on Brandon in the Westcott barn.

"I only checked a few of them," Davis said. "But they're pretty much all the same. The tapes go back years. Of the ones I looked at, Brandon's the only boy I ever saw get away."

"Well, that gives you a motive for Westcott. And presumably Father Holloway—since the tapes are here, I assume they had some twisted little arrangement between them."

"I don't even recognize most of those boys," Davis said. "Where the hell did they come from, and what the hell happened to them afterwards?"

"I wonder if we even want to know the answer to that question," Kowalski said.

Davis thought for a moment. "Okay, the blood upstairs is one thing. But Joe torn to pieces—are you thinking now a person did *that*?"

Kowalski shrugged. "People do crazy shit. We're protected from the worst of it here in the boonies, most of the time. But no—I still believe Joe Westcott was killed by an animal, and we know for certain the two campers were. So whatever happened upstairs must be completely unrelated."

"But Brandon—"

"Yes, the tapes offer a connection between Westcott and Holloway and Brandon. And Brandon may have been at the library shortly before Nola's disappearance. But it's all coincidence until you find something that proves otherwise."

"I saw Brandon fighting with Daryl at the festival in Ferris Park," Davis said. "I was there."

"But, you said yourself, you separated them and sent them on their way. Daryl's free, white, and eighteen, and he's a hell-raiser from way back. He could just be joy-riding around the Twin Cities right now, oblivious that anyone's even looking for him."

"Does he have Nola Fenster with him?"

Kowalski laughed. "I agree you need to find this Turner kid and talk to him. And we need to figure out if the blood upstairs came from one person or sixteen. Or if it even came from a person."

"What else would it be from?"

"I don't know. Maybe some anti-religion nutjob broke in and defaced the hallway with chicken blood, and Holloway is off somewhere wanking to more of his pervy tapes."

"Don't be an asshole, Burt."

"I'm just saying. You haven't found a body, you haven't talked to the Turner kid *or* the priest. Stop conjecturing. You're a better cop than that."

"I'm beginning to think I'm not a cop at all anymore," Davis said. "Perverted shit like this, going on right under my nose for years, and I didn't have a clue. Why the hell didn't any of those boys ever come forward?"

Kowalski placed a hand on Davis's shoulder and gave a firm squeeze. "Go find the Turner boy while I work the samples. We can all beat ourselves up later for our various failings. Maybe even over a beer or six."

Davis nodded. "I'm gonna hold you to that. My guys are here for whatever you need. I'm going to head out and see what Kate has to say about all this—she and her boy have been tight with Brandon for years."

"Plus, it wouldn't hurt to see a pretty face like Kate's right now, I bet."

Davis grinned. "You never miss a trick, do you, Burt?"

"Let's just hope neither of us misses *this* trick, whatever it might turn out to be."

. . .

Davis drove halfway to the Bowman house before realizing he was more likely to find both Kate and Chad at the Wolf Research Center—except for a couple of volunteers who worked in the gift shop, Kate typically gave the rest of the staff Sundays off. He swung his cruiser into a smooth U-turn and let it eat up the few miles he needed to backtrack at a speed that probably wasn't necessary and certainly wasn't safe.

Chad was at the Center, but Kate was out in the field somewhere—she hadn't been able to get a radio signal out of one of the local packs in more than a week and was starting to get worried.

"Does she really think it's wise to be wandering around the woods alone right now?" Davis asked. "She saw those campers."

"Well, she knows her way around wolves," Chad said. "Besides, have *you* ever tried to change her mind when it was set on something?"

Davis smiled, then remembered the reason for his visit. "Is there somewhere we can talk?"

There wasn't much happening at the Center—one sweaty family wandering listlessly through the exhibit area—so Chad ushered Davis into Kate's office. "Is this about Brandon?"

"What in the world would make you ask me that?" Davis said. He sensed that his afternoon—the rest of his summer—was about to get very complicated, very quickly.

"I don't know," Chad said. "He's been acting weird for a while—weird even for him, I mean. And we had a little run-in recently where he seemed..."

"Seemed what?" Davis said.

"Like maybe he was headed for trouble."

"When did this happen?"

Chad glanced at the calendar on Kate's desk. "Last Wednesday. When you and Mom were out at the site where those campers were found." He told Davis about Brandon's visit to the Center, the sudden new aggressiveness that felt so weirdly out of character for his friend.

"Did he actually threaten you?"

"No, it was nothing overt," Chad said. "He just wasn't acting like he usually acts. It's like he was all testosteroned-up or something. What's this all about anyway?"

Davis told Chad what he knew: the church full of blood, Brandon's name on the sheet at the library, Brandon's fight with Daryl, and then, picking his words carefully, something of the atrocities he'd seen on the videotapes in Holloway's study.

Chad was silent for a long time when Davis finished.

"I'm not accusing Brandon of anything," Davis said. "But I do need to talk to him. I was hoping you might know where I could find him."

. . .

Of course it was Benjy Tatum who had the bad luck to find Father Holloway. He'd lobbied to be the one to search the basement—anything to get away from the horror of the upstairs hallway—and then the search itself had lulled him into a false sense of security. He'd been through what he thought was every inch of the basement without finding so much as a drop of blood, and he'd convinced himself that nothing *would* turn up at this point.

But just as he was getting ready to go back upstairs and report his findings (or lack thereof) to Deputy Emory, he noticed a tall metal storage cabinet at the end of a side corridor he'd previously overlooked. He didn't even bother to prepare himself—just walked right up and pulled the cabinet open. What was left of Father Holloway slurped out and landed in a sticky heap at his feet like one of the viscous piles of offal he'd seen on a misguided field trip to a St. Paul slaughterhouse when he was still in high school.

Even before Benjy had finished vomiting—pivoting, at least, to avoid the remains this time—he knew beyond a shadow of a doubt that his career in law enforcement was now well and truly over.

. . .

Chad believed the Turner house was the *last* place Brandon would ever go, but Davis thought they should check with Brandon's father and stepmother anyway. Almost as soon as they'd left the Center, however, the call came in that Benjy Tatum had discovered a body—presumably Father Holloway's, although it was difficult to tell—and Davis flipped on the siren he tried never to use, and turned the car toward Saint Ignatius.

How can something like this be happening in a town like Talbot? Davis wondered. Fewer than thirteen hundred year-round residents, and that number decreasing by the minute. The town had seen its share of violent deaths over the years, but prior to this summer they'd all been accident-related. Drunken car wrecks, snowmobile crashes, hunting mishaps. Now Davis was dealing with animal attacks, missing persons, and something that almost had to be murder, because what *animal* came inside a church, slaughtered a priest, and then hid the body in the basement?

Gripping the handle above the passenger door as Davis rounded a corner way too fast, Chad also wondered what sort of dark cloud had settled over his safe, sleepy home town. None of the recent events made any sense. Wolves didn't randomly attack people, elderly librarians didn't disappear without a trace. And someone like Brandon—someone he considered almost a brother—didn't suddenly become an aggressive, unknowable stranger, possibly capable of murder.

He listened while reports blatted from Davis's radio. *Torn apart...half-eaten...mutilated beyond recognition.* Just like Farmer Joe and the campers, but this time *indoors*—inside the church. Chad thought about the story Brandon had told him back in March. The wolf that had smiled and walked on two legs. He thought of the unseen animal pummeling the back of the van during the howling, how the blows had landed like fists, but then the sharp canine yelp as the glass broke, and what distinctly sounded like a *four-legged* creature fleeing into the forest. The idea in his head was completely ludicrous, and he didn't dare mention it to Davis Langley, but still the nugget was there, tickling inside his skull, rising out of his subconscious like a great glowing full moon.

Hadn't he heard that certain schizophrenics could become so convinced they were some sort of monster—a vampire or a werewolf—that they began to act like one? Howling at the moon, drinking human blood. Had Brandon suffered something so traumatic he'd experienced a complete psychotic break? Something so messed-up it had made him believe werewolves were real—that *he* was a werewolf? Or *had* he actually seen something impossible out on the dark country road last Christmas Eve, something now roaming the countryside, ripping people apart?

They pulled into the Saint Ignatius parking lot and got out of the cruiser. When they were nearly to the door, Davis put out a hand to stop Chad for a moment. "Listen," he said. "It's not pretty in there, but the only thing you're going to see upstairs is a bunch of blood. You're going to be okay with that, right?"

Chad nodded.

"I'm going to need to be here for a bit," Davis continued. "While I'm working with the medical examiner, I want you to call around to see if you can find your friend. Does he have a cell phone?"

"No," Chad said. "And mine was charging so I left it at the Center. Sorry, I wasn't thinking."

"No biggie," Davis said. "I'll double-check with Larry Emory to make sure they're done with the rectory, and then you can use one of the phones over there. And listen, I'm sure I don't need to say this, but don't, you know, talk about any of this with anyone. Except your mom, I guess."

Chad nodded.

They started moving again, and in a moment Davis was pulling open the door and ushering Chad inside. The church foyer was dark and shadowy compared to the brilliant sunlight outside, and Chad felt like he was walking into a cave. *Out of the light and into the dark*, he thought, and when the door whisked shut behind them he jumped a little. He might have felt embarrassed, but out of the corner of his eye he saw Davis jump too.

. . .

Brandon finished with his father and stepmonster and left them in the basement. How many times had *he* been left down there, huddled on the cold cement floor or straining against the nylon rope that had bound his wrists to the beam overhead? *Take some time to think about what you did, you little bastard*— that had been his father's favorite line. He wanted to tell his father something similar now, but his father's thinking days were over. His stepmonster's too. Not that either of them had done much thinking in the first place, even when they were alive.

Brandon ascended the stairs and went to wash away the stink of their deaths with a long, hot shower. *If only I could wash away their years of poison and hatred just as easily*, he thought. He didn't realize it, but he was weeping as he turned on the hot water, and he continued to weep as he toweled himself dry, fell onto his old bed, and sank almost immediately into a dreamless slumber.

. . .

The rectory was deserted and silent and more than a little creepy. The few times Chad had visited Brandon there, the place had felt warm and inviting, with Mrs. McGowan singing softly in the kitchen, and the aroma of homemade soup or fresh-baked bread lingering in the air. Now the building was cool and shadowy, the air stale with a vague mildew smell emanating from the air conditioning ducts.

Chad went first to Brandon's room, but realized that any numbers he might need were stored on his phone back at the Center, and he would need to find either a phone book or a computer in order to call anybody. Plus, it was immediately clear that all of Brandon's clothes and possessions were gone, and this made the room seem somehow...off-limits. He wondered if he should tell Davis that Brandon's things were missing, but realized the police had probably taken them themselves. *Evidence. My best friend is now someone the police are gathering evidence against.*

Chad left the room and wandered down the dim hallway. Even if he found a phone book, he wondered if he would be able to speak, considering the massive lump that had formed in his throat. Besides, he finally had to admit what Brandon had been trying to tell him for years. He truly *was* Brandon's only friend—who in the world could he possibly call?

. . .

The Center regularly tracked three wild wolf packs in the forests surrounding Talbot. Four of the seven wolves in the Damarchan pack had radio collars, so it was extremely unusual for Kate not to be able to raise a signal from at least one of them. She'd been within range of virtually every corner of their known territory over the past week, and hadn't heard so much as a ping. She had one last location to try, much farther than she typically needed to go, and nearly two miles of rough trail beyond where any road would take her. But the sun set late at this time of the year, and Kate figured she had at least three good hours of daylight left. If she couldn't dig up some trace of the pack within three hours, they simply weren't there to be found.

She piloted her Jeep up the narrow, twisty Mini Gizzy Trail, a stretch of two-lane blacktop that ended abruptly in a small gravel turnaround where fishermen and canoeists with day passes could park and enter one of the small tributaries feeding into the Boundary Waters Canoe Area. The name of the road was a bastardized version of an Ojibwe Indian term meaning

"Blueberry Moon," but Kate had never been able to discover how the moniker had come to be attached to this particular stretch of road. There was no concentration of blueberry bushes nearby, no good perch from which to observe the moon. Another random appropriation of indigenous culture by the white man, she supposed, and, typically, he hadn't even bothered to get the name right.

She reached the end of the road and found a parking spot near the foot-trail that would bring her the rest of the way up to the area she wanted to check. The trail was rarely used by anyone besides the Wolf Research Center staff, and she could see from the Jeep that it was weedy and overgrown with the lushness only July can bring to northern Minnesota.

Climbing out of the vehicle, she tucked the legs of her pants inside her socks and sprayed herself liberally with bug spray. She hated wearing any sort of chemical into the woods, but she hated coming home covered in ticks and mosquito bites even more. Grabbing the radio telemeter, a water bottle, and a couple of granola bars, she plunged into the forest and began the long, strenuous hike that would hopefully lead her to some sign of the missing Damarchan pack.

. . .

In Father Holloway's office in the rectory, just down the hall from Brandon's now-empty room, Chad found both a phone book and a computer. But still he couldn't think of anyone he might call who would have any sort of clue about Brandon's whereabouts. He tried the Turner house, but there was no answer. Then, on a whim, he dialed the number for Whispering Pines. He couldn't help but smile when Melissa answered on the second ring.

"Hey you," he said.

"Oh—hi there," Melissa said. "Caller I.D. came up as the church, so I thought this must be Brandon. But hi."

"I'm actually *looking* for Brandon, but since you thought I was him, I assume that means you don't know where he is either."

"No," Melissa said. "I haven't heard a word out of him since that day at the Center with you. I didn't really figure I would."

"Yeah, he did seem a little...*final*, didn't he?"

"So why are you looking for him? And why are you calling from the church?"

Chad wasn't sure how to answer. Not only because he'd promised Davis that he wouldn't talk to anyone about what was going on, but also because some part of him didn't want to betray Brandon any further with Melissa. Wherever Brandon was right now, whatever he might have done—how much of it was because Chad had messed with the one girl Brandon had ever even *tried* to have a relationship with? What if Brandon *had* hurt someone? Daryl, Nola Fenster, Father Holloway. What if Brandon *was* responsible for that insane amount of blood over in the church hallway? Was some of that blood on Chad's hands as well for his part in whatever Brandon had become?

"You still with me?" Melissa said.

Chad pressed the phone closer to his ear and gave a soft sigh. "Yeah, sorry. I guess I can't really say why I'm looking for Brandon right now, except that he may be in some sort of trouble."

"Can I help?"

Chad would have liked nothing better than to have Melissa beside him, holding his hand and listening to his worries over his missing friend, but probably the last thing Brandon needed was to find Chad and Melissa together again if he ever did turn up. On the other hand, what if Brandon turned up at Melissa's, and Chad wasn't there to protect her this time? *Jesus, do I really think Brandon would hurt Melissa? Am I actually starting to believe he hurt anyone, that he had something to do with Daryl's disappearance—or Nola Fenster's? Something to do with the gory mess in the church basement that apparently used to be Father Holloway?*

"No," he said. "I appreciate the offer, and I'd really love to see you, but this is probably something you shouldn't be involved with."

"You're beginning to scare me," Melissa said.

Chad hesitated, weighing different approaches to what he wanted to say. Reasonably straightforward would probably be best. "I don't think you need to be scared exactly," he said. "But I do want you to do me a favor."

"Okay…" Her voice was more cautious now, her natural city-girl wariness obvious even over the phone.

"If Brandon happens to come around, just…tell him you can't see him right now. Don't let him in or anything."

"Jesus—what did he do?"

"Nothing anybody's sure of," Chad said. "But you just need to promise you'll be extra careful until we've had a chance to talk to him."

"Who's 'we'?"

"Well, me and Davis Langley, I guess."

"The cop who was at the Center? This is serious enough for the cops?"

"Yeah, I guess it is," Chad said. "But I really can't tell you any more than that right now."

There was a long silence, and Chad wondered if they'd been disconnected. Then Melissa gave a soft, humorless chuckle. "This is so bizarre," she said. "My parents move here to get away from the violence of the city, and now the police are looking for the very first guy we met on our way into town."

"Yeah," Chad said. "Weirdness abounds this summer, that's for sure. Listen, I need to get going, but promise me you'll be careful, and I promise to call as soon as I know anything more."

"I promise," Melissa said. "Before you go, though, are *you* doing okay? With all of...whatever this is? I know how much Brandon means to you."

The lump returned to Chad's throat and he found himself unable to answer. He wouldn't have known *how* to answer even if he could.

Finally, Melissa broke the silence. "Just be careful," she said.

Chad cleared his throat and returned the phone to its cradle. He leaned back in Holloway's office chair and waited for his voice to come back to him, for his brain to wrap itself around all the conflicting thoughts swirling there. The sunlight streaming through the windows behind him shifted just enough to send a sharp glint of brightness off the commemorative silver letter opener sitting on one corner of Holloway's desk.

Chad leaned forward and lifted the instrument out of its display box. The words *"In appreciation..."* were engraved on one side of the handle, and on the other, in tiny block letters: STERLING SILVER. The instrument looked more like a weapon than an office implement, its point sharp and its blade thin but unyielding. Chad wrapped the blade in the polishing cloth nestled in the top half of the display box and slipped the bundle into the pocket of his jeans. He didn't care how insane it made him look, or how instantly it appeared to validate Brandon's crazy story of the wolf that wasn't a wolf—he just knew that, at that moment, he wanted something sharp and dangerous upon his person. Something made of silver.

. . .

When Chad went outside, Davis Langley was already halfway up the sidewalk that connected the church to the rectory. His expression was grim, and the normal tan of his face had taken on a distinctly ashen hue.

"What's wrong?" Chad asked.

Davis waved the question away. "Any luck finding Brandon?"

"No," Chad said. "I tried his folks, but there was no answer. The only other person I could think of was Melissa—that girl you met at the Center? But she hasn't seen him either."

Davis raised an eyebrow. "That's right. She was with him on the Fourth of July."

"Their second and last date," Chad said. "Things didn't exactly blossom between them."

"But they blossomed between you and her pretty quickly afterwards, it looks like."

Chad nodded, a flush spreading up his neck and across his cheeks. "Kinda makes me look like an asshole, doesn't it?"

"Well," Davis said. "All's fair, as they say."

"Anyway, I told her to be on the lookout for him, and to not let him in if he comes around."

"Did you tell her why?"

"No, we sort of skirted around that issue."

Davis nodded, then shook his head as if to reset his mind to matters closer at hand. "Question," he said. "Did Brandon have a dog, a big dog by any chance? Or did they have one here at the church I didn't know about?"

Chad shook his head. "I assume that means there were bite marks on Father Holloway's body."

"Canine *and* human," Davis said.

Chad felt his stomach roll. He wondered if his face had just gone as gray as Davis's. "Jesus," he whispered.

"Sorry," Davis said. "I shouldn't have just blurted that out. I'm kind of in a state of shock myself. That really *is* information you can't share with anyone, by the way. It may ultimately even be good news for Brandon. I'm almost wondering if we should start looking for one of the *other* boys Farmer Joe...you know... molested out in his barn. Maybe someone who's been harboring a grudge against him and the priest for years, all the while training some big-ass monster of a hound to attack people. It doesn't explain the recent disappearances—Daryl and Nola— but they were only connected to the rest of this by mere coincidence anyway."

Chad frowned. The theory was reasonable enough, he supposed. Certainly as reasonable as his own. He wrapped his hand around the silver letter opener in his pocket and tried to decide if he should risk the ridicule certain to follow if he voiced his theory aloud. He steeled himself against Davis's straightforward gaze. "Before you go in a completely different direction with your investigation," he said, "I need to tell you a story. And I apologize ahead of time, but this is going to sound like some truly crazy shit."

He told Davis about the drive he and Brandon had taken in March, first down to Duncton and then out the dark country roads Brandon had driven on Christmas Eve. He repeated Brandon's story of the wolf that smiled and walked on two legs, and his unsettling impression that Brandon had been less terrified than somehow...excited. Intrigued, at the very least, by the possibility of some mythological monster roaming the countryside outside Talbot. *Damn*, Brandon had said when Chad offered up his alternate, rational explanation. *A werewolf would have been really cool, though, don't you think?*

Davis listened to Chad's story. When it was finished he turned to look across the parking lot, pondering the massive forest that began just down the hill and stretched outward for acre upon unknowable acre in three directions. He didn't smirk, or give Chad an odd look, or offer any of the sarcastic comments Chad had been expecting. He simply stared for a time at the vast expanse of trees before turning back with a question. "So, are you saying you think Brandon *did* see such a creature?"

"No," Chad said. "It's ridiculous." *So why did I steal the letter opener and why am I clutching it now?* "But maybe something happened to Brandon that made him think *he's* a werewolf."

Davis considered the idea. "And the canine bite marks?"

Chad shrugged. "I don't know. I saw a movie once where this guy made himself some dentures to throw the police off his trail, but that doesn't seem like something Brandon would know how to do. Besides, that guy was only biting his victims, he wasn't actually eating them."

Chad realized what he'd said. He stumbled off the sidewalk and vomited into the grass for what felt like days.

Davis waited until Chad was finished, then walked over and placed one hand between the boy's shoulder blades. "Come on," he said. "Let's go find him so we at least know for sure."

Chad rose and took several deep breaths to steady himself. Finally he nodded, and they headed back to Davis's cruiser.

. . .

At the Turner house, Davis knocked loud and long on the front door without even a whisper of response from inside. He and Chad could see nothing but the empty living room from the front picture window, and when Davis surreptitiously tried the front door knob, he found it locked.

"Let's go around to the side door," he said. "Technically, I can't just go in without some sort of warrant or cause, but you can probably get away with it as Brandon's friend. If it were ever to come up later, like in court or whatever, you could just say you were paying a visit, something you used to do all the time, that sort of thing."

Chad didn't have the heart to tell Davis he had never once been inside Brandon's house, even when they were little. Brandon would never allow it. Even as a very young boy, he must have realized how different his house was from other houses—from Chad and Kate's house in particular—and he'd always made certain to either meet Chad someplace neutral or be waiting on the curb well before Chad arrived to pick him up.

As soon as they reached the side door, questions of legality flew out the window anyway. The door opened directly into the kitchen, and even through the dirty mesh of the screen they could tell yet another slaughterhouse awaited them inside. The floor was slick with great swatches of blood, crimson darkening to rust where it had already begun to dry. Blood covered the table, the stove, and great gouts of it had fanned across one wall like some modern abstract painting. The refrigerator door was open and hung slightly askew—as if, perhaps, someone had been slammed against it very hard and then desperately clung to it for protection that had ultimately proven useless. They opened the screen door and stepped inside.

"I don't have the manpower to cover another scene like this," Davis said. "We're going to need to call...hell, I don't know *who* we're going to need to call."

Chad pointed to a pile of torn, ragged clothing in one corner—jeans, white T-shirt now little more than bloodstained strips of cloth, worn sneakers burst at their seams—and then to a distinct pattern within the blood on the floor, where clearly something had been dragged toward the basement stairs. Whoever had done the dragging had left several bare, bloody footprints, but they'd been smeared and distorted until they no longer looked entirely human. Chad and Davis exchanged a look, but each decided on his own not to comment on the clothing or the prints—at least for the time being.

"You should really go wait in the cruiser," Davis said.

"Are you going to the basement?"

Davis nodded, but Chad could tell his heart wasn't in it. Davis's hesitation only made him seem like a *better* cop, in Chad's estimation. "Well, I'm not letting you go down there alone," he said.

Davis sighed—resignation mixed with relief—and took out his gun. He felt around at the top of the stairs until he found the light switch, and together they descended into whatever new hell might await them below.

. . .

Upstairs, in his old room, Brandon was awake. Davis's pounding at the front door had barely penetrated his sleep, but he'd bolted instantly alert and ready the second the side door creaked open. Ready for what, he couldn't say, but he could feel his heart beating powerfully within his chest, and it was a matter of will to prevent the wolf from bursting forth and taking care of the situation just as it had been taking care of so many situations lately.

His senses were wolf-sharp now even in human form, and he could both hear and smell the two visitors below. One was Chad, and although the scent of the other was less familiar, he could smell gun oil and an underlying something that reminded him vaguely of Nikki. *Nikki's father then—the Chief of Police.* So the villagers had come for him even more quickly than he'd anticipated. He wanted to bound down there, rip out their throats and rend their bodies—but Chad was one of them, and Chad had only ever been nice to him. The thought of tearing Chad apart made something very much like a dog's whimper issue involuntarily from his throat.

Of course, what Chad did with Melissa behind my back wasn't particularly nice. Maybe he needs to be taught a lesson right here and now. Maybe he needs to learn about the different sort of alpha patrolling the streets of Talbot these days.

He heard them start down the basement stairs, and he rose from the bed and wrapped a thin blanket around himself. He knew the clothes he'd wrecked during his most recent transformation were still in the kitchen, but in the reddish haze that lingered inside his head, he couldn't remember what he'd done with his duffel bag. He had a couple of changes of clothes in there, but he'd have to learn to be more careful in the future. Clothes were expensive, and he couldn't destroy a whole set of them every time he decided to slaughter someone. That sort of thing was happening on a pretty regular basis these days, after all.

. . .

The scene in the basement was like nothing Chad had ever imagined. Even for Davis, who had seen the damage inflicted on the other bodies, the Turner basement was almost surreal in the intensity of its violence.

The woman—Brandon's stepmother, presumably—wasn't so bad. Her throat had been torn out so savagely that she'd nearly been decapitated, but otherwise her body was largely intact, crumpled like a sack of laundry next to the washer and dryer.

The *man*, however...

Brandon's father had been strung up by his wrists from a large wooden beam overhead. Judging from the wear on the beam, the nylon rope that bound him had hung in the same spot for a long time, and Davis could only imagine what that had meant for the boy Brandon had been inside this house. Another kid who'd never come forward—either here or after his run-in with Farmer Joe. Davis wondered how many more such silent victims Talbot held. And all the little towns nearby. And then the larger towns, farther away, and then the cities, an endless string of victims, and how could anything he ever did, no matter how good a cop he might be, make the slightest dent in such an unbelievable progression of horror?

The hanging man's belt had been removed and used to flay the very flesh off the man's torso. Some of the lashes cut so deeply that the man's ribs were visible in places, and when the belt had finally been discarded—it lay coiled and blood-soaked on the floor like a venomous snake—his tormentor had apparently raked a quartet of razor knives down the man's stomach and back in groups of parallel, gaping slashes. Not knives, Davis realized. *Claws.*

"Jesus," Chad said. "I know they were terrible people—"

Overhead, footsteps pounded down from the second floor and crossed the kitchen in a run. They heard the screen door, and Davis cursed his sloppy police work—*so much for being such a good cop!*—because he hadn't even *considered* checking the rest of the house before heading for the basement.

He pounded up the stairs, Chad at his heels, and was trying to scan every direction at once even as pushed through the door and hit the driveway. Gun raised, helping him focus, he twisted south, west, north, scanning for any sign of movement. The *only* thing moving in Talbot was a large, gray dog loping across a field nearly a quarter-mile away. Davis lowered his gun and stared blankly at Chad, unsure what to do next. The only other time he remembered feeling so at sea was the day his wife died. If anything, he felt even more lost now than he had then.

Chad remained focused on the animal crossing the field, and watched until it disappeared into a stand of trees that would eventually bring it into the forest proper. He turned and met Davis's gaze. "I know you're going to think I'm insane," he said. "But the stride on that animal was all wrong for a dog."

"Don't even say it," Davis said.

"That was a wolf," Chad continued. He sounded almost apologetic. "And a big mother too."

Chad's use of that particular phrase struck them both at once in almost exactly the same way. "Jesus," Davis said. "Your mom's out in those woods."

They raced to the cruiser and peeled out in a screeching U-turn. Davis didn't even bother to call in a report of this newest set of bodies. *What the hell*, he thought. *It's not like either of them is going anywhere anytime soon.*

. . .

Kate had been right about the sun setting late this time of year, but light worked differently inside the woods than it did in more open areas—an expanse of lake, for instance, or a meadow. Within the trees, the light was largely indirect and already full of deep shadows by eight o'clock in the evening.

Even here, in the small clearing she'd chosen as her final test site for the day, the nearby trees were tall enough and thick enough to create an artificial early twilight. This didn't bother Kate—she still had a *few* minutes, at least, before she absolutely, positively had to hit the trail back to her Jeep if she didn't want to stumble through the last half-mile in full darkness—but it did mean that movement within the trees was more easily concealed, obtuse rather than obvious. Brandon was virtually upon her, only twenty yards away, before she even noticed him.

"Jesus!" she said. She stumbled into a jutting mound of granite and nearly lost her balance. Her surprise was so great, it took a moment before she could process what she was seeing. Even when she did, she thought there must be some funny story behind it and she laughed. "Why are you *naked*, for crying out loud?"

Brandon glanced down as if noticing his state of undress for the first time, and then looked at her with an expression she couldn't read. Not embarrassment, exactly. More than anything, the look on his face reminded her of a time when Chad was a little boy, and he'd wandered away from her in a department store down in Minneapolis. When she finally found him, perhaps ten minutes later, he'd looked utterly and uncomprehendingly *lost*. On the verge of tears—he couldn't have been more than four or five—but too overwhelmed even to cry. Brandon had the exact same look right now.

"I...I don't know where to go," he said.

Her first instinct was to run to him, throw her arms around him and try to make everything better. Even if he wasn't actually her son, she'd always thought of him that way, and it had nearly killed her many times over the years to think about what his terrible parents were doing to him inside that terrible unhappy house of theirs. She took a few steps forward, but then the analytical scientist-side of her mind overrode the protective mother-side.

"What are you doing out here, anyway?" she said. "And seriously, where are your clothes?"

"They came too fast and I wasn't ready," he said. Now he *was* crying, although he didn't seem aware of it. Tears streamed down his cheeks, tiny rivers of clean cutting through the dust that had gathered there during his run. "They were down in the basement, and they knew, they *had* to know, they had to have seen the bodies, and so all I could do was run."

Gooseflesh rose on Kate's arms. The clearing suddenly seemed too exposed, her logical avenue of escape blocked by the man standing naked and crying at the edge of the trees. The man who looked like Brandon and sounded like Brandon—a boy she loved almost as much as her own son—but who somehow no longer *was* Brandon. Not entirely, anyway.

She couldn't say how she knew this, but the sense ran so deep and strong within her that she could actually taste adrenaline flooding her system, revving her body into fight-or-flight mode. Only really just flight, because the message her brain kept broadcasting was the same one over and over: *Get away, just get far away right now.*

"Please," Brandon said. He stumbled closer, weaving as if drunk or overwhelmingly exhausted. "I don't know what to do. I thought I could go somewhere in my car, but that's gone now. They were down there with guns and I had to run. I could smell you out here, and I knew you'd help me, so I just ran."

"Who had guns? Who—" And then her brain reprocessed his last sentence. "Did you say you could *smell* me out here?"

Brandon nodded, eager to please as a puppy. "I can do lots of things now I couldn't do before. I'll show you everything— you're going to think it's so cool, I just know. Just, please, take me home with you—you can't let them find me. They'll never understand, but I know you will."

Kate slowly backed away, trying to create additional distance between them without startling him. She knew these woods better than he did, she was certain of that, so if she could get a decent start, she was sure she could lose him in some deep brush and make her way back to the Jeep. He was naked and shoeless, after all, and thorns and the rocky ground would slow him down a lot more than they would her. Whatever had gone wrong inside of Brandon was too much for her to fix on her own. She could apologize to him later, when he was better, when he was Brandon again. Right now she just needed to get far away from him.

"*Please*, Kate. You're the only one who'll understand. I thought Chad might too, but now he's with them, and I don't have anywhere else to go."

"Listen, Brandon," Kate said. "You're scaring me. You know I'll help you in any way I can, but first I need to talk to—"

"*NO!*" His shout was an animal-like snarl, and he grimaced and clutched his stomach as if his organs were shifting inside him.

"I *will* help you," Kate said. "But I need to you to stay here while I go back to the Jeep and radio in. I've got some blankets there—"

"Why won't you help me?" Brandon wailed. "Why are you being like all the rest of them?"

He doubled over in agony, and the twilight stillness of the clearing filled with sharp snapping sounds as if Brandon's very bones were splintering inside his body.

"What is it?" Kate said. "What's—"

Brandon lifted his contorted face toward her and glared through eyes lit with a fiery internal luminescence. "Run," he growled. "That's all you can do now."

. . .

Davis and Chad tried three different spots where Kate *might* have been working, but didn't stumble upon her Jeep at the Mini Gizzy turnaround until nearly ten o'clock. The sky overhead still glowed faintly with a purplish twilight, but the trail leading into the forest was nothing but shadow layered upon shadow.

"She should have been finished by now," Chad said. "Whether she found the pack or not, she should have been done and out of the woods before it got too dark. Why didn't I know where she was working in the first place? Why don't I ever listen when she's talking?"

"Because she's your mother," Davis said. "Anyway, don't freak out on me yet. You know how she is. She'll probably be here any minute." They both knew he was nowhere near as confident as he was trying to sound.

"Do you have any lights in here?" Chad said. "Flashlights, portable spots, whatever?"

"Of course," Davis said. "But I don't know if *us* going after her is the smartest idea right now. The last thing we need is for all three of us to be lost in the woods in the dark."

"Oh, really, is that the last thing we need? What's the first thing?"

"The *first* thing," Davis said, "is for you to calm down a notch. I know you're worried about your mom—I am too—but we're not going to solve anything by taking off in one direction as she's coming back from another. Right?"

Chad slumped and stared out the window at darkness that seemed to be descending exponentially. "So what do we do instead?"

"Does your mom carry a radio or a cell phone into the field?"

Chad perked up. "She may not have brought a radio since no one's at the Center to answer it anyway, but she probably has her cell. Reception's really spotty out here, but it's worth a shot."

Davis pulled his cell phone out of the breast pocket of his uniform and tossed it to Chad. He shook his head. "Do you realize we could have tried calling her at any point in the last two hours we've been looking for her? What a couple of morons."

Chad smiled, and then gave a small laugh. Davis joined him. For some reason, their basic incompetence made it seem as if, of *course*, everything was going to turn out okay. They climbed out of the cruiser and Chad dialed his mom's number. Almost immediately they heard a distinctive jangle and realized she must be coming down the path toward them right now. When the phone continued to ring and she didn't appear, Chad walked over to the Jeep and peered in through the half-open driver-side window. Kate's phone lay nestled in one of the cup holders near the stick shift. As he ended the call on Davis's phone, the phone inside the Jeep gave one last half-jangle and then fell silent.

. . .

Kate ran.

As fast as her legs would carry her—not nearly fast enough.

Through thick groves of pine and cedar. Through stands of white birch straight as prison bars. Through thorny brush and yearling trees that snatched at her face, her arms, her torso.

She ran through swarms of tiny gnats, buzz of their wings first amplifying and then fading in her ears like some bizarre demonstration of Doppler. Ran through mud, through muck, over fallen trees and around enormous, moss-covered jags of granite that might have been ancient idols but were more likely merely rocks. *Too bad*, she thought—she could have used a god just then.

She was forty-eight years old, in remarkable shape. Many women would have added a conciliatory "for someone my age," but Kate Bowman had no time for false modesty—especially now. Strong legs, flat belly, clear lungs, metronome-steady heart. Still, she'd been racing frantically over rough terrain for nearly an hour.

The animal—she couldn't bring herself to think of it as Brandon—was playing with her. Stringing her along. She'd seen wolves do the same thing with rabbits and other small prey, usually when they were teaching pups to hunt but sometimes, seemingly, just for the fun of it. That's what this animal was doing with her. It could catch her any time it wanted, but for now it was just letting her run herself out.

In a clearing she startled a young bobcat. It leapt straight up into the air in a manner that would have been comical under other circumstances, then scrambled into the undergrowth with a yowl of indignation. Kate cursed, a single clipped syllable lost instantly to the enormity of the forest. The bobcat might have offered a momentary distraction at least. *An appetizer*, Kate thought, and immediately wished she hadn't.

The animal was closing in. Or Kate was finally tiring. She could hear its wet chuffs of breath, smell its carnivore musk. A true predator would have moved almost silently until ready to spring, but the thing behind her crashed through the forest like a drunken grizzly.

He's not quite as animal as he thinks he is, Kate thought, but instantly thrust the notion aside. She couldn't let her mind go there, couldn't let herself relive the moment when Brandon had started to writhe and contort in front of her—the moment of his impossible transformation into a creature she refused to name because *it simply could not exist.*

And yet, here it was—chasing her through the dark forest.

The animal put on a burst of speed and Kate heard it move deeper into the shadows on her left. Circling in front of her. Herding behavior—but herding her toward what?

Somewhere overhead a bright half-circle of moon shone down, but within the forest the light was merely a silver glow wherever branches happened to part in just the right way. Kate was amazed she'd made it this far without smashing face-first into a tree or tumbling into a gully.

Now the meager glow was expanding, and it took Kate a moment to understand why. The trees were thinning, the forest falling away. A luminous sky opened before her like an old Cinemascope movie screen, awash with stars.

The animal had manipulated her to the high granite cliff on the western edge of the Damarchan pack territory. Almost the exact spot where she'd first noticed the absence of the pack a week ago. She remembered how surprised she'd been that she hadn't been able to pick up a radio signal for any of the collared wolves even from the highest physical point in their known range.

Now she knew why. The Damarchan wolves had scented the strange new beast in their territory and run like hell. At least Kate hoped that's what had happened. She assumed she'd never know for sure now, but she supposed scientists often died without knowing everything they wanted. Probably everyone did.

Spent at last, Kate stopped running.

She stood on the edge of the cliff and waited.

The canopy of stars was beautiful, the fat half-moon was beautiful, even the animal that was somehow also Brandon was beautiful as it finally moved toward her from the cover of the trees.

Kate was glad to know she could still look at an animal with a scientist's eye mere seconds before it was going to kill her. She could still marvel at the unlikely engineering necessary to create any living creature, still wonder at the complex evolutionary forces that had forged the pathway down through time to create this particular animal, still appreciate the mysterious interplay between predator and prey even when she was half of the equation.

"Can you understand me at all?" she said, mainly to hear the sound of her own voice one last time.

The animal cocked its head as if listening, but Kate saw its muscles ripple in the moonlight and realized it was tensing for the kill.

"I don't know what happened to make you like this," she said. "But if I was any part of it, I hope you know I'm sorry. I always thought of you as my other son, my other little boy, and...well, I'm sorry I was never able to do more for you. I should have done more."

Amazingly, she saw the animal's muscles relax, and the thought flashed through her head: *I'm actually gonna make it out of this alive.* But she had misjudged how far she'd backed away in her fright, and a single careless footfall caught the jut of a rock and sent her stumbling backwards over the edge of the cliff. She screamed—and plummeted like a missile.

In the air, time slowed to a crawl. She didn't see her entire life flash before her eyes, but gravity did prove sympathetic enough to allow her a few select glimpses of the world she was leaving behind.

Mostly she thought of Chad. His cheerful, inquisitive childhood. His surprisingly calm teenage years. The exceptional young man he'd become.

Kate would have given anything to hug him one last time, to look into his eyes, feel his lips against her cheek. She would have happily let the animal on the cliff devour her alive for a single additional minute with her son.

Only the animal above her was no longer precisely an animal. He was reverting back into Brandon again, his almost-human hand reaching out helplessly toward her and his almost-human mouth open in a scream that echoed across the distance as an agonized howl.

Despair pierced Kate like an arrow as she realized what would happen next. Brandon would go to Chad. Just like he'd come to her. Looking for help, but ultimately unable to control the monster he'd become. He would go to Chad, and Chad would take him in, because Chad would be even less cautious than she had been. Nothing but love and sympathy for the boy who had always been his best friend. Chad would embrace Brandon with open, unsuspecting arms, and she was no longer able to protect or even warn him.

At this final realization, Kate felt her heart break.

Then she hit the ground and the rest of her broke too.

. . .

They waited near Kate's Jeep for another thirty minutes. Chad stalked back and forth across the dusty gravel of the turnaround while Davis radioed for updates. Davis had finally sent a team to the Turner house, and they'd secured and photographed the scene and carted away the bodies. He then instructed Pete Jenkins, the night dispatcher, to request assistance from several nearby police and sheriff's departments. Burt Kowalski radioed to say that an additional forensic pathologist would be arriving from Duluth in the morning as well. The machine would grind away on its own steam now, at least for a day or two, and Davis felt the tiniest amount of tension leave his body. Then he noticed the ever-increasing worry and hostility on Chad's face, and the muscles in his neck and shoulders contracted more tightly than before. *Kate is still out there. Out in the dark with whatever the hell we're dealing with now.*

He joined Chad beside the Jeep. "What do you think we should do?"

"I think we should go find her. I've thought that since we got here."

Davis nodded. "This trail. You know where it leads?"

"Of course. I've been up there a thousand times."

"In the dark?"

"Dark or light, a trail's a trail. Let's just *do* something!"

Davis retrieved two big Maglite flashlights from the trunk of the cruiser and gave one to Chad. He tore a sheet of paper from the small notebook he always carried and scribbled a note telling Kate to call his cell phone if she returned before they did, then wedged it carefully under the driver-side windshield wiper of the Jeep. "Lead the way," he told Chad, and together they followed the sharp bluish beams of their flashlights into the forest.

. . .

It took them nearly an hour to hike to the spot where Kate had been working. Davis was impressed by Chad's surefooted confidence in the profound darkness inside the trees—if not for the flashlights, Davis would have thought he'd gone blind. Once they reached the clearing, he was shocked at how light the world appeared once again. The sky thrummed with a velvety navy glow and an extravagant peppering of stars.

"She was here alright," Chad said. He held up the radio telemeter.

They began calling to her, their shouts thin and easily lost against the trees that surrounded the bowl of the clearing. They swept their flashlights in wide, low arcs across the grass, but other than the telemeter they found no sign of Kate. Eventually they circled back to the head of the trail. The night was silent save for a whisper of leaves and the periodic scurrying of tiny creatures foraging the undergrowth for food or shelter.

"Now what?" Davis said.

"I don't know," Chad said. His voice was hoarse from shouting. "She could have gone in pretty much any direction from here. I just don't why she *would*."

"I didn't see any blood or signs of a struggle," Davis said. "If that helps at all."

Chad offered a wan smile. "Yeah, me neither. But why wouldn't she just go back down the main trail? And why would she leave the telemeter?"

Such questions had no answer, and Davis didn't try to make one up. He tried his portable radio, but received only a squawk of static—something had been hinky with his cruiser's relay transmitter for weeks, and now it had either given up completely or just couldn't generate enough oomph to penetrate the dense forest. He tried his cell phone, and the display lit up his face with an unearthly greenish glow. "Here's something," he said. "I've got no signal whatsoever. She could be trying to call us right now and we wouldn't even know."

They started back down the trail, each of them silent and locked inside his own set of worries. They were nearly to the Jeep when the stillness of the night was blown apart by the unmistakable *blatta-blatta-blat* of a helicopter soaring up seemingly out of nowhere and crossing directly over their heads.

"What the hell?" Davis said. He doubted Chad could hear him—he could barely hear himself over the noise of the rotors.

The cacophony passed as quickly as it had arrived, and Chad tilted his flashlight up to illuminate their faces. "Isn't there a medical chopper down in Duncton?"

Davis nodded. "Come on, let's get back into either cell or radio range and find out what the hell is going on."

. . .

The second they left the trees, Davis's cell phone began ringing, and they could hear loud, frantic squawks issuing from the radio inside the cruiser. Davis answered the phone, and Chad watched in the beam of his flashlight as Davis's face went pale in front of him for the second time that day. "What is it?" he said. "Is it her?" Davis held up a hand and continued to listen while the night stretched before them and Chad wondered if his heart was going to beat right out of his chest.

Finally, Davis ended the call and took a deep breath. "It's her," he said. Chad felt his stomach drop. "Some campers down on the Winousak River heard a scream and then what sounded like a fall and went to investigate. They found her at the bottom of the bluff and radioed for the chopper."

"So she's alive, right?"

"Yes, she's alive," Davis said. "But it doesn't look good, Chad. And there's something else, too. Right after the scream...they heard a wolf howling from the bluffs—'like he'd just caught his foot in a beartrap,' they said."

Chad scrambled for his keys and fumbled to find the spare that would fit Kate's Jeep. "Where are they taking her? Duncton Memorial?"

"No, Duncton's routing her directly to Duluth. I guess it's pretty bad."

Chad found the correct key and climbed into the driver's seat, but Davis blocked him from closing the door and planted one hand on the boy's shoulder. "Let me find Emory and turn things over to him. Then I can drive you."

"No disrespect," Chad said. "But I'm not waiting another fucking minute tonight. Besides, you need to go find that 'wolf'...and blow its goddamned head off."

Davis nodded and moved out of the way. Chad started the Jeep and peeled out of the turnaround, gravel dinging the side of the cruiser like tiny pellets of buckshot. "Slow down," Davis called, although he knew Chad would ignore the warning even if he heard it. Davis couldn't fault the kid—had the situation been reversed, he wouldn't have heeded such asinine advice either.

. . .

Brandon lay deep in the forest and howled his sorrow to an unforgiving night. No other wolf answered him, no pack came to investigate. He had no pack—he was as alone as a wolf as he'd been all his life in the human world. At least the boy and the girl in the old Indian story had finally gone looking for the brother they'd abandoned. No one would ever look for Brandon, except to hunt him down.

Maybe that would be for the best anyway. Now that he couldn't control the animal inside, even around someone as important to him as Kate, maybe the best thing he could do would be to throw himself off the same cliff she'd gone over, or wait for some big lumber truck to come barreling down the road and leap in front of it. He thought of news stories he'd seen that talked of men committing "suicide by cop"—creating situations where they knew the police would have to shoot them—but what if they only wounded him and threw him into a cell instead? He could picture himself transforming there, truly an animal in a cage, and then being poked and prodded and *observed* for the rest of his life. In the end, the freak they'd always called him.

No, he couldn't let that happen, and the truth was—he was a coward. That's why he'd put up with his father's bullshit and beatings all those years, why he'd submitted to the name-calling and punches at school. Afraid, always afraid. Only when he became the wolf did he ever stop being afraid, but now he knew the wolf wasn't invincible after all. The beast could feel the same gut-wrenching grief as a person over its role in Kate's fall, and the only way to prevent something like that in the future would be a complete and total eradication of feeling and emotion. The sweet blank numbness of death—why hadn't he chosen differently when Holloway had presented his question back in April? All the pain and heartbreak of his sorry, messed-up life would have been over in a minute, and for all the long months since he would have been gone, at peace, lost in blissful nothingness.

Still, he knew he wouldn't do it himself. *Couldn't* do it himself. The thought of taking his own life was one thing, sad but probably possible, but the idea of taking the life of the creature inside him made his stomach churn and his brain throb as if white-hot needles were being plunged into his skull. The beast grieved for Kate, grieved to depths Brandon almost couldn't comprehend, but still it wanted to live. *Demanded* to live. To run through the woods, to howl at the moon. To hunt. To eat.

Brandon rose and wiped the final gritty remnants of grief from his face. He wondered if he could have it both ways—kill the boy and let the beast do what it would. Transform and then just stay transformed, tamping the Brandon part of him so far down it would never be heard from again. No guilt. No remorse over a life that was never going to be the life he'd imagined anyway. A blankness not of death, but of complete and total surrender.

He trudged through the forest until he found a small break in the trees. Not a true clearing like the one in which he'd encountered Kate, but just a small open area where a fallen tree had created a pathway to the sky that new growth hadn't yet closed. He drew a number of deep, calming breaths. He looked up into the sky, at the multitude of stars wheeling through the vast heavens, and realized, as so many others had before him, how small and insignificant his troubles were in the grand scheme of things. He smiled and closed his eyes. He cast away all the pain of the past and trusted the Universe to handle it now. *God, Great Spirit, whatever,* he thought. He pushed Brandon deep inside, willed the boy's broken soul into some unknowable abyss, and let the wolf consume him.

. . .

At normal speeds, the trip from Talbot to Duluth took about two and a half hours. Chad arrived in well under two, and even managed to avoid any Duluth patrol cars as he sped through one red light after another once he reached the city limits. He found the hospital and parked in the lot outside the emergency room. He burst through the doors and was relieved to find no other patrons waiting at the reception desk, because he most certainly would have pushed them right out of the way.

The nurse behind the desk was expecting him—Davis Langley had called to let the hospital know Chad was on his way. His mother was in surgery, and would be for some time. Numerous broken bones, both lungs collapsed, ruptured spleen, damaged liver...the list seemed endless. The nurse pointed Chad toward a bank of vending machines where he could buy coffee or something to eat, and told him he could use one of the small consulting rooms off the main waiting area if he wanted to get some sleep. Chad told her he wouldn't be able to sleep anyway, but the nurse smiled kindly and said, "You should at least try. She's going to be in there for quite a while. I'll come get you when there's any news, I promise."

He purchased a ham sandwich and a soda from the vending machines, then closed himself in one of the small cubicles the nurse had pointed out. *Consulting room*, she'd called it, but Chad could tell immediately it was a room only for bad news. A tiny space where lives were changed every day, always for the worse. Despite the bad mojo of the place and his earlier protestation, exhaustion washed over him like an ocean wave and he was asleep as soon as he sat down, the food and drink untouched on the table beside him.

He dreamed of nothing in particular—no wolves or rooms filled with blood, no flayed corpses hanging from wooden beams. At some point the kindly nurse crept into the room to cover him with a blanket and turn out the overhead light, but Chad didn't budge—only gave a soft sigh and sank deeper into oblivion.

When he finally awoke, he could tell even before he looked that the world outside the consulting room had changed. He could hear more activity, and bright light cut a fiery streak across the bottom of the closed door. He rose and stretched, his body full of kinks from his awkward position in the chair. He went out into the emergency room, blinking like an owl in the brilliant sunlight blasting through the windows. The clock above the reception desk said 11:13 AM—he'd slept for nearly eight hours.

The nurse who'd helped him the night before was gone, but the young man who'd replaced her offered a sympathetic smile and said, "Hey, we were just coming to wake you. Your mom came out of surgery about twenty minutes ago, and—"

"Is she alive? Can I see her?"

The new nurse hesitated a moment—something Chad didn't like one bit—and then said, "She'll be in recovery for a while yet, but they'll probably let you in for a few minutes at least. Why don't you grab some breakfast and I'll do some checking for you."

Chad thanked the man and headed down the hallway to find a restroom. *They sure are intent on getting me fed around here,* he thought. He wondered if they did that with everybody, a way to distract people from their stress and grief, or if he just looked particularly hungry.

Truth be told, he looked half-dead, even after his long, unbroken sleep. He stared into the mirror over the bathroom sink and wondered what the hell had happened to him within the last few days (although of course he knew). He had a bad case of bed-head that wasn't helping the situation, but even the basic structure of his face seemed to have changed. His blue eyes were sunk into his skull and they appeared darker and more wary than before, staring out over deep hollows that looked like purplish bruises. His skin was pale and stretched too tight across his cheeks, and his jaw was set as if he'd spent the night grinding his teeth and now couldn't stop. He washed his face and smoothed his hair as best he could, and tried to *will* himself to look less cadaverous. The results weren't particularly satisfying, and finally he gave up and trudged back to the reception area.

. . .

They finally let him in to see his mom some twenty minutes later, cautioning him several times that she was in a deep coma, and wouldn't actually know he was there. Also, that she might look a little shocking.

"Shocking" didn't begin to cover it. If Chad had been surprised by his own appearance in the mirror, seeing Kate in the recovery room was like looking at a total stranger—the victim of an airplane crash, or the first raw attempts of some burgeoning Dr. Frankenstein.

Every visible part of her appeared bruised and battered, and what wasn't visible was either in a cast, bandaged, or connected to tubes and wires and pierced by shiny steel rods. Chad choked back a sob, afraid to even touch her, but the recovery nurse took him by the elbow and led him closer. She placed his hand on the one tiny spot on his mother's right shoulder that remained miraculously untouched, and discreetly stepped away to let him collect himself in the face of the terrible, wrecked shell that lay in front of him.

Later, one of the surgeons came in and spewed out a list of everything that was wrong with Kate, and everything they'd done for her so far. Chad barely listened—the details didn't matter, only that she was going to be alright again. The surgeon had no answer for that. "We'll just have to wait and see what the next few hours bring," he said. "And then, assuming those go well, the next few days. She's looking at a long, long road that might not ever circle back to the road she was on before. Do you understand what I'm saying?"

Chad nodded, although deep down he thought the surgeon's words were mostly just condescending blather. He wished the man would go away.

"Is there anyone we should call? Your father, your grandparents?"

Chad forced himself to look away from the bloated purple mess that had once been his mother's beautiful face and stared at the surgeon with eyes stormy and rimmed with red. "No," he said. "It's just her and me."

. . .

From Monday morning, when she came out of her initial surgery, until Thursday afternoon, the doctors and surgeons who wandered in and out of Kate's room remained vague and noncommittal, but at least marginally optimistic. Kate made no sign of either coming out of her coma or going deeper into it, but her brainwaves looked good—or at least she continued to *have* brainwaves. Chad tried to remain upbeat, both for himself and for Davis when he called home each night to report Kate's progress, and Davis, in turn, tried to sound upbeat as he filled Chad in on the happenings around Talbot. No, there'd been no sign of Brandon. No, there'd been no more deaths or disappearances. Yes, the staff at the Wolf Research Center was keeping the place running smoothly, and everyone sent their wishes and prayers.

Chad found a small boarding house across the street from the hospital, and by Thursday night he'd begun to allow the hospital staff to bully him away from Kate's bedside at the end of regular visiting hours. He found himself almost looking forward to a night of lying in bed and zoning out to whatever was on television—sitting beside the broken, motionless form in the hospital was the most exhausting thing he'd ever done. He felt guilty about feeling that way, but the feeling was there nonetheless.

At the boarding house, Chad was just getting ready to head down the hall for a hot shower when his mom's cell phone rang—and instantly he knew. Without looking at Caller I.D., without clicking the button that would connect him to whoever was on the other end, he simply was certain. He sank onto the bed and pressed his thumb and index finger against his eyelids as if he could physically stop the tears before they started. With his other hand, he pressed the accept button and brought the phone to his ear.

For a moment he thought he'd been wrong, because the voice on the other end of the line said, "I'm sorry, Mr. Bowman. We lost her." Then he realized what they meant, and his rage was instantaneous and volcanic. "How do you lose someone who can't even move?" he nearly screamed. "If someone's dead, say they're dead, you stupid fuck!"

The person on the other end of the line hesitated, then whispered a tiny, "I'm so sorry," and disconnected the call.

. . .

And so he was eighteen years old, and his mother was dead. The only parent he'd ever known. He went back to the hospital, touched her dead body, kissed her dead forehead, signed papers officially confirming her deadness, then called one of the funeral homes on the list provided by the hospital to make arrangements for dead Kate to be cremated and her dead remains to be shipped back to Talbot.

Her remains.

He let Duluth disappear from his rearview mirror before he uncoiled the rusty spring inside his chest and let himself sob. First and foremost for his mom, but also for himself—no sense lying about self-pity at this late date.

He felt as if he had a cable of raw, living grief stretching directly from his heart to some unreachable horizon. Periodically, someone beyond that horizon would grab the cable and give it a sharp, breath-stealing twist. Chad wished they would twist hard enough to split his heart right down the middle, and he could just be done with things once and for all. But no such luck.

At a tiny mom-and-pop gas station in the middle of nowhere, he filled the Jeep's tank, bought a mug of strong black coffee, and then let the road spool out before him in a dark blur.

At one point during the trip, Chad swam up out of his thoughts long enough to realize he was driving directly into the moon. It floated low on the horizon, not quite full but very close—bloated like a tick and listing drunkenly to one side. Chad didn't understand the atmospheric wizardry that sometimes made the moon look so enormous or nearby, but he assumed the effect was probably more interesting if you didn't bog yourself down in the science of it.

His mother would have been appalled. For her, the science would have been the magic and the effect merely a byproduct. Chad loved science as much as the next guy—more so, he hoped, since he was planning to make his living at it—but no one loved science like Kate Bowman.

Like Kate Bowman *had* loved science.

A fresh wave of grief washed over Chad, misting his vision and threatening to close his throat. He slapped it away and tried to force anger to take its place.

A fall—she died in a stupid fall.

And had that fall been an accident—or had it been caused, either by someone or some *thing*?

The road shifted definitively northward. It stretched before him like a slow gray river, meandering through a landscape of trees and more trees. Chad slowed to just above the posted speed limit and forced himself to watch for unusual shadows or the flash of luminescent eyes in the ditch. Deer, moose, bear—the forest was filled with creatures large enough to cause serious damage to both vehicle and person if you collided with one of them.

Funny, though—to be worrying about a car accident when your mother was dead and you were basically an orphan and you were returning home to a town so changed within just a matter of days that you weren't even sure you'd recognize it. Chad laughed, but the sound was as brutal as the unexpected snapping of a femur, and he quickly fell silent and remained so for the rest of the drive. Father Holloway's silver letter opener lay on the passenger seat, and Chad wondered if he should chuck it out the window. Stupid, worthless talisman against an even stupider idea. What had he been thinking? The moon wasn't full tonight, and it certainly hadn't been full when Father Holloway was killed—or Brandon's parents. Or his mother.

After a time, he crested a familiar hill and the lights of Talbot swam into view like a mirage, something unreal, one of those miniature replica villages from an antique model train set. No matter how many times he drove these roads, that first glimpse of town was always unexpected.

The sign at the edge of town listed a population of 1,245. Chad wondered how long it would be before someone changed it to reflect Talbot's recent losses. Farmer Joe, Father Holloway, Brandon's father and stepmother, his own mother. Daryl and

Nola? And how many others no one even knew about yet—unmissed for whatever reason and, so, uncounted and unmourned?

Chad slowed the Jeep to a crawl as he glided down Main Street. The clock on his dashboard read just after two AM and the town was closed up tight for the night. "Sidewalks rolled up and all the working lassies home in bed," his grandfather had said once, one summer he'd visited a lifetime ago. Chad hadn't realized until years later that Grandpa Jim had been making some sort of allusion to prostitution, had not understood why his mother had turned red and said, "Dad!"—or why his grandfather had laughed and winked at him in the rearview mirror.

Another person gone from his life, although both of his grandparents had died so long ago that he rarely even thought about them anymore—just a vague, wistful nostalgia around the holidays. Chad had always wondered what it would be like to have crowded Thanksgivings or Christmases like the ones you saw on television. Hallmark cards come to life, with parents and grandparents and aunts and uncles and cousins, everyone gathered around an enormous dining room table covered with mountains of food and flickering candles. All the time he was growing up, his home had been filled with love and laughter, but he and his mom had usually eaten in the living room and their dining room table had typically been cluttered with books, maps, and Ziploc specimen bags filled with fur samples and wolf scat.

At the northern edge of town, Chad turned and let the county road carry him deeper into the woods. Their house was six miles outside of town, nestled in a private pocket of land inside the national forest. Either the state or the national park service attempted to buy the Bowmans out every couple of years, but the distant relative who'd homesteaded the tract had knotted one hell of a grandfather clause into his original land agreement. No lawyer had managed to loosen so much as a single thread in the hundred years since.

To call the Bowman house secluded would have been an understatement. The driveway was nearly a quarter-mile long, and keeping it clear of snow in the winter and basic forest detritus in the summer was a Herculean task. Chad complained about this task endlessly because he knew it drove his mother up the wall. He wished she were there right now, so that he could promise to never complain about such a ridiculously unimportant thing ever again.

The house appeared in the wash of the Jeep's headlights and Chad's heart leapt into his throat—the lights were on in the kitchen and on the front porch.

His mom had been a rabid tree-hugger since before the term was even in fashion. She might have left the porch light burning if one of them was going to be out after dark, but she never would have left the kitchen light on when someone wasn't actually *in* the kitchen.

Chad was out of the Jeep almost before the vehicle came to a complete stop. Maybe it had all been some terrible mistake. Maybe that *hadn't* been his mother's body down in Duluth at all. Maybe he'd been sitting at the bedside of some total stranger for the last four days and his mom had been home and alive all this time. Maybe—

He took the three porch steps in an awkward leap. The door was locked and he fumbled for his key.

"Mom! Mom, it's me, open the door!"

He heard approaching footsteps and the decisive clank of a deadbolt being turned. Then the door opened and Chad's grief flooded back. Not his mom at all—of course not his mom. Melissa.

Chad forgot how to breathe. He felt as if someone had punched him in the gut and now he couldn't remember how to get air back into his body. His grief was a physical pain, jabbing into his torso, his chest, his scalp, his eyelids. He thought of how certain wasps retain their stingers even after a strike. Bees did you the courtesy of disemboweling themselves as they stung you, but wasps kept plunging their venom in again and again. Apparently, so did grief.

He stumbled into the house and Melissa wrapped him in a tight embrace. "Davis let me in," she said. "We didn't want you to come home to an empty house. I'm so incredibly sorry about your mom."

He wept then, wept again—wept within the soft warm circle of her arms as if he were eight and not eighteen—and only after a long time did he quiet and finally, almost grudgingly, pull himself away.

"There's food in the fridge," Melissa said. "These old ladies showed up right after I did and—"

"The Talbot grief squad," Chad said. He summoned up the ghost of a smile. He and Brandon had often laughed about the concept—a group of older women from town who spent their entire lives shuttling comfort food to the families of the sick, the injured, the dying, the dead. Flitting from one tragedy to another like Tupperware-laden sparrows. "I'm not really hungry," he said, but when he opened the fridge and saw the trays of sliced meat and cheese, the casseroles, the pasta and potato salads, he fell upon the food like a ravenous beast.

Once his belly was full, exhaustion slammed into Chad like a speeding train. The stairs to his bedroom felt insurmountable, so he led Melissa into the living room and collapsed with her into the sofa's familiar embrace. "This folds out into a bed," he said, but before he could do anything about it, he was asleep. Melissa spooned into the hollow of his body and pulled the blanket off the back of the sofa to cover them both.

At some point during the night, Chad awoke—or thought he did—and peered through silvery moonlight at an unlikely visitor on the patio. *Wolf's at the door*, he thought, but since he spent so much of his life surrounded by wolves the vision didn't disturb him.

When the wolf began to speak—"*Little pig, little pig, let me come in*," Chad was sure he heard it say—he realized he was dreaming and let himself tumble back toward the depths. The next thing he knew, Melissa's mouth was next to his ear—"Chad, wake up, there's someone out there."—and he woke for real and peered into the inky darkness outside the living room window.

. . .

The wolf knew that Chad had returned to the house, and that Melissa was with him. The scent of Chad's grief was unmistakable. The wolf could smell it from miles away and it made him want to bite out his own insides because, deep down, he knew he was somehow responsible. The wolf could also smell Melissa's warm sympathy, the simple feminine appeal of her caring, and this upset him in a different way. The female should be with him, not with Chad. She should be running by his side through the moonlit forest—he'd seen her first, desired her most. If the wolf was responsible for Chad's grief, then Chad was responsible for the wolf's. And the wolf didn't care what sort of strange beast was clawing at his insides or howling deep in the recesses of his mind, it was time Chad paid for what he had done. Way past time.

. . .

"What exactly did you hear?" Chad said. He continued to stare through the open window, as if by sheer force of will he could filter out the obstruction of the screen and bring the forest into focus.

"First just a rustling," Melissa said. "Like trees in the wind. But then what sounded like footsteps—someone walking through leaves or dry grass."

Chad listened, accustomed to the normal sound of the woods at night in a way Melissa was not. "I don't hear anything," he said—but then he did.

There—a single soft footfall.

Chad held one finger to his lips and dug his mother's cell phone out of the pocket of his jeans. He'd used it the entire time he was in Duluth, his own phone presumably still at the Center. He hit redial on the most recent entry for Davis Langley and held the phone under the blanket to cover the glow from its screen.

Davis picked up on the second ring, as if he'd been waiting for Chad's call. "You made it back okay," he said. "I don't even know how to tell you—"

"Davis, I think he's here," Chad said.

Davis kicked into cop mode without even taking a breath. "I'm on my way," he said. "Make sure your doors and windows are locked and don't do anything else. *Anything at all.* Understand?"

The connection ended and Chad slipped the phone back into his pocket. He slid off the sofa and inched over to the open window. He reached up to slide the window closed, but then paused and cocked his head.

"What?" Melissa said.

"I think someone's crying out there."

Melissa joined him at the window. At first she heard only the woods—wind through tree branches, crickets, the hoot of an owl—but then she caught a distinctive intake of breath and a soft sniffle. "You're right," she said. "And I think it's a girl."

. . .

It *was* a girl—Nikki Langley. She was crying, and also quite drunk. They found her sitting on the wooden bench at the side of the house where Kate liked to have her morning coffee and watch the woods. *Had* liked to, Chad told himself. His life was already a series of events in the past tense.

"Nikki, what the hell are you doing out here?" Chad said. He realized he was shining his flashlight directly into her face like a Gestapo prison interrogator, and he lowered it and knelt down next to her.

"I was just so sorry about your mom," Nikki said. "I didn't want you to be alone. I've been alone since Daryl...you know—went away, and I thought about you being alone, and I just felt so *sad*, you know? Like, this summer was supposed to be so happy but now it seems so sad."

"I appreciate you thinking about me," Chad said. "But you really shouldn't be wandering around alone right now. Especially in the woods, especially at night."

"I know, I know," Nikki said. She spoke with the slurry edge of an exasperated drunk. "The thing no one will really talk about. Even my dad won't talk about it. I know he thinks something happened to Daryl, and I know he thinks Brandon was involved, but he won't *talk* about it. I just want to know what happened to Daryl. And then I thought how you were alone like

I was alone...only I got here and you *weren't* alone. And then I lost my keys somewhere in these stupid woods and couldn't even drive home again."

"You *drove* here like this?" Melissa said.

Chad flashed her a smile and offered Nikki his hand. "Come on," he said. "Let's get you inside and get some coffee into you. Your dad's on his way and—"

"My dad is coming here?" She swatted Chad's hand away. "Don't you know I've been *drinking*? He's going to have about seventeen coronaries."

"I think he'll probably just be glad you're okay," Melissa said.

They got her off the bench and moving toward the front of the house. They'd just rounded the corner and were heading for the front door when Davis's cruiser came screaming down the driveway and settled in a jouncing stop that sent up a spray of gravel and dust.

"It's the cops!" Nikki said. "Everybody run for it!"

And then Davis was out of the car and running toward them, and something *else* was pounding toward them out of the forest, something made of fury and hatred and sorrow and lust, something growling and snarling and snapping aside brush and branches as it loped, bounded, leapt—

Davis pulled his gun from his belt and planted himself in front of the enormous black blur soaring at them from the even blacker maw of the forest. He fired calmly, steadily, shot after shot lighting up momentary glimpses of teeth, claws, fur, terror. Nikki and Melissa screamed, screamed as if they would never stop screaming, and then the night abruptly grew silent.

They stood, ears pulsing with the booming pressure of so many gunshots fired in such close proximity. The smell of cordite hung in the air, along with the adrenaline-tinged sharpness of terror-sweat, and, underneath it all, the unmistakable smell of death.

"Let me have that flashlight," Davis said. Chad tried to hand it to him, but his hand began trembling uncontrollably. Davis touched Chad's shoulder before taking the light. "I think you're going into shock, bud. The girls are going to help you inside and get some blankets around you. I just need to take a look—"

"No," Chad said. "I need to see."

Davis sighed. "Just like your mother." Together, the four of them followed the beam of the flashlight into the forest. They found the body a few yards in, sprawled among ferns and undergrowth, sightless eyes staring up at what was so nearly a full moon. One arm was pinned awkwardly against a tree, fingers grasping upward, reaching for the moon even in death.

The body's wounds oozed rivulets of blood, sluggish as tar now that the heart no longer beat to pump the fluid. Davis knelt and pressed two fingers against the carotid artery to check for a pulse, but there was no need. They all knew the body was dead.

The body was Brandon Turner, simply Brandon—his dark hair shaggy against his forehead, his skin already growing blue under the beam of the flashlight, his teeth just teeth, his nails just nails.

Brandon—just Brandon, Chad thought. *It was only ever just Brandon.*

. . .

The machinery peculiar to this type of death took over, and everyone put themselves on autopilot and let the machine do what it needed to do. The sun came up, and a wagon arrived from the medical examiner's office to cart away the body. Davis determined that Nikki was sober enough to drive and took the spare key for her car off his keyring and sent her home. He gave his weapon to Larry Emory and put himself on administrative leave—standard procedure whenever an officer shot someone, although he was the only one in Talbot who ever had—and then he continued to run the investigation anyway. Melissa took Chad inside the house, made him drink some juice, and led him upstairs to his bedroom. She called her parents to let them know she was okay, then she and Chad fell into bed together fully clothed, and slept the sleep of the dead until late afternoon.

. . .

Davis ran home for lunch and decided to grab a quick nap himself. There was nothing for him to do at the station, at least until the autopsy results came in, and whatever unknowable evil had come to Talbot this summer was presumably gone again. He told himself Brandon had been responsible for all of it, regardless how crazy and unlikely that sounded, and let his mind carry him down into a sweet, dreamless black.

. . .

Melissa woke just after four in the afternoon and found Chad already awake. He was on his back, staring at the ceiling, his expression unreadable. "Are you okay?" she said.

"I don't know," he said.

"How long have you been awake?"

"I'm not sure I *am* awake."

She turned his head toward hers. "You are," she said.

In a moment they were kissing and slipping awkwardly out of their clothes under the confining covers, and then he was inside her, and, for a short time at least, nothing else mattered to either of them.

Later, they moved apart and settled once more into their separate thoughts. Outside, birds called in the trees and insects buzzed against the window screen. Inside, the room was silent save for their soft breathing, the rustle of sheets as one of them shifted position.

When the sun had sunk low enough to cast the room in shade, Melissa propped herself up on one elbow. "I meant to tell you this last night," she said. "But things didn't quite work out the way I'd planned."

Chad turned to look at her.

"My parents...don't really belong in a place like Talbot—especially at the Whispering Pines," Melissa said. "My mom has been popping so much Valium ever since...you know, things started happening around here...she's probably going to have to go to rehab once we get back home."

Chad nodded. He understood immediately where the conversation was heading. "You're going home?"

"We've actually been packed and ready for a couple of days. I just wanted to wait, you know, for..."

"For my mom to die?" Chad said, but immediately regretted it—the expression on Melissa's face was as shocked as if he'd slapped her. "I'm sorry," he said. "I didn't mean it like that. You wanted to wait until I got back here, that's what I meant to say."

Melissa nodded. "I wanted to make sure you were okay."

He pulled her into his arms. "So when are you leaving?"

Melissa gave a soft, humorless laugh. "Tomorrow, no doubt," she said. "I'll never get my mom to stay now that she knows you're back."

"Or once she hears about what happened here last night with Brandon," Chad said.

She snuggled close to him and they made love one last time, slow and more than a little sad, and then Melissa rose and dressed while Chad returned to his absorbed contemplation of the ceiling. At the door to his bedroom, Melissa looked appraisingly at him. "*Are* you okay? Are you going to be?"

Chad shrugged. "Are you?"

Neither of them had an answer. Finally, Melissa turned and disappeared from his life.

Chad thought there was a lot of that going around these days.

. . .

Burt Kowalski's sheep ranch was only a few miles outside of Talbot, but his office—the Minnelac County Medical Examiner's facility—was located fifty miles away in Duncton, the county seat. Kowalski didn't mind the long drive, except when the roads got particularly icy during the winter. But he could always put off going in for a day or two if he really needed to—it wasn't like any of his "patients" were going to complain. He liked to joke that, in his business, "the work will *always* wait."

He'd made the work on Brandon Turner's body wait longer than he'd anticipated. There were so many things to determine in this particular case, so many possible connections—including two unsolved disappearances that might yet turn out to be related—and he wanted to be sure he did everything right.

He'd spent much of the day going over his other recent files from Talbot to make sure he didn't miss any possible leads or circumstances that might connect—or separate—Brandon from any of his presumed victims. He'd need blood and tissue samples, fingernail scrapings and swatches of hair. In this particular case, he'd also need a mold of Brandon's bite—something he'd read about but had never actually done before.

He thought about calling Wayne Kilgress to help—Wayne was his dentist and had certainly done bite molds on *living* people— but Kowalski wanted to try the procedure himself first. For reasons he couldn't quite articulate, he thought Brandon Turner's autopsy might turn out to be one of the most unusual he'd ever conducted, and some selfish part of him wanted to keep the body all to himself, at least for a while yet.

. . .

Inside the refrigerated drawer where Brandon's body was being stored, a small nugget of misshapen metal fell onto the stainless steel platform with a *clink!* that must have been loud inside the drawer, but was muffled and virtually unnoticeable without. Several minutes later a second nugget fell, and the two holes where those bullets had entered slowly knit themselves closed.

Davis had hit Brandon nearly a dozen times, but only five of the bullets had remained inside the body—one in the shoulder, one in the throat, one in the heart, and two in the stomach. The stomach bullets worked themselves out first, followed a short time later by the shoulder slug. The throat took a bit longer to squeeze out its invader, and that slug remained balanced in the hollow just below Brandon's unmoving Adam's apple. The heart took an additional hour to expel the final bullet, and then it was another twenty minutes before the muscle remembered how to pump. It moved sluggishly at first, painfully arrhythmic, but slowly evened out and grew in strength, until finally it reached a smooth, decisive *thump-thump, thump-thump.* A few seconds later, in the darkness of the medical examiner's drawer, Brandon Turner once more opened his eyes.

. . .

Winnie Pettinger pushed her supply cart down the long, narrow hallway of the County building's basement—the only part of her job she didn't like. The basement held the county coroner's office—the medical examiner, they called him now—and, worse, the actual autopsy room. Winnie's job didn't include cleaning the autopsy room, thank the *Lord*, but she hated even having to be this close to it.

Friday nights were worst of all. The rest of the week, there were normally a few hangers-on elsewhere within the building, but on Fridays everyone fled the upstairs offices just as early as they possibly could.

She rounded a corner and breathed a sigh of relief. The lights were still on in Burt Kowalski's office, so she wasn't entirely alone tonight. The lights were also on in the autopsy room, so that meant he was in *there*, but Winnie didn't care so much about the where as the fact that someone else was in the building at all.

Besides, this gave her time to slip into his office to empty his wastebasket and give his desk a cursory swipe with a feather duster without disturbing him. She did just that, and then hightailed it back toward the elevator that would take her upstairs and ultimately toward that most magical of all events—a weekend.

As she passed the autopsy room, Winnie hollered out a quick, "Goodnight, Burt, I'm leaving now!" and expected to hear his usual cheery response. When she didn't, she paused a moment outside the door.

Good Lord, she thought. *It sounds like the man is eating right there in that terrible, awful room.*

She noted a slavering sucking sound that reminded her of the way her great-grandmother used to suck marrow out of any leftover bones on the dinner table. *Right there in the autopsy room—that man must have a stomach of cold steel.* With a shudder, she pushed her cart into motion and hurried toward the elevator.

Because it was Friday and because Kowalski was a widower who lived alone, no one noticed his absence over the weekend. By the time Kowalski's assistant arrived for work on Monday morning, so little of Kowalski remained intact that it seemed silly to even bother with an autopsy.

. . .

Nikki woke in darkness, and realized she'd slept through the entire day and well into the night. The clock beside her bed said 3:13 AM, and she could tell by the way the red digital numbers assaulted her eyes that she'd woken up with one mother of a hangover. *It doesn't seem fair to have a hangover in the middle of the night*, she thought, but realized there wasn't much she could do about it.

She got out of bed and went to find something to eat and drink—especially to drink. *Water, I need lots and lots of water.*

She tiptoed past her father's room and heard him snoring behind the closed door, then made her way downstairs to the kitchen. She filled a tall glass from the filter pitcher they kept in the fridge and drank it down in one long swig. She filled the glass again and replaced the pitcher. She decided she wasn't hungry after all—she'd just take a few aspirin and head back to bed.

Then she heard it.

A whine, a whimper, a gentle scratching at the door.

When she was eleven—shortly after her mother died—her father had brought home a floppy-eared Spaniel puppy she'd promptly christened Ashton. The dog had gone missing years ago (hit by a car on the street right outside their house, although Davis had never told Nikki about that), and Nikki's first thought in her hangover-accentuated daze was that Ashton had finally returned home to her. She rushed to the door and yanked it open, so happy she thought she might cry.

. . .

Davis woke shortly before five and turned off the bedside alarm before it had a chance to ring. He went into the bathroom and peed long and loud, then padded down the hallway toward the stairs. Nikki's door was open, her bed empty and unmade. "You'd better just be up early," he called from the top of the stairs. "If you snuck out again and I'm talking to myself right now, there really *is* going to be some serious hell to pay."

He went downstairs and found what was left of her in the kitchen. *Nikki, his beautiful Nikki.* He couldn't comprehend what he was seeing. The monster was dead—he'd shot the monster. But here was Nikki's beautiful blonde hair, matted with gore. And here were Nikki's heartbreaking eyes, clouded now and focused on some unknown horizon, but still the same breathtaking cornflower blue.

From the hallway behind Davis came the clackety-clack-clack of claws tapping their way across the hardwood floor. *The same sound Nikki's dog used to make*, Davis thought, although this certainly wasn't Ashton—or any dog, for that matter. Davis knew that he should turn and look, give himself first-hand knowledge of the impossible truth before he departed the world, but all he wanted to do was stare at what was left of his beautiful daughter. Love her, mourn her, grieve this loss so inconceivably far and above any other loss he'd ever suffered in his life.

The clackety-clack sound grew closer and stopped behind him. Davis sensed more than felt the motion of something rising, and felt hot wet chuffs of disgusting, meaty-smelling breath on the back of his neck. Still, he didn't turn. *Nikki, my poor baby Nikki. How can I ever mourn you?*

But mourn her he did—just not for very long.

. . .

Bob Henning was a painfully stupid man. His daughter Melissa thought so, mostly privately, and his wife *said* so—as often and as publicly as she could. He was the kind of man who would give up a successful investment business and sell an apartment with a panoramic view of Lake Michigan—*for less than market value*—just to move his family to some half-assed boondock town in northern Minnesota. The kind of man who'd buy a struggling bed-and-breakfast, a business he knew nothing about, simply because he'd driven past it once, almost by accident, and thought, *Yes, now there's the life.*

He was also an easily manipulated man, especially when it came to his wife and daughter, and so he had acquiesced almost immediately when Christine had proclaimed their experiment in hostelry a rousing failure after only six weeks, and told him in no uncertain terms that they were *all* moving back to Chicago—"right the hell now."

Truth be told, Talbot hadn't been the quaint, quiet village he'd envisioned anyway. People missing, campers torn apart by wild animals, the local Catholic priest slaughtered in his own church by...well, no one was actually saying by *who*. And now a young man Melissa had dated a couple of times *gunned down* by the Talbot Chief of Police—just like that!

Like so many things in his life, Talbot had proven a disappointment to Bob Henning, and he didn't mind leaving all that much, although he continued to make halfhearted arguments against the idea even as they were locking up Whispering Pines and settling into their SUV. He'd already contracted with a local realtor to try to resell the place, and he'd agreed to hire a service to pack and ship the rest of their belongings as soon as they were back in the "real world," as his wife insisted on calling anywhere that wasn't Talbot.

The only point he refused to concede was stopping on their way out of town for one last "Fisherman's Breakfast" at Paquette's Family Diner on Main Street, and the delay this caused in their departure proved to be the penultimate stupid thing Bob Henning would ever do. Paquette's didn't open until 6:30, so the Hennings didn't start down the long Whispering Pines driveway until precisely 6:15.

Ten minutes earlier—five—they probably would have been okay, but *damn it all*, Bob Henning was going to have one more of Paquette's famous walleye-and-eggs platters as a memento of their ill-fated Talbot adventure, and Christine and Melissa could both just shut up about it. He piloted the vehicle down the driveway, feeling vaguely vindicated even though neither Christine nor Melissa was saying *anything* at the moment, and watched his bed-and-breakfast dream recede in the rearview mirror.

His reverie was broken by a frantic squawk from his wife in the seat next to him, and he returned his gaze to the road just in time to see a naked man step out of the trees and motion for them to stop.

"Oh my god," Melissa said from the back seat. "Just drive, Daddy. Just step on the gas and drive like hell."

But instead Bob Henning did the final stupid thing he would ever do: he stopped the SUV.

. . .

Chad was surprised when he didn't hear anything from Davis or Nikki on Saturday. If nothing else, he figured Davis would have follow-up questions as to what had happened at the Bowman house prior to the shooting. Or questions about Kate. *Something.* But the land-line didn't ring the entire day, and the only call that came in on his mom's cell phone was from a number he didn't recognize and which he didn't answer.

He spent the day mostly in his room, unsure what to do with himself. Periodically he would run downstairs and grab more of the dwindling supply of grief-squad food, but always he found himself moving quickly back to his room. The house felt too large without his mom, too empty, and he was vaguely afraid to touch anything for fear he might accidentally displace some tiny bit of aura she'd left behind.

Silent morning became silent afternoon became silent night. Well after dark, Chad saw the enormous orb of the moon drag its bloated girth above the treeline. Full at last, disturbingly full, and tinged an anxious pale orange that reminded Chad of Halloween and having a fever and turning over a rock and discovering blind, squirming grubs all at the same time. He was staring at the moon out his bedroom window, marveling at it, despising it—when finally the phone rang. Caller I.D. came up "Melissa Henning," and he smiled.

"Hey you," he said into the handset. "You can't be back in Chicago already."

"No, bud, not in Chicago," said the impossible voice on the other end of the line. "Out here at the Center. Thought you might like to join us."

. . .

Chad screamed through the night, swerving all over the road and speeding even worse than he had on his trip to Duluth. He'd started for his own Jeep, but then remembered the silver letter opener still sitting on the passenger seat in his mom's. "The dealer gave me a two-fer," she'd told him on his sixteenth birthday, as they drove into the dealership to pick up the matching vehicles. He remembered how proud she'd been of such an extravagant gift. Now it was *her* Jeep he was driving like a total maniac, although he supposed both of them were his now, and it didn't matter if he wrapped either one of them around a tree. Didn't matter in so many different ways.

Brandon. At the Center. Alive at the Center. With Melissa.

Chad tried to reach Davis Langley, but there was no answer at the Langley house, on Davis's cell phone, or on Nikki's. He dialed the police station, but Pete Jenkins said, "Nope, haven't heard from him all day. But he *is* technically on administrative leave, so he probably just took Nikki down to the Cities or something."

Chad ended the call and tossed the phone aside. *Moron. Like Davis is going to leave town without telling anyone—especially on the heels of everything that's been happening this summer.*

Chad knew exactly what the silence at the Langley house meant. It was the same silence he'd hear if called the Turner house right now. Or the Whispering Pines. Or his own house. Talbot was becoming a ghost town, and he was apparently the only one who knew it.

He screeched into the Center parking lot and cut the Jeep's engine. He grabbed the letter opener and shoved it into his pocket, then ran toward the front door. He fumbled for the key, but then noticed that the door hung askew on its hinges, and the counter lights in the gift shop appeared to be beckoning him inside.

Inside the foyer, Chad could see that the floodlights were on out in the wolf enclosure. Whenever the enclosure was illuminated, a computerized dimmer turned all of the lights inside the building very low. He walked up the dimly-lit ramp toward the viewing gallery, and his first glimpse of Brandon was as a backlit silhouette, standing at the floor-to-ceiling windows. The pack was nowhere in sight, but Brandon didn't seem to care. Chad wondered if Brandon knew he was there, but then he saw the tiniest shift in the set of Brandon's shoulders and Brandon turned to face him.

Brandon. Alive. How could that possibly be?

Truth be told, Chad thought Brandon looked better now than he ever had before. Leaner, stronger, more confident and poised. His nakedness showed off sinewy, defined muscles, and his skin glowed with exuberant health. *He looks really well-fed*, Chad thought, and immediately made his mind close that path off. "Where's Melissa?" he said.

"Melissa—oh, she's around," Brandon said. "Here and there. And there. And there."

"Jesus, Brandon, what did you *do?*"

"I could ask you the same question," Brandon said. "Only I *know* what you did. I watched you do it—out there after your private tour. She was my girlfriend, and you were supposed to be my best friend!"

He stalked forward several steps, and Chad could tell the animal inside was aching to break free. So close to the surface,

Chad imagined he could see its outlines shifting beneath Brandon's skin.

"She wasn't your girlfriend, Brandon. She was a girl you went out with a couple of times, and it didn't work out. What I did with her afterward was completely and utterly shitty on my part, but she did absolutely nothing wrong. You didn't have to take it out on her."

"A little late for that, I'm afraid. It took you too long to get here, and I needed a snack."

"Jesus, you sick fucking *freak*. You really did kill them all, didn't you?"

"Well, except your mom," Brandon said. "That was an accident, and I would give anything in the world to take it back." He paused, Father Holloway's voice echoing through his thoughts before he physically shook it away again. "The rest— yes. But every single one of them deserved exactly what they got."

"How?" Chad said. "How does *anybody* deserve something like that?"

Brandon smiled, but the pain Chad could see behind it, inside it, made the smile terrible to behold.

"My best friend told me we'd always be friends," Brandon said. "My priest told me God would never turn his back on me. The only mother I ever wanted told me there'd always be a place for me in her house—"

Brandon's voice caught in his throat. For a moment the beast was gone, and Chad could see only the sad, lonely, desperately hurting boy he'd always loved. His Brandon. His brother. He reached out as if he might touch that boy once more, gather him into his arms for an embrace, but Brandon snapped his head up and glared at Chad with eyes now fiery with amber luminescence. "They told me all those things—*you* told me all those things. *But you all fucking lied!*"

Chad watched, in horror and fascination, as Brandon began to transform. *This is what they all saw, right at the end. This is what Father Holloway saw. And Melissa. And my mom. This terrible, impossible thing.*

He turned to run, but the creature that was half-Brandon/half-wolf lunged forward and slammed him against the wall. Chad slumped to the floor, trying to catch his breath, but the animal picked him up and slammed him down—once, twice, a third time—until all Chad could do was lie on his back and watch Death take shape above him.

Completely transformed, the wolf paced back and forth on two legs, saliva drooling from its muzzle and sharp teeth gleaming out of bloody, freshly torn sockets. It couldn't decide what to do with Chad, and such a pointless struggle after all this time made it angry with itself. It reared back its head in an ear-splitting howl of rage.

"Just do it," Chad said. "Just do it and get it over with."

Instantly, the wolf was upon him, its solid weight pressing down on his chest, its musky carnivore odor overwhelming his sinuses. Its sharp, slavering jaws wrapped around his throat, exerting just enough pressure so that Chad couldn't in any way mistake what would happen next.

Some basic reptilian survival instinct took over, and Chad reached down and fumbled the letter opener out of his pocket. The wolf continued to press its teeth into his throat, but still it didn't clamp down in the killing bite. *Playing with me*, Chad thought. *Toying with me like a rabbit.*

Chad brought the letter opener up in a wide arc that glanced off the side of the wolf's muzzle. Instantly, the animal was off him, his throat mercifully free from its jaws, and the night filled with howling and gnashing and screaming. The wolf scrabbled away from Chad, transforming again, half-this, half-that, some terrible deformed *thing* halfway in-between, frantic to escape. Chad struggled to his feet and stalked after it, the letter opener outstretched like a dagger before him.

Down the ramp, into the shadowy recesses of doors—the exhibit area, the ticket booth, Kate's office. At the passageway into the feeding area, Chad caught up to the howling creature and it was merely Brandon again, a gaping red slash down one side of his face. His expression was one of pure agony, and even as Chad watched the wound bubbled and sank deeper into Brandon's flesh.

Despite the clearly unbearable pain, Brandon reached out and pulled Chad toward him until the letter opener pressed against his chest at a spot just over his heart. Another ugly wound opened as soon as the silver touched his skin, but Brandon held Chad's arm firm. "Do it," he said. "Just push in hard and twist. It'll all be over in a minute."

Chad tried. He really did try, but all he could see in front of him was the boy who no one had ever loved quite enough. Not even his mom. Not even him.

"I can't kill you," he said. "I know that I should, I even want to, but I can't." He tossed the letter opener aside and its clatter took a long time to die away in the hollow expanse of the foyer.

They stood for a long time, eyes locked, waiting as some impossible, unrealized lifetime passed between them.

Finally, Brandon moved to the feeding gate and keyed in the security code. He let himself into the wolf enclosure and closed the gate behind him.

"They won't do it either," Chad said. "Nobody ever gets it, but they really *don't* hurt people."

Brandon smiled. He wondered if Chad even remembered the old Ojibwe story. But of course he must—they told it at the Center a hundred times a year.

"*I am a wolf*," he said. He gave a ragged howl.

Chad nearly smiled. He took a small silver whistle from its hook near the security keypad. He put it to his mouth and blew a signal that was out of the range of his own hearing but that made Brandon wince.

Behind Brandon, dark shapes loped out of the forest. Chad could sense their excitement, their thrill as they realized they were finally going to have a real hunt. Without another word, he disappeared down the corridor.

Ten years, Brandon thought. *For ten years the wolves of Talbot have been waiting for precisely this moment.*

God, Great Spirit, whatever, he thought, but no one answered.

He turned and waited for the wolves to come for him.

Epilogue: Even a Man Who is Pure in Heart

Chad lay on his bed and watched the October full moon rise over campus through his dorm room window. His roommate was out partying—Alan was always out partying—but he hadn't asked Chad to join him. He'd stopped asking weeks ago, and now they probably didn't pass more than ten words between them on any given day.

It wasn't Alan's fault. Alan was cheerful and gregarious, friendly with everyone on their floor, and excited to be away from home for the first time. Six weeks in, he was loving every minute of his college experience. Chad, unfortunately, was not.

He'd debated coming to school at all, but in the end what else could he do? He'd barely managed to stay alone in the house for the remainder of the summer—it made him nervous and claustrophobic, and reminded him too much of his mother. The surrounding woods, which he'd previously loved, reminded him too much of everything else. Even his work at the Center had become unbearable. He no longer had any patience with visitors, no longer had any interest in going on howlings, and he could barely stand to look at the Center wolves, much less interact with them.

Brandon's body had never been found. The Center staff had reported a break-in, but nothing had been taken and the only thing out of place was a silver letter opener found in one corner of the foyer. So far as Chad knew, no one had linked that implement to the one missing from Father Holloway's office—

there was really no one left in Talbot who might even be interested in such a link.

Larry Emory was the new Chief of Police in Talbot, and Benjy Tatum had left the force. Chad had heard that Benjy was right here at the university, studying to become a CPA, but he hadn't run into him. A new priest had been installed at Saint Ignatius, but Chad didn't know his name. He'd heard that the videotapes Davis had told him about had mysteriously disappeared during the chaos that followed, but he supposed none of that mattered anymore.

Davis and Nikki had been found and buried; the Henning family had been found and shipped back to Chicago. Melissa's body had been in the vehicle in the Whispering Pines driveway the entire time—she'd never been at the Center with Brandon at all. Burt Kowalski had been found, Daryl Reisling had been found, Nola Fenster had been found. The body of a fisherman had been found in a river some twelve miles south of Talbot, but no one could agree if his death was related to the trouble in Talbot or not—he'd been in the water too long to determine much of anything.

Chad rolled over and tried to ignore the moon. Even with his face to the wall, he could feel the moon's baleful yellow eye on the back of his neck, its soft glow moving up and down his spine. Whenever he saw the moon now, he felt like it was mocking him. His mother gone, his friend gone, everyone gone—and *he* couldn't even focus enough to pass the most rudimentary of his freshman-level classes. Six weeks in, he was already so far behind it was inconceivable he'd last the year. Another thing at which he could fail—like he'd failed to find his mother in time, like he'd failed to save Melissa, like he'd apparently failed Brandon his entire life.

Chad rose and stalked across the room to close the curtains and block out the moon. *Fuck the goddamned moon,* he thought. He paced back and forth between the two beds, but the room was too small to contain his frustration. Soon Alan would be back, and the room would seem even smaller, and that would just make Chad angrier than he already was.

Anger—that was his core emotion now. He felt angry all of the time, betrayed by everyone he'd ever known, betrayed by life itself. He didn't want to be at school, didn't want to be home, didn't want to be working at the Center.

What *did* he want?

That part of his mind was a complete blank. A dead spot, a black hole from which no information escaped.

The only thing that ever made him feel remotely better anymore was to be moving. He needed to move now. Get out of the room, get out of the dorm, get out of his own head for a while. It would mean subjecting himself to the mockery of the moon, but anything would be better than being locked in this tiny cage of a dorm room. He grabbed his jacket and slipped into the night.

At first, he thought he'd just wander campus for a while—the U of M was enormous, sprawling—but it was early enough that there were still people everywhere. He decided to cut down to the river barrens, which should be much quieter. So long as he steered clear of the area where men cruised the trees for anonymous sex, he thought he'd be left alone.

If anyone *did* bother him—well, it would be *their* problem to deal with his anger. Even outdoors, outside of the dorm, the anger boiled inside him. Even as he crossed the wide campus and disappeared into the trees that led down to the river, his anger was like a living thing writhing just beneath the surface of his skin.

He remembered the night he'd left Brandon at the Center. The anger he'd felt that night had never gone away—if anything, it had grown exponentially every day since. He thought of the single drop of dried blood he'd found on the collar of his T-shirt the following morning. As if one of Brandon's canines had just barely punctured the skin of his throat, and a tiny jewel of blood had formed there and soaked into the fabric. He'd examined himself carefully, but there'd been no wound. No puncture, no bruise, nothing to mark his fight with Brandon except the endless, mindless, seething anger.

He reached the river's edge and sat on a fallen tree to watch the moon's reflection shimmer over the black water. Behind him, in the trees, he heard whispers and vague sounds of movement. He frowned. The men didn't usually come this close to campus.

So long as they leave me alone, he thought, but their mere presence worked on him and worked on him until he was aggravated beyond all measure. Until he could no longer think.

He rose and stalked toward the trees. Damn it, this was where *he* wanted to be right now, and they could go find somewhere else.

He started to jog and then to run, the moon opening a path through the trees and focusing his rage into a single piercing beam of golden light. *The moon, the moon, the imperious fucking moon*, he thought.

Woof-man, he thought, but this only reminded him of his mother and made him even angrier.

By the time he was inside the trees, Chad was so full of rage he thought he might bite someone.

Notes and Acknowledgements

First and foremost—thanks for reading my novel!

The text of this edition has been lightly revised from the version that appeared in 2010. I'll talk more about that in a minute. First, some acknowledgements:

Part of this novel appeared, in slightly different form, in the May 2004 issue of *The Edge: Tales of Suspense*. Many thanks to editor (and novelist) Greg F. Gifune, whose acceptance of that tiny piece of the story convinced me to write the rest of it.

The Talbot Wolf Research Center was inspired by, but in no way represents, the International Wolf Center in Ely, Minnesota. The IWC has been studying and protecting wolves for many years, and often takes visitors on howlings even more spectacular (albeit much less scary) than the one found in this book. More information about their excellent work can be found at www.wolf.org.

Talbot was inspired by two of my favorite Minnesota towns— Ely and Grand Rapids. However, Talbot has its own geography, people, businesses, and creatures of the night, and ultimately exists entirely in my imagination.

The song "Who's Afraid of the Big Bad Wolf?" is from the 1933 Disney film, *Three Little Pigs*. Music by Frank Churchill, lyrics by Frank Churchill and Ann Ronell.

The poem from the Ojibwe story, "Sheem, or The Forsaken Boy," was translated by Henry Rowe Schoolcraft and originally published in *Algic Researches* (New York: Harper & Brothers, 1839).

And, of course, the title of the epilogue is from Universal's classic 1941 film, *The Wolf Man*, written by the late, great Curt Siodmak.

I owe special thanks to Heidi Busse, for introducing me to Saint Ignatius and his creepy letters; Mikki Morrissette, for her early marketing advice (even though it didn't work); the late, great Lars and the rest of my pack at the time, for that awesome first trip to Ely and the many wonderful wolf interactions that followed; and the first readers of the original version of this manuscript: Beth DeCoux, Kelly Flanigan, Galynn Nordstrom, and Chris Notsch. Cory Busse gets a special nod, for letting me steal *his* werewolf story, and for providing particularly helpful guidance and support throughout this project's long and bloody gestation. And one final call-out: I'd like to thank author Cameron Chaney for finally pulling me out of a long funk through his sheer enthusiasm for reading, writing, collecting, and all things spooky. Check out his YouTube channel, Library Macabre—and, of course, his books! Thank you, one and all.

Ow-ooooooooooooo!

. . .

Regarding this revision, part one:

In 2004, I wrote a short story called "Brandon Comes Out," about a teenage boy who reveals himself not as gay, but as a werewolf. The story was published in *The Edge: Tales of Suspense*, and normally that would have been the end of it.

But the character of Brandon stuck with me. I wondered, what would happen if an abused and bullied boy suddenly turned into a ravenous beast...and discovered he *liked* it?

I started to expand the story into a novel, originally titled *The Darker Heart*. That also might have been the end of it, but during the writing process, I stumbled upon the Ojibwe legend "Sheem, or The Forsaken Boy." Sheem's story seemed to sync so perfectly with Brandon's that I didn't think twice about making Brandon half-Ojibwe and using the original tale as the core and new title of my novel. Today, that decision makes me a little uncomfortable. As Kate puts it in the book:

> *Another random appropriation of indigenous culture by the white man...and, typically, he hadn't even bothered to get the name right.*

I did try to "get the name right" in the general sense but, as an old white guy, I understand I have nothing to say about Ojibwe culture, nor any invitation to do so. Outside of the original Ojibwe legend, which I found in an 1839 book by another old white guy, Ojibwe culture plays virtually no part in *The Forsaken Boy*.

Here's my lame defense:

One of things I really like about Brandon is that everything is a division with him. He's half-Ojibwe, but has no experience within that culture. He's half-white, but ostracized and hated by nearly every white person he encounters. Later, when his nature splits between human and animal, he isn't sure how to fully embrace either side. He is always the outsider, perpetually the 'other.'

In that respect, *The Forsaken Boy* feels less like cultural appropriation than the story of any 'other' who doesn't fit into a particular time or place or community. At the same time, I realize that's *totally* a massive old-white-guy rationalization.

I apologize to the Ojibwe people and promise to do better in the future.

. . .

Regarding this revision, part two:

The Forsaken Boy was originally published in 2010.

I'd been flirting with a traditional publisher of paperback originals for a couple of years during the writing of the novel, but that company imploded financially right around the time I felt my book was finally ready for the world. I started talking with agents who claimed to represent horror, but every single one of them came back with a similar response: "this story is too dark for us."

I have very little patience for bullshit like that, so I formed Tough Times Publishing and released the book myself. The experiment was weirdly successful, and the book sold well as a trade-size paperback and especially as an e-book. Sales weren't crazy enough to allow me to quit my day job, but they did make me go, *hm*.

Under the Tough Times banner, I published a few books *not* by me, most notably Michael McDowell's 1980's serial novel, *Blackwater* (now available from Valancourt Books). It was a great ride, I made a few bucks, and in the end I can honestly say that doing it myself was one of the best decisions I've ever made.

In 2017, I took *The Forsaken Boy* off the market and put Tough Times Publishing on hiatus. I knew the book would come back at some point, and I always had a fuzzy plan in my head that I would aim for the tenth anniversary and launch a second novel at the same time. Mathematically-astute readers might be thinking: wow, ten years, that second book must be *long*. But no—I am just ridiculously slow. Also, I missed the tenth anniversary—another casualty of the general shitshow that was 2020—and so, what the hell, we'll go with the eleventh. The unusual history of this novel continues down its weird, singular path.

I considered revising the Ojibwe element back out of the story for this version, but ultimately did not. I like the book. It doesn't illuminate any part of Ojibwe culture, but I don't believe it's disrespectful in any way. Going forward, I understand I need to be more aware of these types of considerations ahead of time.

There are a few minor differences between this version of the book and the 2010 version, but nothing that alters the original story.

In recent years, a certain racial slur has become a real gut-level trigger for me. That word appeared three times in the original version of the book, spewing out of the mouth of the 'bad guy' as an indicator of his terribleness as a person, but even in that context it bothered me, and I scrubbed it.

I also turned down the volume on the general level of profanity throughout the book, something which has bothered a number of readers over the years. One of my favorite negative reviews asked: "Does the writer really think people talk this way?" My answer to that is: fuck yeah, I know they do. But I took the point and removed at least a few of my most egregious extravagances. There's still one I'm sure I'll hear about, but it's truly how Brandon was feeling in that moment, so it had to stay.

If you've read this far, thanks for indulging me. I'm still not finished with the new novel I mentioned earlier, but I'm working on it.

Maybe next year?

Stranger things have happened.

About the Author

In addition to *The Forsaken Boy*, Troy Tradup has written plays, screenplays, and short stories, some of which appear in the forthcoming collection, *Protect Me From the Things I Think I Want*.

His plays have been produced in the United States, New Zealand, and Australia, and his stories have appeared in numerous magazines.

Troy lives in a suburb of Minneapolis and is currently at work on a new novel—you can read a short excerpt below.

Troy would love to hear what you thought of *The Forsaken Boy*. He can be reached at troytradup@gmail.com.

Lab Rat
a new novel by Troy Tradup

Chapter 1

He remembered fire, then water, then delicate flakes wafting from a glowing night sky. Snow—or ash? Either way, beautiful. Not just how it looked, but what it secretly meant. The one thing he alone knew, of all people alive on earth.

Fire, water, snow, ash—beautiful.

Terrible, too, but he tried never to think about that part of it.

The world would always find ways to remind you of the terrible.

. . .

"I don't really kiss," the boy said. "Just so you know."

The inside of the van was dark, the driver's expression unreadable. A momentary wash of oncoming headlights revealed a hint of smirk across the man's face, but nothing the boy could interpret.

They'd been driving for twenty minutes and were already farther out of the city than the boy trusted. It wasn't unusual for a trick to want to go somewhere other than the park—back to his apartment if he was single, or to some quiet parking spot if he wasn't—but this guy had a van, one of those vans with no windows in the back, so the boy figured they didn't need to go very far for any extra bit of privacy.

But the guy had started driving, away from the park and out of the city, and now the other traffic had all but disappeared, and the neighborhoods they were passing had gone from urban to suburban to nearly rural. Or what felt like rural to the boy.

He fidgeted, twitchy now instead of when he should have been—before he'd climbed into the man's van in the first place. Vans felt creepy to him to begin with, and this one had a definite vibe about it. But the night was rainy, and the boy was cold, and there'd only been three or four vehicles cruising the park the entire night. In the end, you go with what you're given.

The van's seats were heated, almost to the point of discomfort, but the boy didn't think he should ask the man to turn the temperature down. Dude probably thought heated seats were a status symbol or something, and you didn't want to piss off a trick when he had you twenty miles from nowhere.

"So anyway, yeah," the boy said, thinking he could float his strange nervousness away down a stream of mindless chatter. "Kissing just isn't my thing. With guys, I mean." He knew some tricks got really turned on by the idea of picking up a straight boy doing the whole gay-for-pay thing, and it never hurt to try to goose up the price a little, especially on a slow night.

Another shoosh of headlights revealed a genuine smile from the man now. "Since I'm paying for it," he said, "I don't really care what your thing is."

He didn't sound pissed or anything, just amused. *Probably thinks he's flirting with me*, the boy thought.

They turned off the main road and snaked down a long curve of smooth blacktop. At the bottom of the hill, a concrete cube squatted bunker-like at one end of a small, dimly lit parking lot.

"We're not going to your house?" the boy said.

"Oh, I don't live around here," the man said. "But don't worry. There's no one here this time of night."

"Private," the boy said. Icy prickles spidered up and down his spine.

They cut diagonally across the lot and the man pulled the van into the shadows on the far side of the building. He cut the motor and jerked his chin toward the back. "Shall we?"

"We're not going inside?"

"I don't work here," the man said. "It's just a place I know."

More spiders.

The man slouched out of his seat and monkey-walked into the back of the van. He switched on a battery-powered camping lantern to light the boy's way and the boy clambered to a futon-covered cot that ran along one side panel. The man rummaged in a cooler and brought up a bottle and two glasses. He poured amber liquid into the first glass and held it out. "Drink?"

The boy squinted at the glass and a muscle under his jaw moved like a tiny fist.

"Relax," the man said. "I'm not trying to roofie you." He took a sip from the glass and set it on the futon next to the boy. Then he poured his own glass and knocked back the contents in a single long swallow.

The boy tried to unclench himself, work his way back to some sort of center. *Remember you're the one with the power,* Trev or one of the other guys had told him when he first hit the streets. *You control the situation or the situation controls you.*

He was off his game tonight. Maybe it was the disconcerting drive out of the city, or the van seats that had nearly blistered his ass—or maybe it was just the vague, undefined weirdness of this particular trick. "So, um," he said, "what do you like to do?"

The man barked out a laugh. "How old are you anyway?"

"Eighteen." The stock response.

"How old are you really?"

The boy shrugged. "Fifteen." This was another gambit that sometimes helped loosen a trick's wallet, although on rare occasions it could also shut down the deal completely.

"Do you have a name?" the man said.

Another automatic: "Do you?"

The man laughed again—a sharp, mirthless woof. Not fake exactly, but the boy thought it sounded somehow... premeditated. "Jonathan," the man said.

The boy assumed he was lying—Jonathan as in john as in trick as in *seriously dude?*—but decided to tell the truth anyway. "I'm Eric."

"Well, it's good to meet you, Eric. Now will you please stop looking at me like I'm about to do something nefarious to you and get your skinny ass out of those clothes?"

That felt more familiar, and Eric let himself relax. He felt the situation begin to re-center itself, felt the universe hand the power back to him. In twenty or thirty minutes, they'd be driving back into the city and he'd have cash in his pocket to carry him through yet another day.

He smiled the way Trev had taught him—shy and sort of stupid, like this trick might actually mean something to him, or like maybe he'd never done this before—and then he lowered his eyes to work at the buttons of his shirt in the dim light.

That single, unguarded moment was all the man needed.

He lunged forward and enveloped Eric in a powerful bear hug, pinning the boy's arms against his chest and throwing him off balance. In the dark and cramped space, Eric couldn't establish any leverage to wriggle out of the unwanted embrace.

"Hey," he said. "Hey stop, hey come on now." He cringed at how pathetic he sounded, almost polite, a carryover from his life before the streets.

Jonathan scissored Eric up onto the futon and sprawled solidly on top of him. Eric's foot connected with the glass the man had offered and sent it shattering against the rear door of the van in a whiff of boozy vapor. Jonathan contracted his muscles like an anaconda, tightening his hold whenever Eric tried to draw in a breath. The man's Cheshire grin floated, cat-like and gloating, directly above Eric's face.

"Please," Eric said. "Seriously. You don't have to do it this way. You don't even have to pay. Just don't—"

Jonathan freed one hand and clamped it around Eric's throat. Not playfully, the way some tricks did—teasing and sort of fake-dominant, something Eric almost enjoyed sometimes—but hard and persuasive. *Real.*

Eric couldn't breathe, couldn't swallow. His eyes bulged, leaking irrelevant tears. Snot backed up in his nose and would have oozed down his throat if the man's grip hadn't remained so unrelentingly tight.

Jonathan lowered his face, moving his lips closer to Eric's—*kissing just isn't my thing*, the boy thought inanely—but instead of a kiss the man did something with his free hand that sparked a tiny prick of fire at the side of Eric's throat.

A river of molten lava flowed down inside Eric. Down through his neck, his spine, into his chest and arms and legs. Jonathan was no longer sprawled on top of him, but some other intractable heaviness continued to press down over every inch of his body. He couldn't move, couldn't call for help, couldn't even make his lips form the question he wanted to ask—the question, he supposed, every victim wants to ask his murderer at the end. Eric could only stare, and blink, and try to bring into focus the shiny wavering objects the man was holding in his three right hands.

No—the single object the man was holding in his *one* right hand.

He struggled to pull the word up out of the lava.

Syringe.

A drop of clear liquid trembled at needle's tip.

The drop fell.

Eric fell.

Fire, water, snow, ash.

Beautiful.

. . .

He awoke not to fire in his veins but ice, crystalline cold throughout his body thawing into tiny needle pricks. He could hear his own heartbeat, sluggish but steady, and feel his sludge-like blood liquefy and begin to flow once more.

He was on his back, on some sort of metal table, spread-eagled in a position that seemed unnatural yet oddly, externally familiar. Ill-fitting gears ground together in his groggy brain and finally clicked on a connection: the famous Leonardo da Vinci image, that one sketch or painting that seemed to appear in every art or science program he'd ever watched.

A funny way to wake up—normally he slept like the dead, unmoving the entire night, curled into himself with his head half-buried under whatever he was using for a pillow at the moment. And what had he been doing last night to feel so messed-up this morning anyway? He tried to move, tried to sit up, but—

Man. Van. Needle of fire.

He couldn't move. Or could only barely move. Memory punched in like a fist of migraine.

He found he could shift ever so slightly and when he did the table was cold against his flesh *(I'm naked)*. He could move his shoulders and his pelvis, but his arms and legs seemed far away and beyond any meaningful control. He was covered nearly to his chin in a white sheet and couldn't lift his head far enough to see properly over his chest, but he thought he could feel, through pinpricks of returning sensation, bands of restraint at his elbows and wrists, his knees and ankles. His dick felt pinched and oddly encumbered, and after a moment he realized he could feel a smooth coil of plastic tubing snaking down the inside of one leg.

Oh man, this is so not good.

He tried not to panic. Maybe this guy—this Jonathan or whatever—was just really kinky, and this was some weird new scene Eric had never encountered before.

Sure, right, and maybe Santa Claus is gonna bust through the door and offer me a winning lottery ticket any minute now.

His body loosened, grew a little more flexible, and he was able to lift his head enough to get a better view of the room. Everything seemed to be made of either glass or gleaming stainless steel. The glass consisted of test tubes, beakers, Petri dishes, and what looked to be an entire wall shelved floor-to-ceiling with twenty-gallon aquariums. Funny that he knew the size without even having to think about it—Bobby had always wanted a twenty for his stupid guppies, but their father would only ever let him have a ten. Too much strain on the floor with a twenty-gallon, or some bullshit excuse like that.

Everything else in the room—trays, tables, microscopes, weird-looking implements and instruments—was chrome silver polished to mirror-like clarity. Everything in the room seemed to reflect everything else, and everything ultimately seemed to reflect the man suddenly standing, smiling, just within Eric's field of vision.

"From troubled slumber, young prince awakes," Jonathan said. "And how is my boy feeling today?"

Kinky new scene, my ass, Eric thought. *This guy is plain old batshit crazy. Looney Tunes, gone-to-the-zoo, a-boy's-best-friend-is-his-mother psycho.*

"I'm kind of sore," he said. He tried to keep his voice low and even, because Trev or one of the other guys had told him to never yell at a crazy trick when he'd first started learning the ropes. "And I'm pretty freaked out right now, if you want to know the truth."

Jonathan nodded sympathetically. "I can understand that. But let me just say, right up front, that I'm not going to hurt you. Well, technically, I guess I *am* going to hurt you, but in the end it's going to be so incredibly worth it—for both of us."

"*Jesus fuck,*" Eric said, more exhalation than actual speech.

Jonathan's open palm slammed across Eric's cheek and whipped his head so violently to one side that Eric was afraid his neck muscles might snap. The guy was fast, way faster than Eric would have guessed just looking at him. A stinging fire blossomed across the boy's face. He could feel the exact shape of Jonathan's hand tattooed there in angry red.

"I don't appreciate that kind of language," Jonathan said. "It's very...regressive."

Eric clenched everything tight inside, careful not to show any emotion whatsoever. A single involuntary tear betrayed his resolve by squeezing out of the corner of one eye and plunking down onto the stainless steel table.

"I'm sorry," Jonathan said. "I'm going about this all backwards. I need to get some sleep pretty soon or I'm going to be worthless for the next week, and we have a lot of work to do, you and I. I always forget how long that drive is, and—"

"Drive?" Eric said. He looked around the windowless room, listened for a clue amidst what he suddenly realized was piped-in white noise. Some circadian tickle at the base of his spine told him it was afternoon, and probably closer to dinner than lunch. Which meant he'd been out for...thirteen hours? Longer?

Again: *fuck.*

But he was a fast learner and this time he only thought it.

"So what do you know about starfish?" Jonathan said. He stepped to one side to give Eric a better view of the aquarium wall.

Eric counted thirty tanks, five shelves of six. Each was topped with a hood, and each hood beamed purplish fluorescence into softly burbling water. Starfish of every size and shape clung to tank walls or inched across beds of natural rock and living coral. Some were the dull wash of rock or sand, and several glistened the ivory white of polished bone, but the majority of the creatures seemed to aspire to a sort of crazy Crayola neon— crimson, magenta, cerulean blue, canary yellow. *He needs a black light in here*, Eric thought, but he didn't say it out loud for fear Jonathan might actually have one.

"Yeah, um, those are great," he said instead. "But I have a sense I've been here for the better part of a day already, and I think—"

"Actually," Jonathan said, "you've been here for the better part of *two* days, sleepyhead." He stepped back into view. "But let's not kid ourselves. We both know no one's looking for you. That was part of your appeal. Oh, I suppose the other boys from the park might wonder where you disappeared to, but I seriously doubt any of them is going to call the police, right?"

Eric squirmed against his restraints, but his effort was somewhat perfunctory. It didn't take a genius to see how this was going to turn out.

"I've been watching you, on and off, for several months now," Jonathan said. "Pretty much since you first started hanging around the park, I think. I know you don't go to school. I know there's no one set place you sleep at night. Judging from that sweet little drawl you try to hide, I'd guess Minneapolis is pretty far from whatever home you did have once upon a time. And now you're pretty far from Minneapolis, as well, so..." He shrugged.

Eric swallowed, bitter metallic saltiness slicing like a razor down the back of his throat. His eyes burned, blurred. "Please. Please, mister. Please just let me go."

Jonathan sighed. "I'm so tired. I really meant to handle this differently, but you were out for so long and now I'm just so tired."

"Well, let's just sleep," Eric said. "You can let me loose, and we can both just sleep for a while. It'll be nice. We'll—"

"You see, I wanted to tell you about the starfish first. And the geckos—I meant for you to meet them too. And then there's this plant I don't think anyone else even knows about yet. I wanted to give you this really solid base of knowledge to work from, you know? Because I want us to be true partners in this. I mean that, I really do. This is going to make both of us so incredibly wealthy and so incredibly famous..."

He pulled a rolling cart close to the table and began fussing with something Eric couldn't see. "But who knows?" he continued. "Maybe a demonstration is better anyway. Seeing is believing—that's what they say, right?"

This time, the liquid in the syringe he held up was a pale, milky green—the color of the moth in those old sleeping pill commercials, Eric thought.

"Jonathan, please. Seriously, please just—"

"Don't worry," Jonathan said. "You're going to like this stuff *so* much better than the other stuff."

He lifted the sheet and jabbed the needle into Eric's thigh. Eric felt an immediate electric chill coursing through his veins, and he was higher than a kite before the syringe was even half-empty.

Jonathan was right—he did like this stuff better than the other stuff.

He opened his mouth to tell Jonathan this, but at the same instant Jonathan lifted a gleaming cleaver from the cart and, in a single fluid stroke, neatly lopped off Eric's left hand.

. . .

The first day, Eric screamed and screamed. Not because he was in any pain—Jonathan was careful to never let the pain anywhere near him—but simply to do something, anything, to broadcast his displeasure to a world that clearly could not have cared less.

The loss of his hand seemed negligible, almost superfluous beside the stolid immobilization of the restraints and the sheer impotence of his rage. Not to mention his frustration over his own stupidity, for having allowed himself to be put in such a situation in the first place. To survive everything he'd already managed to survive in his short lifetime, only to end up on this butcher's table...

By the second day, his throat was too raw to even whisper and his rage had dimmed to a tiny, flickering candle flame deep inside him. He battened it down, bricked it up behind a sturdy mental wall with all of the other emotions he'd chosen to ignore or imprison over the past several years.

He took my hand, he took my goddamned hand...

Every few hours, Jonathan arrived with another syringe, another cylinder of milky green fluid that he pumped into Eric's body without comment.

After a few days, the shots no longer made Eric feel high, exactly, but they kept away what he assumed must be a monstrous degree of pain. He stared with dogged focus at one particular square of ceiling tile directly over the table while Jonathan administered the shot and checked the bandages he'd applied *(over my stump)*, but he refused to look at Jonathan or utter a single word in Jonathan's presence. If Jonathan minded the boy's silence, he didn't let on.

This sullen impasse went on for nearly a month, so far as Eric could tell, until one day Jonathan abruptly undid Eric's restraints, removed his catheter, and eased the boy up into a sitting position. As much as he despised the man, as much as he wanted to kill him, Eric was so grateful he wept.

He was surprised to discover he didn't feel particularly weak. Flat on his back for twenty-eight days (that he knew about, that he thought he could account for), fed intravenously because he refused to touch any food or drink Jonathan brought near him, he'd expected to feel numb and jelly-legged if he ever managed an upright position again.

Instead, certain obvious considerations aside *(he took my hand)*, he found he actually felt quite good. Really good, if he was honest about it. He bounced a little on the balls of his feet, full of what his mother would have called—once upon a time— piss and vinegar. Ready to take on the world with both—

"It's your little green friend making you feel like that," Jonathan said. He held up the syringe he'd emptied into Eric's forearm just before removing the restraints, the latest in a veritable parade of little green friends that had come to call while Eric lay prone upon the table.

"It's pretty remarkable stuff," Jonathan continued. "And of course I should have told you more about it before we started, I do realize that. But, what's done is done, and now it's time to get on with our real work. I said before that I wanted us to be partners, but so far I'm the only one doing anything! You can have today to get your bearings, but tomorrow you need to start earning your keep around here."

Before Eric could respond—and seriously, how would a person respond to something like that anyway?—Jonathan had left the room again.

. . .

The door Jonathan used to enter and leave the room was locked, and Eric knew even before he looked that he'd find no other exit.

Of the two additional doors in the room, one opened to reveal a small bathroom and the other what Eric could only assume was meant to be his bedroom now—a narrow cubbyhole containing a bed, a bookcase, a writing desk, and a straight-backed chair. All the comforts of home.

The clothes he'd been wearing the night Jonathan picked him up were stacked neatly on one corner of the bedspread, freshly laundered and neatly folded. On the desk were unopened packages of socks, underwear, and t-shirts, brand-name, all in his size. Several new-looking flannel shirts were draped across the back of the chair, and two new pairs of Levi's, still bearing their store tags, lay on top of the desk itself.

Ignoring the new items, Eric struggled into his old clothes—a much more difficult task with only one hand than he would have anticipated. He had particular difficulty getting his socks pulled up and situated correctly, and he couldn't imagine how he was ever going to get his shoes tied. Jonathan had apparently anticipated this problem, however, because Eric's sneakers were nowhere in evidence and a new pair of loafers was sitting just inside the door. He slipped them on, smooth as butter, as if he'd gone to the store and picked them out himself.

He felt the first whisper of pain when he eased the t-shirt over his bandaged arm *(over my stump, over my goddamned stump)*, and a slightly more insistent twinge as he worked the lumpy bulge of gauze and tape through the arm of his outer shirt. Although he didn't know how he might administer it, or how much might be safe to take *(safe!)*, he wondered if any more of Jonathan's magical green elixir might be hiding somewhere out there in the—

Lab.

He hadn't really thought about it in that way before. That singular, specific word seemed to wink into existence all of its own accord.

I'm in some sort of...laboratory.

I was picked up by some exceptionally messed-up trick, and he drugged me, and he drove me somewhere, and he cut off my hand...

And now I'm apparently supposed to live here in his...lab.

And "earn my keep"—he actually said that!

He went back into the lab and searched for a phone, but found none. Not that a phone would have been all that helpful. Not only did he not know where he was, or who Jonathan was, it wasn't like he could actually go to the police.

Does Jonathan somehow know that? Is that why he chose me at the park, instead of Trev or Grin or Pete?

He knew he was being paranoid, but the question buzzed inside his head like an angry hornet. He was sure he'd only given Jonathan his first name, and he hadn't been carrying a wallet or I.D., so all Jonathan could possibly know about him was that his name was Eric and he sometimes hustled for food money at a park in Minneapolis. He couldn't know about Bowling Green, or the night of the unexpected snow (or was it ash?); couldn't know about Eric's parents, or his little brother Bobby, or—

Unless I said something while I was out of it on his green goo. One drug-induced slip of the tongue, a quick Google search, and he'd know I can never just go to the police.

Or, well, I guess I could go to the police—that would a solve a whole bunch of problems all at once actually—but it wouldn't end any better for me than it would for him.

Fire, water, snow, ash—

But, in this case, pretty much terrible, any way he looked at it.

He looked around the lab for something he might use as a weapon, but the tray with the infamous cleaver was nowhere in sight, and nothing else struck him as particularly threatening.

He supposed he could try to bash Jonathan over the head with a microscope or something the next time he came in, but any direct physical assault would be tricky with only one hand. He also considered just tearing the place up, destroying as much of Jonathan's equipment as possible, but he realized that, while this might make him feel better momentarily, it probably wouldn't help his situation in the long run.

Before he could decide on any particular course of action, he realized he was starting to feel woozy, and his damaged arm was throbbing rhythmically with focused little starbursts of fiery pain that flared and died in time with his pulse.

He slumped onto a small rolling stool beside the table he'd been strapped to for that terrible string of days *(the operating table, he took my hand)* and tried to think.

Yes, he was trapped.

Yes, he was weak, he was sick, he was damaged, he was lost.

But he'd been all of those things before and managed to find a way out, right?

Not an easy way, and certainly not a clean way *(Bobby, damn it Bobby, why weren't you at Kenny's house where you were supposed to be?)*, but a way out nonetheless.

There had to be a way out this time as well. Maybe not a way to fix the damage to his hand *(no worries there, bud, that hand is long gone)*, but some way to get past Jonathan, to get back to the world, to get—

Something in one of the starfish tanks interrupted his train of thought. He hadn't been aware of paying that much attention to the aquariums during his time on the table, but now his eye had picked up something unusual in one of them—some obvious anomaly—all on its own. Maybe because the starfish in that particular tank was an unusually bright shade of crimson, and the contrast with the new object was so obvious. Or maybe because the flow of water through the tank made the object seem almost to be waving at him.

He stood, already nauseated, a scream already building from deep inside his gut, and moved to the tank for a closer look. Not that he needed to look, he knew what he was going to see, knew what he was already seeing, but how could anyone actually believe they were seeing something like that, how could anyone's mind actually process that kind of—

His hand *(his former hand)*, denuded of all but a few tiny scraps of flesh by the hungry starfish, bobbed gently in the artificial current created by the aquarium's air bubbler.

Eric screamed. His throat was raw, his vocal cords constricted from lack of use, and the sound that came out of him was jagged and bestial.

He thought he would be sick and whirled to find a wastebasket, a bucket, something to throw up in, but there was nothing in his stomach to come out anyway. A bitter liquid filled his mouth with vague medicinal acidity, but he swallowed it back down when he heard the voice behind him.

"It's actually kind of ironic," Jonathan said. "But of course there's no way you can know that at this point. You'll see the humor in it eventually."

Eric pressed back against the wall of aquariums and glared at the man standing in the open doorway into the lab. The monster who had done this to him.

"I'm leaving right now, asshole," he said. He raised his good arm, his one remaining hand, and pointed at Jonathan. "I don't care if you like my language or not. I don't give a flying rat's ass what you think about any thing at this point. I'm leaving this place, and if you touch me, if you try to stop me, I will kill you. I will use my one hand, I will use my feet, I will use my teeth. One way or another, I will kill you dead where you stand, you sick freak."

Jonathan considered the boy for a moment, then calmly bent down and propped the door open with a small wedge of rubber. "Down this hall all the way to the end, then take a right," he said. "The door sticks a little this time of year, so you have to give it a good yank to get it open."

Eric stared at him, his chest heaving as adrenaline poured into his system. Was this a trick? Was Jonathan going to tackle him as he tried to pass, jab him in the neck with another of his damned needles?

Jonathan seemed to understand, and moved away from the door. He stood against the back wall, near the makeshift bedroom, and made a noncommittal shrug in the direction of the hallway. "I know I could make you understand if you'd just give me some time," he said. "If you'd just—"

Eric didn't wait to hear another word. He bolted down the hallway, expecting to hear Jonathan's footsteps behind him at any moment, or to feel the bee-sting prick of a needle at his throat.

But the hallway remained empty behind him, and the door leading outside was exactly where Jonathan had said it would be. It even stuck a little, just like Jonathan had said it would. Eric was embarrassed to find himself tugging hard to make sure it shut properly once he was outside. That sappy southern politeness coming out again—what an idiot he could be sometimes.

Forget about that, forget about everything.

What mattered was that he was out—out of the lab, out of the nightmare, outside in a chilly autumn afternoon with the sun already starting to slant low through the trees that surrounded the building.

Eric looked around, trying to center himself, trying to establish any sort of landmark, but there was only the building he'd just come out of—a nondescript, industrial-looking oblong with a single door—and then a whole mess of trees. Trees and trees and more trees—more trees than Eric had ever seen, mostly leafless now because of the season—with a narrow gravel driveway leading down into their depths.

With a final glance over his shoulder to make sure Jonathan wasn't pursuing him *(yet)*, Eric pushed his body into motion and ran for the trees as fast as his legs could carry him.

. . .

Which, unfortunately, wasn't all that fast.

He started to feel light-headed before he'd gone twenty yards, and each footfall sent a laser burst of pain down his left arm. The faster he tried to go, the more intense the explosion at the truncated juncture of his mangled wrist. He wasn't sure what

Jonathan had used to close the wound, but he wondered now if something had ruptured. With each pounding stride, he was certain he could feel thick gouts of blood jetting into the misshapen bandages jutting out of his sleeve.

But the bandages remained white, and when he slowed to a walk the pain rumbled down into something manageable, a muted drumbeat that made his breath hitch involuntarily but didn't actually stop him in his tracks. He lumbered down the driveway, feeling weaker and more nauseated by the minute, and the trees rose around him in a claustrophobic sea of browns and yellows. Here and there a random pine or spruce asserted itself in a shaggy cone of green shading to black in the dimming light.

He shivered. The air was decidedly colder than the last time he'd been outside, and if there had been a jacket among the new clothes Jonathan had set out for him back in the lab, he hadn't noticed it. At least it wasn't raining—or snowing. Considering the temperature, snow didn't seem all that unlikely a possibility.

He wondered how far he would have to walk before he came upon an actual road—a stretch of real blacktop with signs and markers that might offer some hint of where he might be. The gravel that crunched beneath his new loafers seemed to flow through the trees like a slow-moving river, meandering forward without leading anywhere in particular. He was far enough into the trees that he could no longer see the building he'd fled, but the path ahead didn't seem to be opening onto anything else either.

Eric had assumed Jonathan was lying about the long drive he'd mentioned on the first day of his captivity. He'd been certain they were really in the little cinderblock cube they'd parked behind that first night, and if he could ever maneuver his way off the table and somehow get outside, it would be a relatively short jaunt up the hill and back to civilization. Or to the road, at least.

But one step out the door just now had convinced him that wasn't the case. Even the air seemed different here—wherever "here" might be. Colder, of course, because the world had inched a month closer to winter while he was on the table, but also lighter somehow, cleaner. Crisp and sharp, spicy with the smell of dried grass and leaves and tree bark and...autumn. Hallmark Hall-of-Fame autumn—the kind usually encountered only on greeting cards or in television specials.

He'd climbed into Jonathan's van sometime during the first week of October, which meant that now it had to be a day or two on either side of Halloween. *Trick or treat*, he thought. Only this year the trick had pulled a couple of very nasty tricks of its own. *Trick or treat, smell my feet, give the fish my hand to eat...*

The world went dark for a moment and Eric stumbled off the path and into a tree. Thankfully, the impact was on his right side, but the jolt still sent a scream of electricity down his left arm. *Think I just passed out on my feet for a minute.*

The autumn sun was quite low now, little more than a glimmer shooting perpendicular shadows across the path. The light seemed to be pulsating in time with his heartbeat, in time with the pain in his arm, but he realized it was his vision that was blurring rhythmically, causing the world to grow lighter and darker, lighter and darker.

His stomach was churning as well, and a vise was tightening against the base of his skull. The blood in his left arm felt like it was surging against the wall of his wrist and then somehow oozing through. As near as he could tell—the sun had all but disappeared and it was quite dark now—his bandages were still white and unmarred, but he swore he could feel blood pumping forward anyway, pulsing out, finding hidden pathways, creating dimension where none had existed a moment before. The phrase *phantom limb* winked into his head, then dissipated again like smoke.

He slumped against the tree and let himself slide down the trunk to the cold, leaf-strewn ground. He'd rest for just a minute, close his eyes for the tiniest of naps, and then he was sure he could make it the rest of the way down the driveway. How far could it be, after all? Their driveway was only two car lengths at most, maybe just a car length and a half, although right now his view of it was blocked by a big red fire truck and it was hard to gauge the distance with any accuracy.

Somewhere in the depths of sleep or dream or madness—whatever this was—Eric heard the throaty rumble of a large engine and sensed a wash of bright headlights over his closed and fluttering eyelids. *That's my bus,* he thought. *I'm actually gonna get out of here after all.*

He tried to struggle up out of the blackness—he needed to make sure he got a good seat, and that his duffel bag was stowed securely in the cargo hold underneath the bus—but then he realized the bus driver had taken care of all of that for him, the bus driver was carrying him gently toward his seat, and he didn't have to worry about anything anymore.

Not the fire, not the water, not the snow (or was it ash?).

He didn't even have to worry about his missing hand, because he could hear it following along somewhere behind them, inch-worming its way up the steps of the bus and down the center aisle toward him. The pads of the hand's fingers, all clean and pruney from their time in the aquarium *(how did the flesh grow back, I wonder?)*, made tiny squeaking sounds against the rubber pad running between the bus seats as the hand pulled itself forward. Eric understood that this sound made the other passengers nervous, but he found he rather liked it.

Besides, any minute now the bus driver would close the door and start the bus and the sound of the freeway would block out everything else. It might even block out the sound of screaming that seemed to be coming from somewhere very far away.

Eric couldn't determine the source of the screaming but figured it was probably just some fellow passenger on the bus, frightened by his lonely, creeping hand. Or perhaps one of the forlorn creatures trapped in that mad scientist's lab in the hokey movie he wasn't supposed to let Bobby watch. Or maybe it was someone still trapped in that shell of burning house over there at the top of the driveway blocked by the fire truck.

Didn't matter. The bus was moving now, and he could hear nothing but wheels on pavement. The driver seemed to have put the bus on autopilot, and he was carrying a small plastic jack-o-lantern up the center aisle, handing out treats to all the passengers.

When he got to Eric, he bent to retrieve the boy's lost hand from the floor. "Don't want to lose this before you get to Minneapolis," he said. He placed the hand on the seat next to Eric and offered the boy a piece of candy from the jack-o-lantern.

The candy was milky green in color and Eric wondered briefly if it was okay to eat. But when he put it in his mouth it was sweet and smooth and creamy and delicious. It seemed to melt tantalizingly on the back of his tongue like whipped cream, like vanilla cream soda, like Christmas morning, like being tucked into bed at night.

One taste, a single bite, and he couldn't imagine wanting to eat anything else ever again.

Then he realized that instead of him eating the candy, the candy was somehow eating him, and he started to scream all over again.

. . .

"So, what did we learn from our little adventure?" Jonathan said.

He had pulled the desk chair close to Eric's bed, and was gently wiping the boy's forehead with a damp cloth. The soothing wet warmth had pulled Eric up out of sleep like a fairy-tale kiss. He was certain he'd open his eyes and be six years old again, in bed with a fever, but instead of his mother smiling over him—

"First," Jonathan said, "we learned that you're still very weak, and very much in need of my help—or the help of your little green friend, at any rate." He held up an empty syringe and then placed it back on the desk. "Second, we learned that these woods go on for acres and acres. You made it barely three-quarters of a mile and you weren't even into the forest proper yet. My driveway—if you want to call it that—would eventually take you to a logging road, and after eleven or so miles the logging road would take you to a very sparsely traveled country road. That road would eventually take you to the nearest town, another sixteen miles away, but you would have had one very long and very cold walk ahead of you, let me tell you."

"Just kill me and get it over with," Eric said. He closed his eyes and tried to burrow into the pillow. He would have liked to turn completely away, turn his back toward Jonathan, but that would have meant turning onto his damaged side.

"Why in the world would I kill you?" Jonathan said. He sounded so truly perplexed, even vaguely hurt, that Eric had to open his eyes again.

"Isn't that your plan? Keep me locked up here, torture me until you get sick of me, and then—I don't know—bury me out in the woods somewhere?"

(Or feed me to your starfish...)

"Good grief, no," Jonathan said. His expression was so guileless, so seemingly genuine and taken aback, that Eric nearly laughed. "I already told you, I'm going to make you incredibly rich—and famous to boot. Both of us! And you're certainly not locked up here. Look at this nice room I made just for you! You're simply not strong enough yet to go on a thirty-mile hike."

"Because you cut off my hand!" Eric felt a surge of bile rise into his throat, but forced it down again.

"Listen," Jonathan said. "I'm sorry about the way I've gone about things. I just get...overly enthusiastic sometimes."

Eric pushed himself up into an awkward sitting position and thrust forward the white lump of gauze and medical tape where his left hand had once been. "This is not enthusiasm, you—"

A sudden, involuntary sob stopped his voice and his vision blurred behind oily, scalding tears. In a moment he was reduced to a version of his vulnerable six-year-old self for the second time that morning, weeping openly and cradling his bandaged stump close to his chest as if trying to comfort a wounded animal.

Jonathan sat back in the chair and let the boy cry himself out. When Eric's tears had slowed and his breathing had hitched down to relative normal, he used the damp cloth to wipe the boy's face as he would a toddler's, and then he drew the bandaged wrist gently, carefully forward. He worked at a stubborn bit of tape until he found a finger-hold, then slowly unwound the first outer layer of covering.

Eric remained motionless, snuffling a bit, and watched the bandages peel away. He knew he would have to see it sometime—the wound, the abbreviated wrist, the blank space that used to be a hand—and he supposed now was as good a time as any. Get it over with, move on, wait for the next horror this freak could think up...

The final layer of gauze covered a lumpish, jelly-covered glob—some sort of antiseptic goop over whatever horrific, misshapen flap Jonathan had created as a new artificial end to his arm, Eric assumed. As Jonathan peeled away this last bit of gauze, Eric felt a distinct tickle. He was amazed there were any nerves left in the wrist to feel anything at all. He had the same strange sensation he'd had on the path through the woods—that of blood somehow flowing forward into places that could no longer exist—and then the blob on the end of his arm shuddered in a violent, electric spasm. It shook for a moment, trembled, dripping pinkish jelly onto the bedspread, and then suddenly blurped apart with a wet sucking sound.

Slowly the glob unfurled—a flower before the sun, a butterfly oozing forth from its chrysalis—and in a moment Eric was sobbing again, this time with pure, unadulterated happiness. With radiance, with joy. With overly enthusiastic enthusiasm, even.

He sobbed, and laughed, and stared, and gaped.

He held up his perfect new hand, and wriggled his perfect new fingers.

He turned toward Jonathan with a look of wonder and amazement. A look very much like the first raw beginnings of religious fervor—or love.

"Dude," he said. "Who *are* you?"

Made in the USA
Middletown, DE
06 February 2022

60605510R00187